THE HOUSE SWAP

MIRANDA RIJKS

INKUBATOR
BOOKS

Published by Inkubator Books
www.inkubatorbooks.com

ISBN (eBook): 978-1-83756-477-4
ISBN (Paperback): 978-1-83756-478-1
ISBN (Hardback): 978-1-83756-479-8

Miranda Rijks has asserted her right to be identified as the author of this work.

THE HOUSE SWAP is a work of fiction. People, places, events, and situations are the product of the author's imagination. Any resemblance to actual persons, living or dead is entirely coincidental.

PROLOGUE

There's something magical about Provencal nights. The sweet, perfumed scent of the air; the faintest hint of salt mixed with lavender and pine. The clicking of the cicadas and the hum of distant giant water sprinklers cooling down rows and rows of vines. So very different to London where the air is always heavy, laden with fumes and the unsavoury scents of the city, any stillness pierced by the sounds of sirens and the thrum of traffic. That's why I love the South of France. Beauty permeates every one of our senses.

I didn't plan any of this. At least I didn't mean to. But sometimes our lives thread off into directions we never anticipate and although we think we're masters of our own destinies, of course we're not. Paths get blocked, avenues that were once throbbing with possibilities become empty of choice. And so we have no alternative. We must choose survival. In fact, us humans are programmed to choose survival.

I thought I understood fear, how to harness it, how to rise above it. People look at me and see strength, inspiration even.

So when all my plans come together, so very carefully plotted, I am ready. Strike while they're relaxed, and no more perfect time than a holiday. We all love a luxury villa or a sumptuous town-house, a swimming pool or a cinema room. They're the things we aspire to, what most people never experience. Except I'm not most people and nor are they. We're the extraordinary. And I will fight for that, to the death.

I hear the footsteps, but I am ready. What takes me by surprise is the scent of fear; how my nose is able to sniff it out, how I wait for it to emerge from the shadows of the night. I am stealth and patience, ready to strike. But despite all the planning, the careful examining of every nuance, every possibility, circumstances change. My heart is thumping so hard, my breath heavy and frustratingly loud. Yet I must be calm. There it is again, the whiff of terror. My nose twitches. I turn around, thinking I'm ready.

And then she screams.

CHAPTER ONE

ELODIE

'I think it's the next turning on the left,' I say, squinting at the map on the dashboard. The sun is so bright it makes the screen hard to view.

'You think or you know?' Lewis is snippy. He took the wrong turning out of Nice Côte d'Azur Airport and now there is tension oozing from his every pore. It had been a stress-free trip with a flight that took off and landed on time, and a car upgrade, but Lewis doesn't like driving in Europe, where we're on the 'wrong' side of the road. He's wary of going around a roundabout the wrong way, not that he'd ever admit it to me or agree to me driving.

'Slow down,' I say. 'Yes, it's here.' I scroll through the instructions that Susan Lester emailed me, stating in block capitals that we must ignore the Sat Nav otherwise we'll end up at the rear entrance of a local winery. There's a little white post at the side of the road exactly as she described.

Lewis indicates to the left and turns the car onto a chalky track. The scenery is stunning now we're up in the hills, surrounded by thick woodland that every so often opens up to vistas of rolling hills dotted with pale stone-walled villas with terracotta roofs and shutters painted in the prettiest of lilacs and turquoise. I can't wait to breathe in the warm air fragranced with pine, lounge by the beautiful azure pool and drink rosé from the local vineyards. This holiday is very much overdue.

The rental car bounces over potholes, jerking us from one side to the next, the tyres throwing up powdery white chalk that settles as fine dust over the bonnet of the dark grey vehicle.

'You'd have thought they might have filled in some of the potholes,' Lewis moans. 'It's not going to be easy to cycle on this.'

I don't say anything as I have no intention of cycling. Road biking is my husband's thing.

It was back in May when Lewis pointed out we hadn't booked a summer holiday, and as we wanted to go away during the last two weeks in June, any decent hotel or villa would already be fully booked. I'd been so busy with work, I simply hadn't had time to research a holiday. And then my business partner, Niall Hutchinson, suggested we do this house swap, a trial for the new venture we're setting up. Lewis surprised me by leaping at the idea. I suppose the photos of the fancy Provencal villa swayed him. And who wouldn't want a free holiday in the South of France? This seemed like the perfect solution.

We were sitting in our London kitchen, eating a Chinese takeaway. 'It's less than thirty minutes to the coast and surrounded by vineyards,' my husband enthused, as he shovelled food into his mouth with one hand while browsing through Susan Lester's blog with the other. 'Some of the best restaurants in Provence are within spitting distance and fine weather is a dead cert. Niall sold the chateau to the current owners. Don't you remember?' he asked. No, I didn't. Between us, Niall and I have sold hundreds of houses. I run the UK arm of Hutchinson Brown Properties and leave the European side to Niall, who sells fancy houses predominantly in France and Italy.

'But strangers staying in our house,' I murmured glancing around at my white marble kitchen with its gold taps and accessories. I wondered for a moment whether my concerns about strangers staying in our home might echo other luxury homeowners too. Was the house-swap business even viable?

'Niall says Susan and Piers Lester are lovely, really respectful of other people's properties, and they're looking to come to London with their seventeen-year-old son, who's staking out universities over here. They're not hoi polloi like me; they're educated posh folk like you, my darling.' Lewis put his chopsticks down and snaked his thick arm around me, pulling me into a strong hug. The bulk of him makes me feel safe and loved and I realised we hadn't had nearly enough physical contact recently. When we first got together, Lewis described himself as my bit of rough. It's not true that I'm posh; we're both from working-class backgrounds but we've done extremely well for ourselves. Extremely. 'Besides, Teresa will keep an eye on them, make sure they look after this place.'

'It sounds like you've already made up your mind,' I said, wriggling from his grasp. 'You and Niall have been plotting against me.'

'I just think it's a great opportunity, and you know me. Never one for passing up on a freebie. And if you want to set up the house-swap arm of Hutchinson Brown Properties, then you at least have to try it yourself.'

AND SO, here we are. Doing a house swap, and I still have butterflies about it, despite having had numerous emails with Susan Lester, plus a FaceTime call where she introduced Lewis and me to her husband Piers and son, Rafael, a delightful, well-spoken young man. Apparently, we met the Lesters at Niall and Danielle's wedding in Monte Carlo some months ago, not that I actually recall them. There must have been five hundred people at the most sumptuous wedding we've ever attended, so I suppose I can be forgiven.

Despite locking everything valuable into the safe in our master bedroom suite and making sure our reliable part-time housekeeper, Teresa, is fully briefed and ready to step in, I am wary at the thought of strangers inhabiting our beautiful Knightsbridge home. I reassure myself that everything is insured and it's not as if we have any irreplaceable family heirlooms. The only thing I cherish from my childhood is a bottle of Badedas bubble bath given to me by my grandmother, her very last gift to me before she passed away, a bottle that undoubtedly would be rancid if I was to open it now.

And then I mentally kick myself. I'm being so precious when really that's not me at all. I grew up with nothing. Home was a two-bedroom semi in a poor part of Stoke-on-Trent. Mum and Dad didn't have two pennies to rub together but what they weren't able to give us in terms of material wealth, they made up for with emotional support and love. The bedroom I shared with my younger sister Ottilie was too small for a normal mattress, so Dad sawed off the end and wedged it between the two walls. We slept head to toe on that lumpy mattress until I was fifteen. Dad tried to make that room homely for us, painting the room in a lurid pink, and placing stickers that he bought at the pound shop over the ever-increasing patches of damp.

My sister and I were ribbed at school for having ridiculously posh-sounding names. It wasn't until I was in my teens that Mum told me she chose the French names Elodie and Ottilie because they both mean prosperity, and all she wished for us was to accumulate greater wealth in life than she had. Mum didn't live long enough to see my success, but I think she would have approved. Although as she never even visited London, let alone France, perhaps she'd be telling me that I'd got too big for my boots. Too materialistic and precious. I stare out of the car window as we bump along the track, blinking tears from my eyes at the thought of Mum. But goodness, she'd love this scenery, the rolling hills covered in vines as far as the eye can see, the scent of lavender and the pink oleander that seems to be growing like weeds.

I rub my eyes and let a smile edge at my lips as I realise that Susan's photos don't do this scenery justice. It's breathtaking. And then we wind to the right and up ahead is a stone wall with a wide opening, olive trees lining the entrance. Lewis slows the car, edging it through the open gates. In front of us is the villa, pale honey-coloured stone walls rising up to a long, pitched terracotta-tiled roof. A huge arched front door is in the centre, with eight windows framed with shutters painted in a pretty lavender blue, and to the left another building, a square tower, adjoining the main house. The tower and the lower half of the villa are wrapped around with scaffolding. It's a bit of a stretch calling this house a chateau, but it's certainly a very fine villa.

'Wow,' Lewis says. He parks the car next to a silver Renault, which looks battered and well-used. I climb out slowly, the hot air hitting me like a hair dryer, a scent of eucalyptus and jasmine making me inhale deeply. The property is exactly as it looked in the photos, as it looks on Susan Lester's website, www.ChateauLesterLiving.com, which she's set up like a blog and where she posts effusively about the delights of Provencal life. It's just a shame about the scaffolding.

'Hello! Welcome!' And there she is, striding out of the front door, her arms stretched out in front of her. She's wearing a billowing floral dress, her mahogany hair swept up into a chignon, huge dark sunglasses swamping her small face. 'Elodie, Lewis?' She makes a beeline for me, placing her hands gently on my upper arms and leaning in for an air kiss. She's wearing a floral-scented perfume that I can't place. But for a moment I'm confused. I wasn't expecting Susan to be here, thought that she, her husband Piers and son Rafael would be on a flight en-route to London Heathrow right now, ready to install themselves in our house. She must notice my frown, the slight tension in my body.

'We thought we'd take a later flight so that we could welcome you to Chateau Lester. We've got a buffet lunch ready for you on the veranda.' She glances at Lewis, who has one hand on the handle of the car boot, and throws him an awkward smile. 'Why don't you leave your luggage for now? Come and have a glass of vino. You must need it. How was your flight? Did you find us okay?'

Susan is a whirlwind. Lewis throws me a look, raising an eyebrow, an expression of amusement on his face. I can tell straight away that Susan is too flowery, not his type. He locks the rental car and we follow our host. As we pass the front door, I see three suitcases and a couple of bags, luggage labels attached, ready for their trip to London. In contrast, Lewis and I have just the one case; then again, packing for England will always be more tricky, requiring clothes for all weather. I expect Susan to lead us through the imposing front door, but she doesn't. We walk around the side of the house towards a garden with a sun-scorched lawn, and then turn to see a stunning veranda covered with another roof of terra-cotta tiles, with three open arches looking onto a large cerulean swimming pool surrounded by lush lavender and the garden beyond. Underneath the arches is a long wooden table, stacked with bright yellow, red and blue earthenware, salads in large circular dishes, and heavy cut-glass wine glasses. It reminds me of jauntily taken photographs, the hints of the perfect life in a sun-kissed paradise that fill up Susan's blog.

'Oh wow!' I say, any concerns about staying in someone else's house immediately forgotten. 'You really didn't need to go to so much trouble.'

'It's nothing,' Susan says, waving her hands around again. 'We wanted to introduce you to the joys of Provence, but now I'm worried because I didn't check if you have any food intolerances.'

'No, we don't, and this looks absolutely amazing.' I had assumed that the photos on her WordPress website were staged; a blog featuring little snippets of perfectly ripe toma-toes piled on a floral tablecloth, freshly baked cakes placed on glass stands and fresh salads covered with waxed paper, but perhaps the Lesters really do live like that.

'Right, why don't you take a seat and I'll call my boys.' She glances at a small watch on her wrist. 'We haven't got long. If we're going to catch our flight, we have to be out of here by 2.30 p.m.'

Susan disappears into the dark interior of the house and I raise my eyebrows at Lewis, but he's more interested in looking at the view, over the tops of trees to the vineyard-encrusted hills beyond, and somewhere, far in the distance, the shimmering azure Mediterranean sea.

'Welcome, welcome!' A man appears, his limbs bronzed, his skinny legs in faded navy shorts. In contrast to Lewis, he's tall and willowy, wearing wire-framed glasses, his face all sharp angles. He strides up to me and holds out his hand, shaking mine with vigour. 'So lovely to meet you again. I'm Piers and you must be Elodie. What can I get you? Red, white or rosé?' I'm slightly embarrassed by the 'again,' because that infers Piers recalls meeting us at Niall's wedding, when I definitely don't recognise him—or perhaps he's referring to our Zoom call.

'A glass of rosé would be lovely,' I say, as I sit in the chair Piers pulls out for me.

'And you, Lewis?' Piers asks.

'More of a beer man, myself,' he says. I pull an apologetic face but Piers doesn't seem to mind.

'Coming right up.'

A couple of minutes later, the four of us are seated at the table, Susan sliding dishes of fresh-looking salads and dried meats towards us, wooden serving spoons wedged into each bowl. 'Raf will join us in a moment. He's upstairs with his girlfriend, Lucille, and I can't tell you what a fuss he's made about going to London. First love and all that, not wanting to leave her behind.'

And then there is the clatter of footsteps and Raf appears followed by the girl I assume is Lucille. He's tall like his dad with gazelle-like limbs, a body he hasn't quite yet grown into, and unlike either of his parents, he has reddish hair. A mixture of his mother's dark tresses and father's blonde mop, no doubt. In contrast, Lucille seems older. There's a reassurance about her, a confidence in her braided hair and the glittering diamond in her nose, her fraying shorts so skimpy her buttocks show underneath. She's busty too, and her sleeveless crop top leaves little to the imagination. I notice Lewis look her up and down and I wish he'd avert his eyes.

'Right, kiddos, you need to eat up,' Susan says.

It takes me a moment to realise that Rafael hasn't sat down but is staring at Lewis. This happens sometimes, but less frequently as every year passes.

'Are you Lewis Brown? *The* Lewis Brown?' he asks.

'As in the boxer?' Piers adds, removing his glasses, wiping them with the bottom of his linen shirt and putting them back on again. 'Good heavens! So you are!' Piers turns towards Susan. 'Did you know we were having a celebrity to stay in our humble chateau?'

'Sorry, I...' For the first time, Susan seems a little flustered. That's what notoriety can do to you. All eyes are on Lewis and I notice how he puffs his chest out, how his face is ever so slightly flushed.

'I am indeed, although I'm a "has been" these days.' Lewis laughs.

'But you're a legend,' Rafael says as he sits down.

'Busted. That's me, and it's very kind of you to say so, but my success was a long time ago. I'm surprised someone as young as you would have heard of me.'

'I've seen some boxing videos on YouTube. Didn't you reach the semi-finals of the World Amateur Boxing Championships and now you have these really famous gyms in London that all the celebrities go to?'

'Famous gyms? If you say so.' Lewis chuckles, puffing out his chest. It does his confidence so much good to be recognised. That's the trouble of being famous in your youth.

Unless you're world class and become a highly paid pundit, it's generally downhill thereafter, and in Lewis's case, I worry that his confidence is knocked a little more with every passing year.

'Oh my goodness, that's so cool,' Rafael exclaims.

An awkward silence falls, where the only noises are the singing birds and the clatter of cutlery.

'Right, I need to introduce you to the most important person in the household,' Susan says. I wonder for a moment whom she's referring to. She clicks her fingers. 'Pushkin!' she shouts. A moment later, a black Labrador hurtles from the interior of the house, his paws scuttling on the paving stones, his amber eyes framed with long black lashes.

'What a beautiful dog,' I say, only now remembering that one of Susan's house-swap stipulations was for us to be dog lovers. This swap is also a dog swap and I just hope that our bichon, Muffin, will be well-behaved for them and not too yappy. I rub the top of Pushkin's head and he sinks to the floor next to my chair.

'Doesn't he bark at strangers?' I ask, wondering why he didn't come out to greet us when we arrived.

'Only when he feels threatened, but fortunately he seems to like you. Anything we need to know about your dog?' Susan asks.

'If you wouldn't mind collecting her from the neighbour's son when you get there, that would be great. Hugo is looking after Muffin until you arrive. I've left lots of notes for you in the kitchen.'

'It'll be such a joy to be in the hustle and bustle of central London,' Piers adds. There's a wistfulness in his voice. 'It's been too long.'

'And what are you going to do in London?' I turn to ask Rafael.

He shrugs his shoulders and doesn't answer. I don't have much experience with teenage boys, so perhaps that wasn't a sensible question. Lewis and I don't have children. I would have liked to, I think, but we were both working so hard in our thirties, the years slipped past, and now, although theoretically it might be possible, it's really too late. I don't mind. Our lives are full.

'Raf hasn't decided yet,' Susan answers for him. 'Although there are a couple of museums we want to visit and we've booked to see a West End show.'

'And you, Lucille. Are you studying?' I ask the young woman, only then wondering if she speaks English.

'I'm going travelling,' she says, with a strong but charming French accent.

'Lucille has just finished her baccalauréat. She's the year above Raf at school, although technically she's left now.' I sense a tension between Susan and the two youngsters and wonder if perhaps she doesn't approve of her son's girlfriend.

'You mentioned you have a couple of bikes I can borrow,' Lewis turns to Piers. 'That still okay?'

'Of course,' Piers replies. 'There's a road bike and a mountain bike. If they're not up to scratch, there's a bike rental shop in the village, but feel free to use ours.'

The food is simple but excellent and after a glass and a half of delicious rosé, I'm feeling sleepy. Our 4.30 a.m. start is catching up on me. I stifle a yawn and Piers glances again at his watch.

'We really need to be getting a move on,' he says, pushing his chair back. For a moment I think what a shame it is that the Lesters aren't going to be staying; that I would have enjoyed their company, particularly Piers's, who seems an amiable man.

'Come on, Raf,' Piers says. The Lesters rise to their feet and Susan starts to collect the dirty crockery.

'Let me do that,' I say. 'You go and catch your flight.'

After some more air kissing, we follow them back around the side of the house to the cars. Piers hauls their suitcases into the rear of the Renault while Lucille and Rafael embrace overenthusiastically under the eaves of the roof.

'Hurry up, Raf,' Susan shouts, a sharp edge to her voice. Rafael disengages himself and lopes towards the car, his shoulders rounded, a look on his face suggesting he's not far off bursting into tears.

Piers reverses the car and then accelerates away down the drive, sticking his arm out of the driver's window waving goodbye to us. A moment later, Lucille appears on a bike, pedalling furiously as if she's trying to keep up with the Lesters. And then they're all out of sight and Lewis and I are left alone, almost bereft. It feels mighty strange to be standing on the steps of someone else's house while the owners disappear into the distance.

'Right,' Lewis says, breaking my reverie. 'Let's have an explore, shall we?' He puts his arm around my shoulders and I lean into him as we turn around and walk through the open front door.

THE INTERIOR OF THE VILLA – or Chateau Lester, as Susan grandly calls it – is a stark contrast to the exterior. The downstairs floors are all brown tiles, some chipped, all of them mismatched. The rooms are large, stripped back, with exposed beams. Some walls appear to have been freshly painted, others are literally crumbling, chunks of plaster loose or missing, window frames with peeling paint. I'm silent as we wander through the many rooms, two lounges, an impressive wood-panelled library, a long, thin dining room and into the square kitchen. In here, the walls are painted white, but the kitchen equipment is freestanding, with the huge range cooker taking pride of place. It's a dark maroon colour with several doors, one of them hanging at a jaunty angle. There's an old butcher's block in the centre of the room and a long wooden dining table covered with watermarks and rings from decades of use. Although the windows look onto the beautiful veranda and garden beyond, the views and light are diminished by scaffolding that wraps around this end of the house. There's a slight dank odour throughout – damp, I presume – masked with lavender.

'Not exactly the deluxe accommodation the exterior promised,' I murmur. 'So much for the camera never lies. Her website makes this place look stunning but it's obvious now why all the photos are close-ups.'

'Oh come on, it's not that bad,' Lewis says, nudging me. 'It's lovely that they're making the effort to bring the chateau back to its former glory. There's something special about being the custodians of history.' I think of our perfect London home, the designer wallpaper, the hand-made kitchen and the shining marble bathrooms, and then I hear Mum's voice in my head. *Stop chuntering and being such a cade, lassie. It's who you are, not what you have, that makes you a good 'un.* It took me a while to realise the slang she used, such as cade meaning a spoiled child, and chunter for moaning, was a local dialect and not widely understood.

'It's rustic,' Lewis adds. 'And besides, we're going to be outside most of the time.'

'I suppose so,' I admit.

'I'll grab the suitcase and let's have a look upstairs.'

The staircase is stone and the handrail is made from wrought iron in an intricate curling pattern. I recognise it from a photo that showed the shadows of the design on a white wall. Upstairs I count six bedrooms, but only three of them are in use as bedrooms. The master has a king-sized bed and it's made up with cream and blue linen, the pillows neatly plumped up and a vase of flowers on the painted chest of drawers opposite the bed. This room seems fresh and the temperature is cool, the surfaces spotless. At least our bedroom is welcoming. I sit on the side of the plump bed and let out a sigh.

It isn't until a few long seconds later that I realise there is no en-suite bathroom. I get up again and walk along the corridor. There is one bathroom at the far end, a large, echoing room with a wide shower, sink and WC and the scent of floral chemicals. The bathroom is quite a walk from our bedroom and I'm glad we're staying here alone. The second lived-in bedroom is clearly Rafael's, full of book-shelves, a large computer screen, a black gaming chair posi-tioned under a shelf full of computer games, and three skateboards hung on the wall as if they're pictures to be admired. The third bedroom simply has a large bed made up and a single chair, with a small en-suite shower room, barely big enough for Lewis to step inside. The paper is peeling off the walls and there's a dank smell. The other three rooms are empty bar a few boxes that look like they've never been unpacked since the Lesters moved in. I wander back to the master bedroom where Lewis is unzipping our suitcase.

'I'll unpack,' I say. 'And then I might take a nap.'

Lewis stands up and flexes his back. 'Alright. I'll check out those bikes Piers was talking about and, if they're up to scratch, I'll go for a bike ride.' He gives me a quick peck on the lips and I listen to his heavy footsteps as he disappears downstairs.

Five minutes later, I'm lying on the comfortable bed. The villa might be run-down but I'm in desperate need of relaxation, a chance to switch off from my hectic business life. A chance for Lewis and I to spend some time with each other. A chance to get our lives back in balance. It's only as I'm drifting off to sleep that it crosses my mind I didn't expressly tell Susan she couldn't take photos of my home; that under no circumstances could she share details of our lives for her blog. But she wouldn't. Surely not.

CHAPTER TWO

PIERS

It's a shock landing at Heathrow Airport, taking the tube into central London, being assaulted by the overwhelming bustle of people, sights and sounds that have been completely missing from our tranquil Provencal life. I feel like an alien that has landed in the most foreign of lands, which is the strangest feeling considering I spent the first thirty years of my life in this city. The air smells rancid, heavy with fumes, claustrophobic even.

We exit the underground at South Kensington tube station, weaving between the hordes of people as we pull our suitcases, wheels crunching noisily along the pavements, winding our way past rows of elegant town houses in the direction of Knightsbridge. Me leading the way, followed closely by Susan, with Raf dragging his heels some way behind, as if he wants to pretend that he's not associated with us. Poor Raf. I know how badly he wanted to stay in France, to spend these next couple of weeks with Lucille, and go off travelling with her around Europe. Susan was having none of that. He hasn't muttered a word since we left

France, and I sense that his sulkiness is grating on Susan's nerves.

I don't mind Lucille. I'm certain she's a temporary fixture, and despite Raf thinking he's met his soul mate, it's obvious that she's just his first experience of sex and what he assumes to be love. I remember my first girlfriend and how convinced I was that she was the one for me. That was until she met my cousin Andy and ran off with him. At the time, I thought she'd broken my heart, but with the benefit of hindsight, I realised I felt humiliation rather than heartbreak. It's been a running gag between Andy and me for years, our similar taste in women.

Over the Easter weekend, Raf asked if Lucille could stay over – code, of course, for *can I bonk my girlfriend in my bedroom?* Susan was having none of it, so I brokered a compromise. Lucille could stay so long as she slept in a spare room. Needless to say, Susan was like an alert prison guard, and when she heard the creaking floorboards at some ungodly hour, she was out of our bedroom ready to accost the night-time lovers. Except, strangely, Lucille wasn't creeping into Raf's room. Susan found her wandering around the living room. 'It's like she was snooping,' Susan explained. I suggested that perhaps she had been sleep-walking but Susan was convinced the girl was up to no good, not that we found anything missing, or have done since.

We turn onto Font Street. Number 34 is similar to the other houses, with a white stucco facade and black wrought-iron gates that open to white marble steps that lead up to the shiny black front door. Perfectly round bay trees with curly trunks stand in black planters either side of the door, and up above are two storeys. The first has three windows, and on the top floor are another three dormer-type windows surrounded by grey hanging tiles. I open the gate and lug Susan's and my suitcases up the steps.

'Have you got the key?'

Susan rummages in her handbag and hands it to me.

'Remember the code?' she asks, recalling how Elodie explained that we have twenty seconds to disarm the alarm system otherwise security will be called out as a matter of urgency, swiftly followed by the police. I glance at my phone, checking the six digits, and then turn the key in the door. Immediately the alarm panel beeps, but I locate it behind the door and plug in the numbers. It's a relief when it falls silent. The moment I step inside I realise how very different the Browns' house is to our own sprawling yet modest property. This is proper grown-up living, with smooth marble floors and mood lighting that flicks on as we walk through the hall. There must be some sophisticated lighting system linked to hidden sensors. There's a scent of jasmine – expensive, not like the floral chemicals that Susan sprays liberally in our bathrooms to mask the scent of old drains.

'Wow!' Susan exclaims, glancing around the hallway, noting the beautiful inlaid satinwood console table and the magnificent floral display in a heavy crystal vase. To the left is a feature glass staircase that seems to defy gravity by hovering midair. We leave our suitcases in the hall and wander into the house, stepping first into a living room that looks like it's come out of a fancy club. The floors are dark wood, the pale beige sofas curved into a U shape, opposite a mirrored wall that houses a huge fancy fireplace, one of those that likely flick on with the switch of a button. In the centre of the ceiling there's a feature crystal chandelier, and back lights behind the shelves of the bookcase, lending everything a subtle glow. Speakers are recessed into the ceiling. A Juliet balcony looks onto manicured gardens beyond the house, a square of grass edged by flower-filled borders that is apparently a private garden for the houses that surround it.

'This is something else,' Susan says, in a whisper. 'Un-bloody-believable.'

'I feel really bad about our place,' I say, guilt weighing on my shoulders. Our unfinished house may be sprawling but it's like a slum in comparison to this. We turn and walk into the kitchen, which is all shiny white marble streaked with pale grey veins, on the floor, walls and units, and highlighted with sparkling gold taps and gold handles on the cupboards and range cooker. I let out a slow whistle. 'I'd be scared to cook in here,' I mutter.

'Yeah, you'd probably break something,' Susan says, somewhat unkindly, I think.

'This place is dope.' Raf appears behind us. 'There's a cinema room for four people downstairs, and a gym.'

'Don't touch anything,' Susan says. Raf rolls his eyes at her.

'What's the point of a house swap if I can't touch anything?' he asks. Neither of us replies.

We turn to go back to the hall and pass two further rooms — a dark-wood, book-lined library and a dining room with silver wallpaper and sconces on the walls. There's modern art on every wall and tall sculptures stand in corners.

'They must be bloody loaded,' Raf articulates what I'm thinking. More than loaded; literally dripping in cash. How much is this place worth here in the capital city's prime location? North of ten million, I suppose? We got really lucky for our house swap, embarrassingly so.

'I did alright, choosing this for our house swap, didn't I?' Susan grins at me.

'Better than alright.' Raf and I follow her back into the kitchen.

'Oh look. Elodie has left something for us.' She lifts up an envelope addressed in cursive writing to: Piers, Susan and Rafael. Slipping her index finger under the flap, Susan slides out a card that says, *Welcome* across the front. She reads it out aloud. '*Dear Piers, Susan and Rafael, Welcome to our home. Inside the folder you'll find all the important things such as the Wi-Fi password, where I shop for groceries and the like, our favourite restaurants and details of our GP in the unlikely event you'll need him. Don't hesitate to call or email me if you have any problems. Also, our housekeeper Teresa will pop in three times a week to clean the house and change your linen. Teresa has made up a bed for you in our principal guest suite and Rafael's room is on the other side of the corridor. Please can you call Hugo, the son of our next door neighbours at number 32 on 07987543696. He'll drop Muffin back home. Her food is in the fridge, all marked up. I hope that you have a wonderful fortnight! Items in the fridge are for you. Best wishes, Elodie and Lewis.* Well, that's kind of her,' Susan says. 'Do you think she'll be charging us for Teresa's time? I hope not.'

'Surely she would have told us,' I say, wondering how much an hour a cleaner charges in this part of central London.

'Why is the dog's food kept in the fridge?' Rafael asks.

I open the enormous American-style fridge and see a drawer full of pouches marked "Muffin". 'It's some fancy fresh food for a spoiled pooch,' I say, noting that the huge

THE HOUSE SWAP   23

fridge is completely empty bar a bottle of white wine, a half
pint of milk and a pack of butter, with a handful of vegetables in one of multiple drawers. We didn't empty our fridge,
but just shoved all of our old bottles of condiments and the
like onto the bottom shelf.

'We'd better call this Hugo,' Susan says, glancing at her
watch. It's getting late. 'Raf, can you do it?'

'I'll take our bags upstairs,' I say. I tread carefully,
worried about scratching a bag against the flawless walls.
Upstairs it's as glamorous as downstairs, each bedroom made
up as if it was a room transported from a designer boutique
hotel, pillows plumped up, cashmere blankets in neutral
colours placed over beds, heavy curtains in pale grey and
taupe silks, walls lined with wallpaper in gentle hues and
delicate patterns, the air lightly scented with delicate florals.
The three bathrooms are sumptuous, double sinks, marble
floors, rain showers, a jacuzzi bath, and mirrors with func-
tional and mood lighting. White fluffy towels hang from
sparkling radiators, not the normal types of towel rails, but
their metal arms have been shaped into sculptures,
rectangular and bold. Just stepping in this place makes me
scared of tainting it. Perhaps I've become too accustomed to
living amongst rubble and ruins.

The doorbell rings and awakens me from my reverie. I
leave the bathroom and return to the top of the stairs. Susan
opens the door and I pad down the glass staircase, my damp
socks leaving smudges. A boy stands there, perhaps a year or
two older than Raf, a small white fluffy dog under his arm.

'You must be Mrs Lester,' he says stepping into the hallway. He speaks with rounded vowels and the innate confidence of a privately educated young man. 'This is Muffin.'

He places her on the ground and unclips a pink sparkling lead, handing it to Susan.

'And you must be Hugo,' she says.

'Guilty as charged.'

'Raf!' she shouts. 'Our son must be a similar age to you.' Raf doesn't appear.

'Why don't you come into the kitchen and meet him,' she says to Hugo. I imagine if this conversation had been in reverse, if Raf was talking to this stranger's mother, and how he would likely shrink in on himself, shoulders curved, unable to meet a stranger's gaze. But this lad is nothing like our son.

'Sure,' he says. 'It would be great to hook up. Perhaps I can show him some of London's hotspots.'

I follow them into the kitchen, where Hugo strides up to Raf, his hand extended, and shakes our son's hand, pumping his arm up and down. 'Fabulous to meet you,' he says. 'We need to hang. I'll give you a bell tomorrow or the next day,' Hugo says. Raf mumbles something and I notice how his gaze runs over the other boy's clothes, the designer gear with logos proudly on display, the slicked-back hair, the chunky gold watch on his wrist. Perhaps it will do Raf good to spend time with Hugo, let some of that confidence rub off on him.

'Right, better be getting back. Mummy has made apple crumble and insists we eat it. She's a terrible cook and I'll have to slip it down the waste disposal when she's not looking.' He laughs but our laughs in response sound forced and awkward.

Susan sees Hugo to the door, whilst I lean down and stroke Muffin, who is looking around as if she's confused to find these strangers in her home.

'What a jerk,' Raf mutters under his breath.

I don't reprimand him but then wonder if I should.

THAT NIGHT, we're lying on the softest marshmallow-like mattress I've ever lain on, tucked under cool linen sheets, the faint hum of London's traffic in the distance. I can't stop thinking about the Browns in our run-down chateau, which isn't a chateau really but Susan insists that's what we call it.

'Switch your brain off,' Susan says, nudging me with her elbow at my waist. That's the joy of an eighteen-year marriage. You almost intuit what your partner is thinking.

'I'm just concerned about the state of our place, and that we didn't tell them about the break-in.'

'Stop worrying. The police said it was nothing, just opportunism, and why worry the Browns unnecessarily?'

'Yes, but I still think we should have mentioned it.'

'If it'll put your mind at rest, I'll message Elodie in the morning, but I really don't think we should be worrying them. These things happen, and it's not like anything was taken or there was much damage.'

We lie in silence for a couple of minutes.

'Are you worried about tomorrow?' Susan asks, taking my hand in hers. 'Is that what this is all about?'

'Yes. But at least we'll know one way or another soon.'

She kisses the side of my neck. 'I'm sure it's nothing. Dr Reinhard didn't seem too concerned.'

I don't say anything because she's right. I've been displaying all the classic symptoms of prostate problems: needing to pee multiple times in the night, the feeling that I'm not emptying my bladder properly, and the occasional lower back pain. And the most worrying thing, my dad died of prostate cancer aged just fifty-five, so I've always assumed I'm high risk. Either I'm being a hypochondriac or my fears are well founded. I've taken the opportunity of being in London to book myself in to see a leading Harley Street urologist, and Susan's right. I'm absolutely terrified.

CHAPTER THREE

ELODIE

The next morning I'm awoken by the sound of hammering. Slow, methodical bangs that echo not only around the room but also inside my head. I groan. Last night, when Lewis returned from his bike ride, we polished off a bottle of rosé – or more to the point, I did, as my husband was drinking beer. I didn't sleep well and now my head is sore. I force my eyelids open and blink at the sun rays pouring through the bedroom window. Unlike our curtains at home, these are white muslin, their Ikea labels visible through the fine fabric, and they do absolutely nothing to block out the light.

'What's going on?' I groan and turn towards Lewis, but his side of the bed is empty. I glance at the clock. It's only 7 a.m. I try to turn over, pull the pillow over my head, but the banging doesn't stop. Eventually, I swing my legs out of bed and walk to the tall windows. The left side is partially open so I swing it open further and peer outside. There are four vans parked next to our rental car. One has a large ladder on its roof, the others are white, although they look as if they could do with a good clean. A man appears, wearing a navy

T-shirt and grey shorts, a worn leather tool belt around his waist. He looks up and waves at me. I feel self-conscious, aware I'm wearing a thin cotton nightdress that could well be see-through, my hair mussed up from sleep. I step backwards, out of view. What the hell is a team of builders doing here? And more to the point, why didn't Susan tell us?

I feel a churn of annoyance in my belly and grab some clothes. And then realise I don't know if the builders are inside or outside the house. The bathroom is all the way down the corridor and I don't fancy running into any of them. I pull a cotton dress over my nightdress and grab some clean underwear. Fortunately I don't run into anyone inside the house and twenty minutes later, I'm showered, dressed and feeling vaguely ready for the day. I find Lewis downstairs in the kitchen, the wide doors flung open. He's talking to the builder I saw out of the window.

'What's going on?' I ask.

'This is André,' Lewis says. 'He's the site foreman.'

'For what?'

'We're working on the renovations of the villa.' He speaks with a heavily accented voice.

'But we're staying here on holiday. Susan didn't mention anything about building work.'

He shrugs, in that very gallic way that I normally find so charming. 'We need to switch off the water for a few hours.'

I frown at Lewis but he just says, 'I'll take myself off for a bike ride then. Pick up a couple of bottles of water on the way back.'

I feel a surge of annoyance. This is meant to be our holiday, a peaceful fortnight in the beautiful South of France, not a couple of weeks being disturbed by builders.

'How long are you going to be working here?' I ask.

'Pff. Je ne sais pas.' André shrugs his shoulders again. 'Two weeks, two months, two years. We'll see.'

I have absolutely no answer for this. How could Susan and Piers, in all good faith, organise a house swap in the knowledge that we're meant to be co-existing with builders? This isn't going to be a holiday.

'I'll fill up some jugs with water,' I say, trying to control my annoyance. As much as I feel like shouting and stamping my feet, this predicament isn't André and his team's fault.

'Thank you,' he says, nodding at me before turning around and exiting the kitchen via the open arched patio doors.

When he's gone, I turn to Lewis. 'I can't believe it! We need to call the Browns and tell them to halt their builders whilst we're here, otherwise I'm going home and they can get out of our house.' I'm not sure why the disappointment is so overwhelming, why I'm just a beat away from bursting into tears. Maybe it's because I didn't sleep well last night, or perhaps it's simply because I need a holiday more than I'd imagined. The past few months have been relentless, workwise, and this is the first time I'm truly able to switch off.

'Alright,' Lewis says, putting a calming hand on my shoulder. 'Take a deep breath, love. I'm sure there's been some misunderstanding. Do you want me to call them?'

'If you would, yes, that will be great. If you're going for a bike ride, I think I'll take myself off to the local town for the morning, do some shopping, calm myself down.'

'Excellent idea. You don't mind me going out for a bike ride, do you?'

I kind of do, but this is as much a holiday for Lewis as it is for me, and exercise is his way of relaxing. 'I'll pick up some fresh food and we can have a lovely lunch,' I say. 'But call the Lesters. Tell them to send their builders packing.'

AS I GET into the rental car, my phone rings. It's Niall, my business partner.

'How are things in Provencal paradise?' he asks.

'The exterior is somewhat better than the interior,' I say. 'And did you know that their building works are ongoing? I mean, you can't accept guests if you've got the builders in.'

'Oh,' Niall says. 'I thought they'd be done for the summer. We'll have to add a clause into our agreement that our future holiday swap hosts don't have any ongoing building works. Honestly, that would never have crossed my mind.'

'I've asked Lewis to have a word with the Lesters.'

'Good idea,' Niall says. 'Anyway, just wanted to wish you a lovely holiday, and if you need any advice on where to visit, just give me a call.' He hangs up, and I smile at his familiar mixture of charm and abruptness.

Niall and I met at the graduate training scheme run by my first employer, an American investment bank housed in a gleaming glass and metal building in the city of London. Whereas I was completely out of my depth, putting on the acting role of my life, pretending that I knew what I was doing and absolutely deserved to be there, Niall really was at ease. With his foppish hair, sparkling mind and charming manners, thanks to his expensive private education, Niall was everything I assumed I disliked in men. Seemingly entitled, chauvinist and so very pleased with himself, I tried my hardest to avoid him. Except after the first fortnight, I stumbled across him sitting on the steps of a fire exit at the back of

the building, puffing furiously on a cigarette, his head literally in his hands. To my astonishment, I realised he was
crying.

'Are you alright?' I asked, standing there awkwardly.

'Not really.' He sniffed. 'I'm completely out of my depth
here. I'm not clever enough, I don't understand a fraction of
what people do in this place, and I should have never been
accepted onto the scheme. I'm a fraud and my family will
never forgive me.'

Stunned, I sat down on the cold concrete step next
to him.

'You wouldn't have got onto the training scheme if they
didn't think you were up to working here.'

'You clearly don't know how the machinations of power
work,' he said, his shoulders slumping. And back then, Niall
was right. I had no clue how the old boys' network operated.

'Anyway, I've made up my mind. I'm quitting, relin-
quishing my graduate training place to someone more
deserving.' He stood up abruptly, grinding his cigarette butt
with the heel of his expensive-looking leather brogues,
wiping his eyes with a fine cotton handkerchief.

'Hold fire,' I said, grasping his arm. 'Just think it through.
Why don't we go for a drink after work and you can tell me
everything.'

He paused for a moment, as if to really look at me.
'Okay,' Niall said slowly.

'And you won't do anything rash until then?'

'I'll hold fire,' he promised.

That first drink cemented our friendship, however
unlikely a friendship it was. Despite the assured façade,
Niall was an unconfident kid, desperately trying to live up to
his father's lofty ambitions for his only son. Niall remained

at the bank for a year, just long enough for it to not look too flighty on his CV, and shortly afterwards transferred into selling property. His father never forgave him. Niall told me that Niall senior declared that 'Property is for the nouveaux riche. Not for people like you or me.' Niall was and still is a great mimic, and although I never met his father, I could envisage exactly how pompous the man was.

The two of us have remained friends for the past couple of decades, and while I settled down with Lewis, I was convinced that Niall would never marry. His relationships normally lasted about six months, and then he'd find a younger and prettier version. Always chestnut or blonde with long legs, normally rather vapid. Except then he met Danielle, and although she was physically his stereotype, she was intelligent, with a string of financial qualifications and a high-flying career. When they announced their engagement, Lewis and I were equally staggered and delighted. Despite his flirtatious manner and jet-setting lifestyle, I've always felt Niall would make a great dad.

Their Monaco wedding was something else. Danielle's parents seemed understated – her dad a retired taxi-driver and her mother a beautician – so Niall and Danielle must have paid for the wedding themselves. It was a weekend I will never forget. The wedding itself took place on the veranda of one of Monte Carlo's most iconic hotels. Rows of white chairs bedecked with shimmering silvery white bows and fountains of white and pink roses faced the azure Mediterranean sea. The ceremony took place under a vast arch of pale pink and white flowers cascading like a waterfall, conducted by a man wearing all white. Danielle wore a princess-style white taffeta gown covered in Swarovski crystals, with a train that must have been eight feet long, her hair swept up in a chignon with loose tendrils of curls and little crystals fixed to her long, dark eyelashes. She looked breathtaking. Danielle and Niall read each other love notes, and there wasn't a dry eye amongst their guests. It was honestly so beautiful, I struggled with the fact that the Niall I thought I knew so well was the emotional, gushing groom. His elderly mother attended, but it was perhaps just as well that his father had passed away a few years earlier. I doubt Niall would have wanted Niall senior at his wedding.

Later, there must have been four hundred guests seated at tables of ten in a circular domed room, where the ceiling opened up to the sky and stars twinkled above. I've never seen so many roses and flickering candles in small cut-glass bowls. There was an army of waiters dressed in starched white linen, who carried in silver-dome-covered plates laden with partridge and lobster, placing the plates on the table and lifting the domes off in perfectly synchronised moves. I didn't count how many tiers the wedding cake had, but it was at least eight. It towered upwards, and the bride and groom had to stand on chairs in order to cut it.

The evening was simply dazzling, helped of course by copious amounts of Cristal champagne and Chateauneuf du Pape. We danced into the early hours to a bespoke playlist put together by some leading DJ I hadn't heard of. I don't remember meeting the Lesters, but we may have done. I just recall having an amazing time, dancing with men I had never seen before and will never see again. And now, a year on from the most opulent wedding I have ever attended, Niall and Danielle still seem blissfully happy. So happy, I sometimes have little pangs of envy, wondering if Lewis and I were ever that much in love.

SAINTE-CHOUETTE, the local town, is just five kilometres away and it is utterly charming, with pale cream buildings all clustered together perched on the top of a hill, again recognisable from the photos on Susan's blog. I follow the signs to a large outdoor carpark on the edge of the town. It is busy, despite the early hour, full of locals dressed in linen carrying wicker baskets and canvas carrier bags, all hurrying in one direction. Not knowing where I am, I decide to follow the groups of mainly women, walking along cobbled-stone streets, weaving between ancient houses wedged in tightly, their tiled roofs hanging low, doors and window frames in creams and pastel blues. I pass small courtyards with Juliet balconies and wrought-iron lamps, window boxes overflowing with geraniums, pink roses climbing up doorways, dense lavender bushes in planters next to steep steps. In recognition of its name – the saint of owls – there are depictions of owls everywhere, on signs and on the front of buildings. And then the street opens up onto a square packed with stands piled high with fresh fruit and vegetables. I'm utterly delighted that it's market day. It's not a big market, perhaps thirty or so stands, fresh fruit and vegetables down one row, fresh fish and condiments on the next, and clothes on the final aisle. People are jostling to get to the fresh produce stands, where the vegetables are brightly coloured, and the odour from the fish stands brings a hint of the nearby ocean. I only hear French spoken and there's something comforting to know that this is an authentic market, not one created for tourists.

An hour later and I am laden down with shopping bags bulging with fruit and vegetables, a true smorgasbord of the local delicacies. I'm not ready to return back to the chateau yet so I wander along a narrow street, finding a coffee shop with a couple of empty tables outside. I've chosen well. There's a snippet of a stunning view, a peek between ancient buildings giving a vista onto the steep hills beyond the town. There's something familiar about this view and I wonder if it was featured on Susan's blog.

A server appears at my table, a woman probably mid-forties, with frizzy hair tied back in a low ponytail. She asks me something in rapid French, which I don't understand.

When I ask her to repeat herself, she grins and says, 'Ah, you are English! You like a tea?'

'No, thank you. A coffee, please,' I say.

She nods with approval. 'With pleasure.' She disappears inside. I glance at my phone and am a little dismayed to see I have no phone reception, which means I haven't got a clue where I am. I certainly wasn't paying attention when I was striding into town. When the lady arrives with my small cup of extremely strong coffee, I ask, 'Would you be able to point me in the direction of the main car park?'

'Of course. Where are you staying?'

'In a chateau... well, villa really, about five kilometres north. Next to Vineyard La Mette Charme.'

She claps her hands together. 'Mais non!' she exclaims. 'Are you the friends of Susan Lester?' She pronounces Lester as Lestaire. 'Did Susan tell you to come here? Did you read about my coffee shop on her website?'

I'm about to be honest and say no, it's a coincidence that I stumbled across it, but I check myself. It will be kinder to tell a white lie. 'Yes, she recommended your coffee.'

'That's very nice of her. You know them well?'

'No, not at all. We're doing a house swap and met them for the first time yesterday.' I don't bother to say that we met them at Niall's wedding because I have no recollection of it. 'They're having work done on their house.'

'Pff,' she exclaims, throwing her hands in the air. 'Susan is a...' She stops herself from saying any more and I wonder what was about to tumble from her lips. She leans forwards and speaks in a conspiratorial whisper. 'They're not very good at paying their bills, you know. This is their third set of builders. Unfortunately that doesn't do much for the good reputation of the English, you know. A shame because she's a nice lady.'

I squirm slightly because really this is nothing to do with me. 'Are you familiar with their house?'

'Bien sûr. My friends live in Vineyard La Mette Charme next door. We hear a lot about the Lesters. They take a long time to do the renovation works, but I mustn't gossip. I hope you have a lovely time here in Provence. Can I get you anything else?'

'No, thank you. Just the bill.'

I leave a healthy tip but as I'm making my way back to the parking lot, my arms weighed down by the shopping, I wonder about the Lesters. The lifestyle that Susan painted in her emails, the one she depicts in her photographs on her blog, seems to be a facade and that makes me feel very uneasy.

CHAPTER FOUR

PIERS

I don't sleep well, despite the comfortable bed and exquisite surroundings. Susan is up at the crack of dawn as she always is and when I eventually emerge into the sparkling white kitchen, she looks up and smiles.

'I need your help. Can't get the fancy coffee machine to work. Elodie didn't leave us an instruction manual.'

I peer at the contraption. It's large and full of levers and buttons, like one of those machines that baristas use in upmarket coffee shops. In France, we have an old-fashioned cafetière which does the job just fine. 'I'm not sure,' I say. 'I'm worried I might break it.'

Susan sighs melodramatically.

'I'll go out and get us coffee,' I suggest. 'We passed numerous coffee shops on our way here last night.'

'Thanks, love,' she says, distractedly looking at her phone.

I have two hours until my doctor's appointment and I know the time is going to drag, so this is a good excuse for me to do something. I shrug on a jacket and head out of the house. The first coffee shop I arrive at has tables and chairs outside, hanging baskets either side of the door and a canopy in pastel green and white stripes. The women queuing are all in athletic wear with expensive hairstyles, and the men have cashmere jumpers tied around their necks. The coffee menu is vast and I realise how very out of touch I've become living our modest lives in France. When it's my turn, the young woman turns to me with a smile.

'Just two standard coffees please.'

'Flat white, flat black, cappuccino? Dairy milk, full fat or single, oat or almond milk?'

'Um just a plain white coffee. Normal milk, please.'

'Two flat whites coming up.' I watch her pull out two china cups and saucers.

'It's to take away,' I add.

She sighs slightly. 'Two flat whites to go.' I'm not sure if she's saying this to herself or to the young man operating the machines behind her. 'Anything else?'

I stare at the vast array of pastries and point at three cinnamon buns, one each for Susan, Raf and me.

'That'll be £12.60 for the three buns and £10.20 for the coffees. Total £22.80, please. Apple Pay?'

I stare at her open mouthed. Over twenty pounds for two coffees and three buns! I try to calculate how much that would cost us in France. Perhaps five euros maximum. The woman behind me shuffles impatiently and I hurry to pull a couple of twenty-pound notes from my wallet. Our money will be gone in two days at this rate. I know London is expensive, but this is quite crazy.

'Sorry, but we don't take cash,' the barista says.

What? No cash. I've read all those articles suggesting the UK will be moving to a cashless society, but I didn't think it was already a thing. I fumble for a card and hand it over, wondering how these people manage to live in such an expensive city.

I carry the coffees back to the house carefully, eager not to spill a drop. On the doorstep to number 34, I ring the bell, realising I forgot to slip the second key into my pocket. After a long wait, I hear Muffin yapping and Susan opens the door.

'Your coffee, ma'am,' I say, deciding not to tell her how outrageously expensive they were.

Raf is sitting at the breakfast bar, slurping cereal, which he must have found in one of Elodie's cupboards.

'I'm taking Raf to the British Museum this morning,' Susan says, sipping her coffee.

'I don't want to go. It's boring,' Raf speaks with his mouth full. He doesn't say thank you when I hand him his cinnamon bun.

'I'm sure it won't be,' I say. 'It'll be great for your history course.'

'Can I spend the day with you, Dad?' Raf asks. My heart jolts slightly, because Raf never chooses to be with me. I'm just his annoying, geeky dad. And yet this morning is the only time he can't come with me. We haven't told Raf that I'm seeing a doctor as we don't want to worry him, so I say I've got a business meeting. He eyes me suspiciously because I never have business meetings. Not anymore. These days I run a garden maintenance business for wealthy British expats, but the business isn't doing well; a result of Brexit or the economic downturn, I'm not sure which. Or perhaps second-home owners prefer a well-connected local to be doing their gardens. I only manage a couple of bites of my cinnamon bun, nerves fluttering unpleasantly in my stomach, so I put it to one side and retreat upstairs.

Susan and I are both getting ready to go out. 'Where's the doctor's appointment?' she asks. 'You don't want me to come with you, do you?'

I would, but it's clear she's got better things to do this morning. 'Harley Street,' I reply.

Susan stops still. 'Harley Street? Bloody hell, Piers. Are you going private? I thought the whole purpose of coming back to London was to use the National Health Service.'

I'm a bit taken aback. Surely Susan knows that now we're living in France, I can't just pop back for an appointment with the NHS. It never even crossed my mind that I could do anything other than pay to see a doctor. 'Where's the money coming from?' she asks. 'It's all earmarked for the chateau.'

'I'll find a way,' I say curtly. A flash of anger passes through me. Surely my health is more important than her bloody window frames? It would never cross my mind to question her if she spent money on checking out health worries. Besides, if I really do have something seriously wrong, we'll need to take stock and decide whether to stay in France or return to the UK.

She must notice my stony face because she walks over to me and places a kiss on the side of my face. 'Sorry, love, I'm sure it'll all be fine. Call me when you're done.'

THE CLINIC IS PLUSH, looking more like a hotel than a hospital. I'm directed to take a lift to the third floor where I follow a thick-carpeted corridor to another small waiting room. After completing a form and waiting a nervy ten minutes or so, a nurse beckons me to follow her. Dr Gupta stands up when I enter his square consulting room with a

large window looking out onto Harley Street and expensive
art on the walls. He seems a warm man, with an over-enthusiastic handshake and kindly eyes. I explain my health
concerns, that we're living in France and I'm only in London
for a fortnight. He reassures me that all the tests can be done
today and he'll have the results of the blood tests and scans in
a couple of days. It's never pleasant having intimate check-
ups but he is swift and gentle. He sends me back to the
reception area where I'm directed to the basement for blood
tests and an ultrasound. I sit for about twenty minutes
flicking through pages of magazines, the words swimming in
front of my eyes, before another nurse comes to collect me
for the ultrasound. I'm directed into a small, dark room. The
sonographer doesn't have the kindly bedside manner of Dr
Gupta and I close my eyes, willing the awkwardness to be
over as quickly as possible. But he takes his time, pressing a
button with a click over and over again. By the time he's
finished, fear has gripped my throat and I feel like the walls
are closing in on me.

'All done,' he says, handing me paper to wipe myself dry.

'Is everything alright?' I ask.

'I'll be sending the results to Dr Gupta, who will talk you
through it.'

Of course. I need to be patient. This is a process. Except
no, it's my life in the balance and I need to know whether I
have some incurable disease. The not knowing is eating away
at me. After having several vials of blood taken, I'm directed
back to the reception desk. I make an appointment to return
to see Dr Gupta in three days' time to get the results. I wish
it could be instantaneous.

AS I WALK SLOWLY down Harley Street, shiny brass plates above most of the doors listing the highly qualified doctors that work within each property, I can't stop thinking about my father. He was too young when he died, in the very prime of his life, newly appointed managing director of the travel agency where he worked. He and Mum had plans to move to France when he retired and often I wonder if I'm living his dream because he couldn't. I think back to when we moved to France. I was so desperate to leave my corporate job, to start a new, gentler life, and Susan, who initially wouldn't countenance the idea, swiftly changed her mind when Niall sent us the details of the villa that is now known as Chateau Lester. To think that for the price of our four-bedroom new build on a modern estate on the outskirts of Crawley we could have a sprawling Provencal villa, it seemed too good to be true. Of course, the property needed lots of work doing to it, but we had such lofty dreams. Susan would start a blog and document our new life. We'd get sponsorship deals, like Dick and Angel in the television show *Escape To The Chateau*. I'd be a stay-at-home dad, raising our son in the sun, learning how to do stone masonry and plastering. Except nothing turned out the way we'd imagined. And if I'm dying, what then?

Will Raf suffer the same fate as me? Will he have to live my dreams because I'll be dead in a box? But I'm not sure what my dreams really are. When it became obvious that I didn't have the skills or aptitude for renovations, and that it would take me a lifetime to get everything done, we had to employ proper tradespeople. And when the money started to run out, I had to find something that I actually could do, a job that didn't require me to speak fluent French – another thing I'd failed to grasp. I never had a burning desire to do garden maintenance; I don't even want to become a garden designer, which is surely a more lofty ambition. Instead, an opportunity arose and I grabbed it. It pays a few of our bills although, worryingly, not nearly enough. Does lacking any great ambition make me a lesser person? Is it all right just to bumble along and be grateful for your wife and child and easy life? And how will Raf cope without me?

That question hurts most of all because sometimes I think Raf would barely notice if I wasn't around. We don't have the close relationship that we used to have before he hit the surly teenage years. Once upon a time, I could do no wrong. I was my son's hero, but the last couple of years, that has changed. He's rude and disdainful towards me and I get the feeling that I'm not good enough for him. I struggle to understand that, because it's Susan who is tough on our boy; she sets the rules and admonishes him, yet even though he mutters 'I hate you' under his breath, I wonder if her tough-ness makes him respect her. But where is the love in all of this? I hope that beneath everything, the love the three of us have for each other will supersede any superficial frustration. I suppose I want to feel confident that Raf will miss me, that I make a fundamental difference to his life, and that somehow a lack of a father will be as devastating to him as it was to me when Dad died. Yet at the same time that is such a deeply selfish thought. Of course I don't want my boy to suffer. I want him to have a loving, secure life, and I'm desperate to be there to support him as he launches himself into adulthood.

With these melancholy thoughts filling my head, I find myself in Cavendish Square and wander into John Lewis. The huge department store is bustling, full of colour, beau-tiful clothes and busy shoppers. After wandering around for a bit, I telephone Susan. Perhaps I can meet up with her and Raf at the British Museum; we can have a relaxing family outing all together. Except she doesn't pick up, and surprisingly for someone who is umbilically attached to his phone, neither does Raf.

I find myself outside the sprawling restaurant on the top floor and choose the cheapest drink on offer, a very British cup of tea. As I sit at a sticky-topped table, I stare at all the other patrons, smiles on their faces, seemingly worry free. But all I can do is think about my mortality and wonder how long I've got. Needing to distract myself, I flick through my phone and navigate to Susan's website. To my surprise, there's a new post.

'Hello, darlings!' she exclaims, as if she's some celebrity with millions of subscribers. 'Me and the fam are on holiday – doing a house swap! And look how lucky we got. Knightsbridge, no less! Harrods around the corner, a cinema room in the basement and a kitchen to die for.' I swallow hard. She's posted photographs of the stunning interiors of the Browns' Knightsbridge home. I sincerely hope that Elodie and Lewis don't mind.

CHAPTER FIVE

ELODIE

Back at Chateau Lester, Lewis has returned from his bike ride and is leaning against a pile of bricks, chatting to André. Perhaps it's unfair of me, but I feel a surge of annoyance. I don't want my husband schmoozing with the builders; I want them to finish their work and leave us alone. I carry the shopping bags into the kitchen and turn on the kitchen tap. The water spurts out in bursts, leaving sand and dirt in the white butler's sink. I leave the water to run while I unpack the fresh fruit and veg. Lewis saunters in as I'm making a salad. Cooking is not my forte; in fact, neither of us bother much. It's really not necessary when you have Harrods food hall as your local supermarket and are surrounded by excellent restaurants. And these days we tend to use Uber eats and get take-ins. Yes, that might sound indulgent but both of us work crazily long hours, earning very healthy incomes, and the last thing I feel like doing is cooking or housework when I get home in an evening. I know how incredibly lucky we are and I've promised myself I'll never take it for granted.

'I see you've hit the market,' Lewis says, opening the fridge and removing a beer.

'Have you spoken to Susan about getting the builders to leave?'

'Yes. She was deeply apologetic and said she'll speak to them about doing quiet work whilst we're here.'

'But I want them gone!' I exclaim. 'This is meant to be our holiday.'

'I know, love, but she explained what hell they've had finding and retaining good builders. It sounds like this renovation has been a complete nightmare. If she asks them to leave, she's worried they won't come back.'

'She should have warned us,' I say. I take out my annoyance by noisily and quickly chopping raw carrots.

'I've spoken to André and he's a good chap. Said he'll try not to disturb us.'

AFTER A SIMPLE SALAD with cheese and freshly baked baguettes, I'm feeling tired. The stress of the last few months is catching up to me and combined with the hot weather, I can barely keep my eyes open.

'I'll take off for another bike ride,' Lewis says, as he helps me put the crockery into a very old and manky-looking dishwasher. I wonder if it actually works.

'In the heat of the day?' I ask.

'I'm fit and I love this heat. Remember I did that marathon through the Sahara?'

I don't mention that was fifteen years ago.

'Take a bottle of water with you,' I say.

'Don't worry so much, Elodie. Why don't you relax by the pool? It's gorgeous out there.'

As Lewis disappears, I saunter upstairs and change into my swimming costume. I've put on a good stone over the past year and I'm the heaviest I've ever been. To be blunt, I don't feel great about myself. Lewis, bless him, hasn't said anything, or maybe he hasn't even noticed, although for someone who takes excessive pride in his own personal appearance, I doubt it. Perhaps I need to ask my husband to become my personal trainer. He'd love that, except I can't think of anything worse.

I fling a cotton kimono over my costume, find a couple of towels in the airing cupboard and head back outside, sunglasses perched on my head, carrying a paperback that I picked up at the airport. I can't see any of the workmen but I can hear them. They must be inside the strange brick tower that's adjacent to the house, or around the front of the building.

Lewis is right. It's beautiful by the pool. Thick bushes of lavender edge the patio and let off a heavenly scent. Behind them are tall pointy Cupressus and an ancient mulberry tree with a thick, gnarled trunk. I put up a large parasol and pull a sun lounger underneath it so I'm in the shade, and sink onto it. The air is completely still and the heat infuses my bones. I drop off to sleep. When I wake up, my feet feel like they're burning. No longer in the shade, they're turning red, so I remove the thin kimono and head for the pool, gingerly walking down the steps as the shock of the cold water makes me shiver. It really is beautiful, and now I feel bad about my negative thoughts towards Susan. If every day is like this for the next fortnight, I'll certainly be returning home feeling refreshed. I swim slowly up and down the pool, easy breast-strokes, my head out of the water, sunglasses protecting my eyes from the bright glare. It isn't until I'm getting out of the pool, hauling myself up using the metal steps, the water pouring off my body, that I glance upwards towards the house. There are four men lounging against the side of the building staring at me, two of them smoking, one drinking from a flask. André gives me a thumbs-up and I want to squirm with embarrassment. All the good of my swim seems to vanish in an instant as I hurry back to the sun lounger, whipping a beach towel around my torso, my cheeks aflame. I can't stay out, not with all their eyes on me. With gritted teeth, I walk back into the house. The men seem to disperse into thin air, but I know they're around here somewhere and it makes me feel awkward.

Back inside the house, I lock the bathroom door and take a quick shower, dressing in a loose, flowing sundress. It's a huge relief when I hear the starting up of engines and watch the builders' vehicles disappear down the drive. I glance at my watch. It's just 3.45 p.m. At least we'll have solitude towards the end of the day. I make myself a freshly squeezed orange juice and head out to the patio. Lewis has been gone for a couple of hours and I feel a bubble of nerves. I hope he's all right and hasn't got heat stroke.

I'm just settling down to read my novel at the table under the pergola, when I'm startled by a female voice.

'Hello! Anyone here?'

I jump up as a woman rounds the corner of the house. She's probably mid-forties, with thick, black hair held back with a tortoiseshell clip. She's wearing three-quarter length beige chinos and a white smock-like shirt, and carrying a wicker basket.

'Bonjour. You must be Elodie Brown.' She speaks excellent English but with a strong French accent. 'How are you?'

She proffers a hand, which I shake, and then she places the basket on the long table and removes a bottle of wine, a pot of olives and a bag of nuts. 'I've brought you a few goodies to welcome you to our special corner of Provence.'

'Thank you,' I say. 'That's very kind.'

And then she gently slaps her palm against her broad forehead. 'Silly me, I haven't even introduced myself. I'm Colette Moreau. My husband Didier and I own the vineyard just over there.' She waves her hand out towards her left. 'We were wondering if you would like to come for a wine tasting.'

'Goodness, yes, we'd love that. It's terribly kind of you,' I say. I can't imagine our London neighbours, most of whom we've never even met, extending such friendliness towards the Lesters. 'I suppose Susan has told you about us?'

'She just said you were doing a house swap, so I'm afraid I know nothing more. But you can't come to Provence without sampling our produce. Would 6 p.m. be convenient?'

'Today?' I ask with surprise.

'Yes. Didier and I are both available this evening.'

I don't particularly feel like going out and Lewis isn't even home yet, but it feels churlish not to accept, so I smile at her and thank her profusely.

'We are Vineyard La Mette Charme. You take the Lesters' drive and when you get to the main road, turn left. We're the first turning on the left, about two kilometres along. There's a large sign on the roadside. Right, I must hurry now as I have a few errands, but we look forward to seeing you and your husband a little later.'

'Thank you,' I say, and watch as Colette Moreau disappears in a whirlwind.

I TELEPHONE Lewis and to my surprise and relief, he answers. Normally, when he's taking a bike ride he has his phone turned off, using it only in the case of emergencies.

'Where are you?' I ask.

'Should be back in about an hour.'

'We've been invited to go wine tasting at the local vineyard for six p.m. Can you hurry back?'

'I certainly can,' he says and I can hear the smile in his voice. Lewis may prefer beer, but he's never one to decline a decent bottle of red.

Ten minutes before six and we're both ready, Lewis showered and dressed in a bright, flowery shirt and navy shorts. He's already looking tanned. I've fed Pushkin and given him a short walk up and down the drive. He's a well-behaved Labrador and when I tell him to go to his bed, which is a large flat mattress in the corner of the kitchen, he does as he's told. I hope Muffin is being as compliant with the Lesters, but somehow I doubt it.

'Got the car keys?' he asks as we walk downstairs.

'I assume you'll want me to drive so you can drink,' I say.

'You think wrongly, my lovely wife. Tonight you can indulge and I'll drive.' I wonder whether it's because he prefers driving or whether he's being genuinely considerate towards me.

VINEYARD LA METTE CHARME is a wide stone barn with a huge double-door entrance. It's a stunning, ancient building that has been renovated with care, so it's a surprise that the house set to the right is a simple concrete rendered square, basic and modern, rather out of keeping for the style of the local Provencal houses. As Lewis turns off the engine, Colette appears and welcomes us.

'Come in, come in.' She holds Lewis's hand for a fraction too long and it reminds me that many women find my husband very attractive. He's your typical alpha male and sometimes it surprises me that he chose me, because I'm no pushover. But Lewis respects me and our relationship is balanced in that regard.

We follow Colette into a large barn-style room, ancient wooden beams spanning the width of the space, the far wall covered in a vast wine rack, every space filled. There must be literally hundreds of bottles on that wall, the bottoms of the bottles facing outwards. In the centre of the room are wooden wine barrels used as high tables, with simple stools dotted around. The name of the vineyard is burned into the wood on the side of all the barrels. The opposite wall looks more like a shop, with wooden shelves and bottles of wine standing, small price labels attached to each. It's an impressive space.

A man strides through a doorway, his tanned face weathered and lined, his blue eyes sparkling, even from a distance.

'My husband doesn't speak such good English,' Colette says.

'Bonjour. Didier Moreau.' He shakes my hand first and then Lewis's. 'Welcome.'

'We've chosen ten of our most popular wines, but if there's anything you'd like to try in addition, then don't hesitate to ask,' Colette says. She beckons towards a wine barrel nearest to the shop area and I see that she's laid out a large silver platter piled with charcuterie and there are many empty glasses on the adjacent table.

'This is so kind of you,' I say, wondering whether we are required to pay for this tasting. Perhaps this is normal and they just expect us to buy some wine. That won't be a hardship. Didier speaks in rapid French, with Colette expertly translating as they explain the different grapes, the process of wine making.

'How long have you had this winery?' I ask, sipping a delicious rosé.

'This land has been in Didier's family since 1760. His family has been growing wines for so long, and that's what makes our vineyard very special. The skills of growing have been passed down from generation to generation. It is said that the grapevine was introduced to Provence by the Phocaeans around Marseille two thousand six hundred years ago, which makes Provence France's first wine region. Then the Romans cultivated the vines and spread them throughout France. During the Middle Ages, the abbeys produced the wine, and then some of France's most noble families started purchasing vineyards. Our land extends to thirty hectares, but just twenty hectares are of vines in production. This is a good size for us and we produce 130,000 bottles each year. Our wines are labelled AOP, which is Appellation d'Origin Protégée, which means we are subject to strict laws that control the origin of our grapes, the minimum alcohol levels, the methods of production that we use and how much we produce per hectare. This maintains the high quality.'

'Have you got children to take over the winery?' Lewis asks. It's a surprising question from my husband. Lewis has been diligently spitting out the wine into a silver spittoon while I have been drinking it, relishing the smooth, fragrant notes. I feel a little woozy already.

'We have a son and a daughter. Lucille is showing the most interest, but they are still young. Just eighteen and twenty.'

I hear footsteps behind me. 'In fact, Lucille is here now.' I turn around and see the girl we met yesterday, Rafael Lester's girlfriend.

'Hello. Lovely to see you again,' I say.

She just nods at me, her face impassive. Clearly the sentiment isn't shared. She speaks rapidly in French to her father and I can't follow what she's saying. She then turns towards us.

'Dad has to go and deal with some urgent business so I'm going to take over from him. I hope that's okay with you.' She is strangely expressionless.

'Of course,' I reply. 'Your parents were just saying that you were interested in possibly taking over the vineyard.'

'Maybe.' She shrugs her shoulders 'But first I'm going travelling and then perhaps I study viticulture at college. I would like to go to the University of California but it's very expensive.'

'We can never afford it,' Colette says, with a hint of rue. 'She needs to get a scholarship or marry a very wealthy American.'

'Tais-toi, Maman,' she mutters.

'Where do you intend to travel?' I ask.

'Asia, India. I will backpack and just decide from one day to the next. As Susan Lester tells me, you're only young once, so I will make the most of it.'

I note a brief scowl pass over Colette's face.

'And Rafael? Will he join you?'

'He's too young. We will see.'

My heart contracts slightly because I wonder whether Rafael is more infatuated with Lucille than she is with him.

'Have you known the Lesters a long time?' I ask.

'Since they arrived here.' Colette pours us both a glass of wine from a fresh bottle.

I've lost track. Is this the sixth or seventh glass I've had? I really must spit out the wine now otherwise I won't even be able to walk back to the car.

'This is a beautiful red from 2019, a very good year for us,' Lucille explains. 'It is quite bold and dry, with hints of blackberries, plums and an oaky note, even a hint of chocolate. It is my father's favourite.'

'You're really good at this,' Lewis says. 'I mean, in England, you'd only have just been allowed to drink wine at your age. And in the States it would be illegal.'

'We are brought up with wine here in France. It's like eating chocolate for us. We enjoy it. We don't drink to get drunk.'

Colette smiles wryly, but she looks proud of her daughter as she steps away towards the shop area.

'It must be nice for you having a friend living so close by,' I say, and then I feel stupid, realising I'm talking to her as if she's a young kid, when she seems much more mature than her years.

'It was hard when the Lesters arrived,' she murmurs.

'Why's that?' I ask.

'My parents wanted to buy the house and the land. It was originally in our family a long way back, but Susan and Piers offered too much money to the sellers. It was very disappointing for my parents.'

'But I assume you're all friends now,' I say, getting the hint that Lucille is talking out of turn.

'I guess,' she replies unconvincingly. It strikes me that the Lesters are not particularly well liked around here. I wonder whether that's a general feeling of xenophobia or whether they, in particular, are unpopular. I sympathise with the Moreaus – it must be galling to be out-priced by foreigners, but hopefully the Lesters have made an effort to integrate with the locals.

When we've finished the tastings, Lucille takes us on a short tour of the winery, but much of it passes me by as I concentrate on putting one step in front of the other, hanging on to Lewis's arm in order to stay upright. Despite nibbling on the charcuterie, my stomach is largely empty and I have definitely drunk too much. I'm annoyed with myself.

The machinery is huge and modern, massive metal vats, room after room of equipment, everything temperature and humidity controlled, and then finally a vast cellar filled with oak barrels. Even in my inebriated state I can appreciate how impressive this setup is. Fortunately Lewis is able to ask plenty of sensible questions. At the end of our tour, I want nothing more than to lie down and sleep, but Lewis is in buying mode. I remind him that we can't take the bottles home – or at least they would have to go in our suitcases, which would be highly precarious, but he promises we'll drink them over the next fortnight. Colette seems delighted when my husband extracts his American Express card and purchases several hundred euros' worth of wine.

'Well, that was a good first day,' Lewis says as we climb into the rental car. 'Well done you for organising the wine tasting.' I just smile, or at least attempt to smile, because it wasn't me who initiated it. By the time we're driving along the bumpy track towards Chateau Lester, the wine is becoming increasingly acidic in my stomach and I'm feeling more and more nauseous. And when, just a few minutes later, Lewis has switched off the engine, I'm feeling feverish, my body clammy, my stomach clenching painfully. I make it to the bathroom just in time.

Lewis finds me on the black-and-white-tiled bathroom floor, my forehead leaning against the none-too-clean ceramic pedestal of the sink, shivering uncontrollably despite the warmth of the evening.

'Bloody hell, Els,' he says, leaning down and levering me up by slotting his strong arms under my armpits.

'I'm not well,' I murmur.

'I can see that. Let's get you to bed. Too much booze?'

'Possibly, and combined with the sun... I don't know. I just feel really sick. The bathroom's so far away; can you find me a bucket or something?'

'You've probably got sunstroke.'

Lewis settles me back into our bed and after much huffing and puffing he returns with a large plastic bowl, a glass of water and some towels. I hope I'm not sick again.

'If you don't mind, Els, I'll sleep in the spare room. Can do without you chucking up all over me.'

I'm too tired to object. 'I'll leave the door open so if you need me, just shout.' Lewis picks up his phone, alarm clock and pillow and trots out of the room. With him being a heavy sleeper, I very much doubt he'll hear me through these thick stone walls.

I lie in bed shivering for a long time and I'm hit, not just by waves of stomach cramps, but intense loneliness. I'm really regretting coming to France, away from my friends, away from my work. I sound like a spoiled child, yet I realise how much I'm dependent upon my friends and colleagues to keep my mind occupied. How, despite the superficial cordiality, how distant Lewis and I have become. I don't blame him for not wanting to sleep with me as I'm throwing up, but I crave his reassuring presence next to me. As I eventually sink into a restless sleep, I wonder how long ago Lewis became not enough. And I wonder how is it possible to feel so very lonely in a marriage that from the outside appears utterly perfect.

CHAPTER SIX

PIERS

It's our second day in London and I'm feeling pleased with myself. I've got Raf a present that I just know he's going to be over the moon about. When he eventually emerges for breakfast, I sit down opposite him at the breakfast bar and slide the envelope towards him.

'What's this?' he asks. His hair is standing up on end and he's wearing the oversized grey T-shirt that he sleeps in.

'Open it.'

Raf undoes the envelope and slides out the tickets. Susan was unimpressed when I'd told her I intended to take Raf to his first football match at Stamford Bridge. It's a big deal attending premier league games, and when I discovered that Chelsea was playing Manchester United whilst we were in London, well, I couldn't miss the opportunity. The cost of the tickets is outrageous, well beyond what we can comfortably afford, but Raf has missed out on things growing up in rural France. It's a rite of passage for a dad to take his son to watch the footie, something I did with my dad but haven't yet been able to do with Raf. The fact that Raf supports Man U whilst I support Chelsea makes it even more opportune.

I expect Raf to be excited, or at least show an element of appreciation. I get nothing. He puts the tickets back into the envelope and slides it across the marble counter towards me.

'What? You don't want to go?' I ask, pulling my head back in bemusement.

'Yeah, it's not that. It's just that Hugo has asked me to watch the match in his cinema room. It's in the basement of their house and the screen is the whole width of the wall. The chairs are like beds. It's seriously cool, way better than the cinema room in this house.'

'But these are tickets to see the game live! There's nothing that beats a live match.'

Raf shrugs and I feel a surge of annoyance. I can't even say our boy is spoiled because he's really not.

'How about you go with Hugo? He can have my ticket and the two of you can go together.'

Susan glances up and throws me a look as if she's about to contradict me but I get in there first. 'I'll take you to the game, see you through the gates, and I'll be there waiting for you when it's over. You and Hugo will have a great time.'

'I'll have to ask Hugo,' Raf says. I'm tempted to tell him how much the tickets cost, how much I was looking forward to going with him, but I don't. What's the point in having an argument, making him feel guilty? It's not going to achieve anything. Our relocation to rural France wasn't Raf's choice; we were the ones who forced him to up and leave his old friends, to start again in a country where he knew no one and didn't speak the language. And we've all had to make compromises.

'Do you want to call Hugo or drop by his house?' I ask.

'I'll call,' Raf says, picking up his mobile phone. 'Hi, Hugo. My dad has got tickets to see the game tonight at Stamford Bridge. Do you want to come with me?' I can't make out Hugo's response.

After a moment, Raf turns to me and asks, 'What seats have you got?'

'Um, I'm not sure,' I say. 'But they're high up in the stands. I mean, I only got them last week so there wasn't a lot of choice.'

'Did you hear that?' Raf speaks into the phone. There's a beat of silence. 'Yeah, I agree. Okay. See you later.'

I look at Raf expectantly. 'Hugo only goes to matches when he's in his dad's box. We'll watch in his cinema room.' He must note my fallen face. 'You could go with Mum, though,' he suggests.

Susan scoffs. 'Good heavens! Don't you know me at all? I'd rather be run over by a bus, thank you very much.'

I'm disappointed, of course I am, but I put myself in Raf's shoes. If I had just made a new, rich friend, I'd rather hang with him than with my dad. And it's not like Raf knows anyone like Hugo in France. I'm also conscious of not imposing my expectations on our son. My dad was old-school and he expected me to become his mini-me. Even years after his death, I have to stop checking myself, wondering if he'd approve of what I'm saying, what I'm doing. I don't want that for Raf. He's growing into his own person. I want him to be free, not weighed down by his parents' fears and expectations.

'Don't worry, I'll sell the tickets,' I say.

'Will you get the full amount back?' Susan asks.

'I'll do my best.' I go online and have a look at the various ticket resale websites. Most of them only offer a percentage of what I paid for them, so I decide to try Facebook Market-place. Within ten minutes of placing the listing, I've had two offers to purchase at the price I paid for them, both people local to where we are here in Knightsbridge. I guess that's the bonus of living in such a built-up, well-heeled location. Feeling pleased with myself, I agree to meet someone called Will in an hour's time at Starbucks on the other side of the road to Harrods.

'What are you doing this morning?' Susan asks, 'other than flogging the tickets?' She's dressed in smart linen trousers and a white cotton sweater, her large handbag open on the countertop.

'I'd hoped we could spend some time together, go and visit the Saatchi Gallery perhaps. There's a wonderful botanical exhibition where my favourite photographer, Juli-ette Scott, is exhibiting. Perhaps we could take a river trip afterwards.'

'Oh, sorry,' Susan says. 'I've got other plans. Later this afternoon perhaps?' She turns to Raf, who is surprisingly rinsing his cereal bowl in the sink. 'And you, love?'

'I'm heading over to Hugo's. I'll spend the day with him.'

'Right,' I say, feeling superfluous. I should have pinned Susan down before we left home, created an itinerary for all of us, rather than deciding what we're doing on the hoof. I know my wife – she'll be busy catching up with old friends, visiting the shops, even if it's only to window-shop.

As I leave the house, I wonder whether I'm being naive. What if this Will gives me counterfeit money? How will I actually know? And then I stop myself from catastrophising. I know what's really going on – I'm terrified about getting the results from the doctor. At 10.30 a.m. I walk briskly onto the Brompton Road, past early shoppers – who really aren't that early at all; it's just that the shops don't open here until 10 a.m. – and realising I've got twenty minutes to spare, slip into Harrods. There is something so rarified about the interior of this shop, and it's not just the crazily high price tags. It must be the lighting and the way the air is ever so slightly scented, or perhaps it's just how the products are merchandised with so much space around every bag or perfume bottle, as if each item is a masterpiece deserving its own display cabinet. Or maybe it's the shop staff who seem to me as if they're acting more like curators of the world's finest things rather than shop assistants. I've never bought anything here and I doubt I ever will. Not on my paltry income. Sometimes I regret leaving my well-paid job in sales and moving to France for the simple life, which hasn't turned out to be so simple after all. After a few minutes of aimless wandering, and inevitably getting lost, I emerge, blinking hard, onto Knightsbridge and hurry to Starbucks. I must look like the hickish man I've morphed into because a young, dark-haired swarthy man in startling white trainers, wearing a gold necklace, approaches me immediately.

'Are you Piers?' he asks in a deep baritone voice.

'Yes,' I say, fingering the envelope in my pocket.

'Let's move over there.' The man tilts his head to the far corner of the coffee shop, near the sign to the toilets.

'You got the tickets?' he asks.

'Yes. And you've got the money?'

He shoves his hand into the rear pocket of his designer jeans and removes a leather wallet. He must have hundreds of pounds in cash and I try not to stare. He peels away a couple of notes and hands them to me.'

'Keep the change,' he says. 'I'm in a hurry.'

'Right,' I say, holding the notes up in the air, but goodness knows what I'm actually looking for.

'They're the real thing.' He's laughing at me and I try not to feel like an idiot. 'I'm hardly going to scam you out of a couple hundred quid, mate.'

'Sure, sorry,' I say, hastily handing him the envelope. He takes the tickets out, has a quick look at them and shoves them back in the envelope. 'Are you selling them on?' I ask.

He laughs even louder now. 'I'm not a tout!' he snorts. 'They're for my nephew. I forgot to get him a birthday present and my sister will murder me if I don't produce something he actually wants. You're really cynical, mate.'

'Sorry,' I say, wishing I didn't have a propensity to think the worst of people.

'Thanks for saving the day, though.' He pats my back before hurrying away.

As both Susan and Raf are out, I decide to pootle back along Knightsbridge and visit the Victoria and Albert Museum. I lose myself wandering from exhibition to exhibition, moving through the history of artefacts, staring with awe at paintings. Eventually, I find myself in the museum cafe, housed in the most stunning room, The Gamble Room, with ceilings and walls covered in intricate mosaics of ceramic, enamel and gold. It's almost dazzling as I sip my over-priced coffee. I'd like to visit the Science Museum on the other side of Exhibition Road, but deciding that perhaps Raf might be up for joining me, I postpone that for another day. Slowly, I wander back towards the Browns' house.

The house is quiet and for a moment I wonder if I'm alone. I head upstairs and notice that the door is ajar to the master bedroom.

'Susan?' I ask as I step inside. I gasp. My wife spins

around, a startled expression on her face. She's wearing a full-length mauve silken dress that's a little too large for her and a garment I certainly don't recognise. 'What are you doing?' I stare at the pile of clothes on top of the king-sized bed and the high-heeled shoes scattered across the thick-pile carpet. It takes a moment for me to decipher what I'm seeing and then I blurt out, 'Bloody hell, Susan.'

'Yes, I'm trying on Elodie's clothes.' She holds my gaze defiantly. 'I've never seen such a closet full of designer dresses and the shoes. They're stunning, aren't they?' She holds up a pair of black patent shoes with gold stiletto heels.

'But you can't do that!' I exclaim. 'It's a gross invasion of Elodie Brown's privacy. What if they've got hidden cameras or something in here?'

'Don't be silly. Of course they don't. It's just I haven't seen such lovely things for years and I wondered if I could still carry off clothes like this. It's not like I'm going to post photos of me wearing her designer gear on the blog.' She must notice my stoney, horrified stare, because she slumps down onto the side of the bed and puts her head in her hands. 'I know I shouldn't be doing this but I couldn't help myself.'

I grit my teeth to prevent myself from saying, *of course you could help yourself*. I'm appalled and shocked. I didn't know Susan had it in her to do something like this. Trying on another woman's clothes. And then I wonder if I'm overreacting. No one will ever know.

She stands up suddenly and turns her back to me. 'Unzip it, will you. None of this stuff fits me anyway. Elodie is at least one dress size bigger than me and her feet are smaller. I'll put it all back the way I found it.' She sounds like she's close to tears and I wonder what has prompted this.

Living in luxury, I suppose, far beyond anything we will ever be able to afford. And then I feel a pang of guilt. Of course it's hard for Susan. I couldn't care less about designer clothes or fancy kitchen appliances, but I know she does. I try to ignore the feeling that I've let her down. When we got engaged, I could only afford the tiniest diamond and I promised her that I would replace it with a bigger gem when I got rich. Except I never did. Instead, we've sunk every penny we have on the chateau and unless I magically win the lottery, I doubt I'll ever be in a position to fulfil that pledge. I thought that the beautiful French house was what she wanted, that it would be enough. But perhaps I'm wrong.

I unzip the dress as she requested and put my arms around Susan's shoulders, hugging her from behind, except she feels tense and then wriggles out of my grasp.

'Do you want to talk?' I ask.

'No, Piers. I don't. Go downstairs and leave me, please.'

I stand there hopelessly for a moment, and then do as my wife has asked.

WE DON'T GO OUT for the rest of the day. Somehow the hours pass with me watching the game on the giant television in the basement and Susan on the phone to friends. It's late when the doorbell rings and Raf is standing there, swaying as he props himself up by leaning against the doorframe. He's drunk. Completely out of it, sniggering to himself as he weaves into the hall. Fortunately Susan is in our ensuite bathroom, soaking in some designer bubble bath, and she won't have heard Raf's homecoming.

I support him up the stairs and into his bedroom.

'I'll get you a glass of water.'

'You gonna tell Mum?' he slurs.

'No. But only if you don't throw up and make a mess. And tomorrow you're going to be well behaved and do what we want to do. Got it? Otherwise you won't be allowed to spend any more time with Hugo. This isn't acceptable behaviour, Raf, and besides, you're under age. No more booze, okay?'

'Oaky, Papa,' he says and bursts into laughter. At least my son is a happy drunk, I suppose.

THE NEXT MORNING, I awake late and, to my surprise, discover that Susan has already gone out. She's left me a note on the kitchen counter saying, 'Will be back for lunch. Can you get something in?' This annoys me. Aren't we meant to be on holiday together, as a family? It's like we're ships in the night, all doing our own thing. Frankly, we might as well be at home. I let Raf sleep, as I'm sure he'll be nursing a dreadful hangover. Better that he's allowed to sleep it off. And then the doorbell rings. I hurry towards it, except the door is already opening. A woman steps inside. She must be mid-fifties, with a worn face, neat clothes.

'Oh,' she says. 'I didn't want to disturb you. I'm Teresa, the housekeeper. I'm here for a quick tidy up but I'll come back later. You're on holiday, and the last thing you need is me buzzing around you. Are you planning on going out at all?'

'Um, yes,' I say awkwardly. I'd forgotten that the Lesters mentioned that Teresa would clean a couple of times during the week. 'We will be out this afternoon.'

'In which case I'll come back then. You have a lovely day.'

And she's gone, before I can tell her that really it's fine for her to clean around us.

With a few hours to spare and nowhere to go, I wander down to the basement to Lewis's home gym. It's packed full of equipment, most of which I haven't got a clue how to work or what it's meant to do. I switch on a running machine that has an integrated television screen where I can select any place in the world I wish to run. I choose the Grand Canyon, somewhere I'd love to visit but I doubt I ever will. Money is much too tight for a long-distance holiday. The default settings, which I assume are Lewis's, are for someone with a degree of fitness I can only dream of, so I adjust them and set off. To my surprise, I lose myself and run for close on an hour. At the end I'm exhausted, but the endorphins make me feel so much better. En route to the bathroom, I gently open Raf's door and peek inside. It's gone 11 a.m. but he's still fast asleep.

I take Muffin for a short walk around the block, and while she's a sweet dog, I miss our Pushkin. An hour or so later, the front door opens. I step into the hallway and see my wife, literally laden down with shopping bags, several with the recognisable olive green and gold from Harrods and a couple from Harvey Nichols.

I can't help myself. 'What have you got in the bags?'

'I've been shopping.'

'So I can see. For what?'

'Clothes.'

'Clothes!' I exclaim. 'Where's the money coming from?'

'I put them on the credit card.' She heads up the stairs, the bags over her shoulder. I follow her into our bedroom.

'Susan, are you out of your head? As you said yourself, we can barely afford for me to see a private doctor, let alone for you to buy clothes at two of the most expensive shops in the country! Our credit card is already maxed out with builders' merchant materials for the chateau.'

'You're shouting at me, Piers,' she says. She shrinks in on herself slightly.

'I'm sorry, but what were you thinking?'

'I was thinking that for a short while it might be lovely to not worry about money, to live a life like the Browns'. To feel good about myself, because I never feel good about myself, Piers. I hate the way we have to scrimp and save, how I'm wearing clothes that are a decade old, how we're everyone's poor relation.' Her voice catches and she turns away from me, but not before I see the tears in her eyes.

'We can leave France, come back to the UK where I can return to sales and earn a proper salary. We'll definitely sell the chateau for more than we bought it for.' I step towards my wife, but she edges backwards.

'But you don't understand!' Susan's voice has risen several pitches. 'I love the chateau. I want to stay in France. It's home now. It's just you–' She stops talking suddenly, as if she's catching herself.

There's a horrible pause which eventually I break. 'It's me. It's because I'm not earning enough. Is that what you're trying to say? And what about you and your blog and the six-figure income that you were meant to bring in? The blog that has earned all of five euros from Google ads. You can't put it all on my shoulders.'

She collapses onto the bed, her shoulders shuddering. I walk over to her. 'I'm sorry, love. I'm sorry it hasn't worked out the way we wanted.' I put my arms around her but she pushes me away.

'Just leave me alone, Piers.' She sniffs.

I hesitate. My wife is a mess and I feel like I should stay and comfort her, try and work out a plan so that we can live comfortably within our means.

'Just go!' she yells at me.

I leave the room.

And walk straight into Raf.

'What's going on?' he asks, narrowing his eyes at me.

'Mum is...' I'm not sure what to say.

'It's you, isn't it?' He glowers at me, before pushing past. 'You made her cry, didn't you? It's because you're pathetic.' He slams his bedroom door closed. I stand in the corridor of this beautiful house staring at the closed doors. My wife and my son loathe me and I've no idea what to do about it. And for a fleeting moment, I wonder if they're right. Whether everything really is my fault.

CHAPTER SEVEN

ELODIE

I wake up feeling remarkably better. It's early, so I swing the window open and breathe in the cool air. The sun is rising and the sky is a pure aquamarine. Pulling on some chinos and a T-shirt, I wander downstairs and am greeted by Pushkin who is so happy to see me. I wonder if his tail will wag off. I miss my little Muffin, but this boy is a good substitute. After feeding him and making myself a cup of tea, I carry it outside and sit, enjoying the solitude and the quiet early morning.

Except not for long. About ten minutes later, there's the crunching of tyres on the gravel drive, the slamming of car doors and the chatter of the workmen. And a few moments later, the drilling starts.

We cannot stay here. What sort of a holiday is this, with all the noise and the mess from the builders? So much for André promising not to make any noise. I'm just about to pick up the phone to call Susan when Lewis appears, his hair still mussed up from sleep.

'If the builders don't scarper by lunchtime, we're moving

to a hotel,' I say, thumping my empty mug on the table. 'I'm calling Susan.'

'It's 7 a.m. in the UK; a bit early to call when they're on holiday, don't you think?' Lewis says, scratching his head. 'And we do need to think about this from the Lesters' perspective. I mean, we don't want to be rude about this place. It's a bit run down on the inside but the setting is beautiful.'

'Fair enough,' I concede. 'I won't be rude, but we're here on holiday. This can't go on. Either the builders go or we're moving to a hotel.'

'Good luck with that, in the height of summer,' Lewis murmurs before turning back to go into the house. I find it interesting how my husband, who appears so very much the macho man, for whom combative boxing was his early life, absolutely loathes confrontation. Lewis has a tendency to bury his head in the sand, to walk away from difficult situations, or to palm them off to me to deal with.

I ignore him, take out my phone and start searching online for boutique hotels near Sainte-Chouette. Frustratingly, Lewis is correct. Everything half decent is already booked. I start looking further afield but either the hotels are ridiculously expensive (which of course we could afford but frankly I think it's a waste of money) or they have lousy reviews. Maybe we'll have to bite the bullet and go for somewhere expensive. In the meantime, I'm going to talk to André myself. Perhaps he didn't understand Lewis's request for silence. Perhaps Susan hasn't spoken to André yet. I sigh. As normal, it's up to me to actually get things done. Sometimes I wonder how or even why Lewis and I are still married. I try to imagine my life without him, but weirdly, I can't. Despite everything, I love my husband.

André is up a long ladder but when he sees me, he smiles broadly and scoots down it.

'What a beautiful day, non? As beautiful as you are, almost.'

I restrain myself from spurting out some sarcastic retort. 'Lewis told me that you would be silent for the rest of our stay. Is that possible?'

'Oui, oui. But this morning we need to cut the stone and then from this afternoon we will be as quiet as possible. Like little mice. You won't even notice we're here.'

'For the next ten days?'

'Don't worry, you will have a tranquil holiday. I promise.' He places his hand on his heart and bows his head theatrically. I can't tell if he's being genuine or somewhat contemptuous. I send Susan a message, rewording it several times so it doesn't sound too rude.

> Hi, Susan. We're finding it a little hard to relax with your builders being here. Is there any possibility they could take a break or at least do silent work during our holiday? I hope you're having a great time in London. Best, Elodie.

AFTER TAKING a long walk with Pushkin, I return to find Lewis doing laps in the swimming pool. He hauls himself out.

'I've booked us a table at one of the best restaurants in the area,' he says. 'Thought that might cheer you up.'

I'm surprised, as Lewis isn't known for his proactiveness, normally leaving our social life to me to organise. But this is exactly what I'd hoped for during this holiday and I'm thrilled. I check my phone periodically for a reply from Susan, and although I can see she has read the message, she hasn't responded to me. I hope this isn't going to become awkward. The builders are still here, but at least the noise levels have reduced. And then, when we're eating a salad for lunch, I hear the revving of engines and, to my delight, all the vehicles leave. Susan must have spoken to them. I'm so relieved and spend a relaxing few hours reading by the pool.

I'm not a frequent user of social media but I am aware that as a business, Hutchinson Brown needs to up its game. So many of the leading estate agents are using Instagram and Facebook to promote their properties with massive success. We need to follow suit. With my sunglasses on, I flick through various realtor accounts and then, to my surprise, I see that Instagram is suggesting I follow Susan Lester. I click on her account and for a moment I can't make sense of the pictures that I'm seeing. It's the familiarity of them that is so confusing. And then it's as if a switch has flicked in my head and a fury races through my veins. Susan Lester has posted photographs of my house with twee little captions such as, *Knightsbridge nights in with the fam,* and *Luxury London living my style,* and *Thanks to EB for this awesome house swap. #Loveurlooks.* Even though, rationally, no one will be able to link these photos to me (I mean, there must be plenty of people with the initials EB), it feels like a gross invasion of my privacy. My home is my sanctuary, the place I retreat to from the outside world, where I feel safe and secure. And now it's been exposed by a stranger.

I'm not prone to angry outbursts or impulsive reactions, so I know that I need to take a breath and take time to decide how to react. I'll discuss it with Lewis, see if he thinks my fury is irrational.

LE JEUNE HIBOU – which I discover means the little owlet – is a delightful restaurant perched on the top of a hill with breathtaking views. The tables are all outside, underneath fancy umbrellas, a stone-built barbecue to our left and servers that are overly attentive. We choose the tasting menu and the food is utterly delicious. I keep the wine to the minimum, not wanting a repeat of last night. Lewis and I talk about our respective businesses and plans for the rest of the holiday, and surprisingly the conversation flows easily. So often I've found that Lewis only half-listens to me and consequently hears what he thinks I've said rather than what I've really said, so to have his full attention takes me back to the early romantic days of our marriage.

'I've missed you,' I say, reaching across the table for his hand.

He throws me an uncomprehending glance. 'Haven't gone anywhere.'

'I don't know. I just feel we've drifted apart of late, haven't made time for each other.'

A strange look passes over his face and he stares off into the distance. 'Well, let's make up for it now,' he replies, squeezing my hand in return.

I then tell him about the photos that Susan has posted on social media, the pictures of our house and our belongings. His initial reaction is one of confusion.

'Why does it upset you so much?' he asks, a deep frown on his forehead, as if he genuinely doesn't understand. 'She hasn't mentioned our names or our address, and isn't blogging what she does to earn money?'

'But she didn't ask permission,' I say. 'And it's our house. It feels like she's inviting the world in to view our home.'

'Right,' Lewis says eventually. And I'm annoyed that he

doesn't sense the intrusion of our privacy the way that I do. 'If it upsets you that much, then we can ask her to take the posts down, can't we?'

Later that evening we make love. I can't remember the last time we did that, and although there is nothing particularly romantic about it, at least I feel that Lewis and I are taking strides to rebuild our connection.

SOME TIME LATER, I awake and need to go to the bathroom. I grab my travel clock with its inbuilt torch and make my way down the corridor, the moon throwing shadows through the window in the hall. Suddenly, there's the sound of breaking glass. My first thought is, has Lewis accidentally smashed his water glass, but then Pushkin starts barking. There's another crash and my heart leaps into my mouth. Without thinking, I run back along the corridor, careening into the bedroom. Lewis is still fast asleep.

'Wake up!' I say, shaking his shoulders. 'Wake up!'

'What is it?' he asks groggily.

'Didn't you hear?' I whisper. 'The sound of breaking glass, and the dog is barking. I think someone is inside.' My stomach clenches.

Lewis swings his legs out of bed and pulls on some clothes, but there's silence now. 'I'm going to investigate. Stay here and lock the door.'

'Please be careful, Lewis. Call the police.'

But he's gone, closing the door behind him, and I don't even know if he's taken his phone with him. I switch a bedside light on and creep to the door. So much for locking it. There's no key or keyhole. I grab a chair and wedge it up underneath the door handle.

The dog has stopped barking now and Lewis must have switched some lights on because as I stand at the window and look outside, a pale glow spills onto the patio below. My heart is hammering, my breathing shallow. I realise I don't even know what the number is to call the French police, and my hands are shaking too much to navigate my phone. I strain my ears to listen out but hear nothing.

A couple of minutes later, Lewis knocks on the door and says, 'No one here, Elodie. Open up, love.'

I hurry to remove the chair.

'They must have gone,' he says, as he strides into the bedroom. 'Someone has broken a window in the library. Looks like they climbed up the scaffolding but you and the dog probably scared them away. I've had a good look around and can't see anyone.' Pushkin trots into our bedroom and comes up to me, nuzzling his wet nose against my bare leg. I stroke his soft fur and feel grateful that he's here to protect us.

'Should we call the police?' I ask.

'If it makes you feel safer.'

'What's the emergency number?'

Lewis shrugs his shoulders, so with quivering fingers I search on my phone and discover that 112 is the emergency number across Europe.

After a lengthy conversation, the operator, who fortunately speaks fluent English, tells me that he will pass on the details of the incident to the local police but as the imminent danger has passed, we might not hear from them until the morning. There's nothing we can do about the broken pane of glass in the library so we, along with Pushkin, shut ourselves into the bedroom, pulling furniture across the doorway. Not surprisingly, sleep is elusive.

THE NEXT MORNING, I'm awoken from a confused nightmare to the sound of a car horn. Lewis's side of the bed is empty, so I pull on a kaftan and hurry downstairs. The front door is wide open and a gendarme in full uniform is gesticulating at Lewis in the hallway. I run down the stairs to join them.

Between Lewis's few words of French and the gendarme's broken English, we manage to decipher that this is not the first time there has been a break-in at the chateau.

'One month ago, someone entered the property and this was reported by the owner, a mister Piers Lester. Nothing was taken. Was anything taken this time?'

'I'm not sure,' I say. 'We will have to check with the Lesters.'

'I think the dog and I scared them away,' Lewis adds. 'I couldn't see anyone or anything.'

We lead the gendarme into the library and show him the broken window, but he barely glances at it, let alone dusts for fingerprints or looks outside for footprints. 'Pff. Probably just children,' the gendarme says. 'They see the scaffolding and think it fun to climb it.'

As he leaves the property – without any investigation – it doesn't make me feel reassured. I'm also annoyed with the Lesters. If they had a break-in less than a month ago, why didn't they mention it to us? Did they think it might put us off, stop us from wanting to do the house swap? If so, they were right. I don't feel safe here now. As I return upstairs to get ready for the day, there are uneasy prickles at the back of my neck and a sensation that all is not what it seems.

CHAPTER EIGHT

PIERS

I can tell the moment I answer the phone that Lewis isn't happy.

'There was a break-in at yours last night. Glass broken in the window to the library.'

'Are you alright?' I ask. My heart sinks. *Not again.*

'Yeah. Fine. Didn't look like they took anything but obviously I can't be sure. The dog barked and Elodie woke up so we probably scared them away. The thing is, the gendarme said it's the second time this has happened in a month. Why didn't you tell us?'

'I'm sorry,' I bluster. 'We just assumed it was our last lot of builders. We had a bit of a falling out with them and some words were said. We assumed it was done out of revenge. The police told us not to worry.'

'And this time they said it was probably kids. What's the truth, Piers?'

'I don't know and I'm really sorry. Do you want to leave?' My heart sinks at the prospect, but perhaps it would be for the best all around if we return to our respective homes. I can stay in London for a couple of days for my appointment with Dr Gupta, and Susan and Raf can return home.

'No need for that,' Lewis replies. 'We're enjoying the sunshine. But I trust you'll keep the builders away, because my wife isn't keen on having them around. Not very relaxing with all the banging.' He pauses and then adds as an afterthought. 'Oh, and the wife isn't happy that Susan posted photos of our house on social media without asking permission. Best you get her to take them down. Okay?'

What on earth did Susan do that for? I know she's still hopeful that she can boost her numbers and monetise her social media efforts, but even I can see that was out of order. I sigh. 'Susan has spoken to André so hopefully you won't be disturbed any more. I'm sorry about that. And for the break-in. And I'll get her to take down the posts. Again, my apologies.'

'Alright, mate,' Lewis says gruffly, and hangs up on me. I'm not sure I'd be so sanguine if the shoe was on the other foot.

SUSAN HAS BEEN inside the bedroom for the past hour, so I go upstairs and knock on the door, gently opening it, and then wonder why I'm knocking on my own door. She's lying on the bed, texting on her phone, which she immediately places face downwards as if she's hiding something from me. I note that all the clothes have been removed from the bed and there are several bulging shopping bags standing next to the door.

'I'm going to take them back,' she says, without looking at me. 'It was stupid. Of course it was.'

'Oh darling,' I say, as I stride towards the bed ready to

give her a conciliatory hug. But she holds her hand out as if she doesn't want me anywhere near her.

'Please, Piers. Just leave me.'

I hesitate for a moment. 'I'll take the shopping back, so you don't have to. Are all the receipts in the bags?'

She nods and then mutters something under her breath, which may be a thank you.

'Will you keep an eye on Raf?' I ask as I pick up the bags.

'He's not a child, Piers.'

There's a sharp retort on the end of my tongue, but I swallow it. Susan is no doubt feeling humiliated, an idiot for buying clothes well beyond our means, but there's no point in escalating things into another argument. 'I'll see you later. Oh,' I add as if it's an afterthought. 'The Browns have asked if you'll remove your posts showing the photographs of their home. They're a bit paranoid about privacy and all that.' I know I'm pandering to my wife, tiptoeing in an effort not to start a fight, and I hate myself for that. I'm not a weak man, except around my wife I often feel that I am. Sometimes I feel an overwhelming resentment towards Susan for the tiny little cuts she makes in our relationship. The eye rolls, the sarcastic retorts and the sighs laden with disdain. Yet I still love my wife, the way her smile lightens my heart, her passion for Provence and her determination to restore the chateau to its former glory despite the sacrifices we're having to make.

I STRIDE QUICKLY TOWARDS HARRODS, weaving between loitering tourists, entering the ground floor and then promptly getting completely lost. The store is enormous, apparently one of the largest in Europe. I ask an assistant where I need to go to return clothes and she directs me to the escalator in the Egyptian Room where I'm bemused by the massive gold pharaoh and the ornate columns. On the third floor, I follow signs to Customer Services.

'I need to return everything,' I say, placing the two large heavy cardboard bags in olive green with the distinctive gold Harrods insignia on the counter top.

'Any particular reason why?' The server has a strong accent that I can't place.

I can hardly tell her the truth. 'I bought the items for my wife but they don't fit.'

She takes out item after item: dresses, silk blouses, a pair of shoes and a silken scarf. I pick up the scarf and look for the price tag. £75. That's so expensive for a scarf, but I put it to one side. 'I'll keep this,' I say.

'Of course, sir. Is it a gift? Would you like me to wrap it?'

'Yes, please.' At least Susan can keep one item, something beautiful and extravagant that hopefully will bring her pleasure.

I'm in Harvey Nicholls getting refunds for the items Susan bought there when my phone rings.

'Mr Lester?'

'Yes.'

'Hello. This is Dr Gupta's secretary. He has a cancellation this afternoon and was wondering if you might be free to attend his surgery.'

My heart stops for a moment. 'Have you got all the results?'

'Yes, we do.'

It must mean bad news. Why else would the doctor ask me to come and see him sooner than the diarised appointment? My knees feel weak and I have to remember to breathe. I try to remind myself that medicine has improved dramatically since my father died so prematurely. That a positive test is not necessarily a death sentence. I agree to be in Harley Street within the hour.

I barely notice my surroundings as I get on a bus that takes me up Park Lane and along Oxford Street. I hop off and walk the rest of the way. My heart is pounding by the time I arrive.

DR GUPTA SMILES BROADLY as I enter the room and pumps my hand enthusiastically.

'I assume it's bad news,' I say, as I sit down heavily in the leather chair opposite his desk. 'That I've got prostate cancer.'

'Not at all,' he says, with an expression of surprise. 'You categorically do not have cancer or any life-threatening illness.'

'Oh thank goodness.' My shoulders ache as I release all the tension and lean back against the chair.

'Varicocele can often cause azoospermia, which, as I'm sure you know, can be genetic. I suppose that's one thing you don't have to worry about – passing it on.'

I lean forwards. 'I'm sorry, I don't understand a word of what you're saying.'

Dr Gupta looks a bit surprised. 'When the veins around the testes are blocked and enlarged, then it stops you from producing sperm, which of course means you can't impregnate a woman.'

'Well, that's okay. We don't want any more children. Does it cause any other problems?'

There's a long silence as the doctor glances down at the

notes on his desk and then looks back at me, a frown on his face.

'You have high-grade varicole, which you will certainly have had all of your life. I assumed you knew – that you have a zero sperm count, meaning you're completely infertile and always have been.'

There's a thrumming in my ears and my chest constricts. 'Sorry?' I say it as a question. 'What do you mean always have been? I've got a son.'

I stare at him, trying to process what Dr Gupta is telling me.

'I've always been infertile?' I repeat the question. I can't process this. I assumed that when I had to give a sperm sample it was to check for cancer cells or the like.

He shuffles uneasily in his chair, the frown deepening between his eyes. 'Mr Lester... Piers. I can't be one hundred percent sure, but I certainly believe so. In your case it would be highly' – he stresses the word *highly* again – 'unlikely for you to produce sperm. You have a zero count. Now, if you want to address the infertility, then we can perform surgery. There's no guarantees, of course, but we can explore the options.'

'No, no. You don't understand. I've already got a son. He's seventeen.'

Dr Gupta bites the side of his lower lip and holds my gaze. I can tell that we're both thinking the same thing and for me it is the most terrible shock.

'Are you sure?' My voice comes out as a croak.

He nods. His lips are a thin line and I see something that might be pity in his eyes.

'Could this have developed recently, perhaps?' I lean far

forwards, my hands tightly gripping my knees, my head over the side of the doctor's desk.

'I'm sorry, Piers, but no. You will have been born with this condition.' Dr Gupta hands me an envelope. 'Your results are inside, along with some information on varicocele and the treatment options,' he says. I shove it into my jacket pocket without looking at it, as if it's a bomb that has already exploded once and might detonate for the second time.

The realisation spears me like a dagger.

Rafael is not my son.

CHAPTER NINE

RAFAEL

This holiday sucks. I mean, who goes to central London with their parents for a holiday? We should be at the beach, surfing, ideally somewhere cool like Ibiza where I can go partying. I miss Lucille so much. My body literally aches for her. But no. My parents think swapping your house with some strangers is a good idea for a holiday. The only positive thing is Hugo.

We watched the match at his place yesterday and that was something else. Hugo's family must be stinking rich. Their house is huge, with this vast cinema room in the basement and a swimming pool with waves. When we were sitting – or really lounging – on the comfy sofas, their maid came in and gave us beers and popcorn. Who actually has a maid? I felt sorry for the woman, dressed up in a black and white uniform with an apron. I hope they treat her well. I thanked her profusely but Hugo barely glanced at her. It was sick that she gave us beers, though. She probably didn't realise I wasn't eighteen yet, but even if I was, the thought of Mum handing beers to me and a mate is laughable.

Anyway, the game was awesome. The screen was so big and, with its crazy surround sound, it was way better than actually being in the stadium. We chatted for a bit at half time and when Hugo asked me where I lived, I told him in a chateau in France. He seemed really impressed by that and asked to see photos. I showed him the photos on Mum's blog which make the place look like a proper chateau. It's a joke, because it's not a chateau at all, just a big house or a villa, and it's totally run down. Nothing like Hugo's fancy place. I wonder what he'd think if he actually visited it.

Hugo has just finished school and is waiting for his A Level results. He went to Eton. I've never met anyone who has been to a boarding school, let alone a school as posh as Eton. It explains why he talks like he's got a boiled egg stuck in his throat. Not that I care. He seems like a good guy and he's promised to introduce me to his friends. He asked if I had a girlfriend and when I showed him photos of Lucille, his eyes nearly popped out of his head.

'She looks a bit... I dunno... Is she older than you?'

'A year,' I said, feeling proud.

'Yeah, she's cute. Good figure. Great tits.'

'Have you got a girlfriend?' I asked.

'Got a few on the go. You know what it's like.' He winked at me. And no, I didn't know what it was like. I just felt happy that he approved of Lucille.

AND NOW IT'S another day with my boring parents. We're going to a musical on Shaftesbury Avenue. I mean, how old do they actually think I am? A musical! I might have wanted to see *The Lion King* when I was ten years old, but give me a break.

'Can I hang with Hugo instead?' I ask Mum.

She glowers at me. 'No. The tickets are expensive and I want to go. You've already screwed things up for your dad by not going to the football, so the least you can do is come with us this afternoon.'

She's in a really foul mood. The atmosphere between Mum and Dad is horrible, all strained, as if neither of them wants to be with the other. It's like London has brought out the worst in them both, which is ironic because we're meant to be on holiday. Joke. I think Mum's been crying because her eyes were red. And Dad. He's been acting super weird. They fight from time to time, but never like this, with this horrible atmosphere. Whilst they're getting ready, I call Lucille.

'I miss you,' I say and then regret it, because my voice sounds all whiny and that's not cool. 'Can you come to London? There's space for you and I've got some new friends.' Not strictly true; I have one new friend, but hopefully I'll meet more soon.

'I can't, Raf. I haven't got enough money.'

'Can't you ask your parents to lend you some? You just need enough for the flight to get here.'

'It's not possible, and besides, I'm in the middle of something. I can't just drop it and disappear for a few days.'

'In the middle of what?' I ask.

Mum shouts upstairs. 'We're going now.'

'Let's speak again in a few days,' she says. 'I've got to go now. Je t'aime.'

'Me too. Bisous.' And then she's gone.

It isn't until we're on the underground train that I think back over my conversation with Lucille. What did she mean when she said she's in the middle of something? Does it mean she's met someone else? If she really loved me, she'd make an effort to come to London, surely? Or is it because I've got no money and I can't afford to pay for her? I wonder for a moment if I could ask Hugo to lend me some cash and I could send Lucille a ticket. But what if she still said no? That would be so humiliating. I really love Lucille and think about her every single moment of every day but now I'm doubting it's reciprocal. So much for distance making the heart grow stronger.

'What's up, mate?' Dad prods me with an elbow.

I don't know why he calls me mate. I'm not his bloody mate, I'm his son, and sometimes – no, a lot of the time – I wish I wasn't. Dad's not like Didier Moreau, Lucille's father, or like Lewis Brown. He's tall and skinny and he cries if we watch a sad movie. Mum walks all over him, yet he doesn't seem to mind. Or if he does, he's just too weak to say anything. Mum drives me mad but at least she's a strong person.

Soon we're sitting in the plush gold-ceiling theatre and the musical begins, over-enthusiastic actors dressed up in stupid costumes singing stupid tunes. I shove in my ear buds and before long, I'm fast asleep, dreaming of Lucille.

CHAPTER TEN

ELODIE

'We've got surprise visitors,' Lewis shouts. I'm lounging by the pool, reading a book, enjoying the peace now that the builders have gone. Lewis spoke to Piers, who promised that they wouldn't be back during our stay and apologised profusely for the break-in, which is strange, because it wasn't his fault. Perhaps he felt bad for not telling us about the previous break-in. I'll see if I manage to sleep tonight, and if I don't, then I'm booking us into a hotel tomorrow, regardless of the price.

I glance up, holding my hand over my forehead so I can make out who the two people are standing next to my husband. I grab my kaftan and hurriedly pull it over my swimsuit.

'What are you doing here?' I ask, as they pace towards me.

'We're en route to Cannes.' Niall smiles broadly, his arm flung casually around Danielle, who is dressed in a gauzy, long dress. 'And Lewis mentioned that you've had a few issues with Chateau Lester. Sorry to hear about the break-in.

Sadly, security is becoming more and more of a problem in the South of France.'

I'm happy to see Niall. They say you shouldn't go into business with friends, but honestly, it was one of the best decisions I've made. Niall is like a brother to me and we've supported each other through the ups and downs of the years, both in our business and personal lives.

Just over six years ago, I was exhausted from years of working crazily long hours and the stress of managing corporate finance deals. The time had come for me to leave investment banking, especially as I'd accumulated a fortune thanks to my enormous salary and even larger annual bonuses. It's obscene, really, how much I've been paid over the years, and I'm often sad that Mum and Dad didn't live long enough for me to ease their money worries. I've been supporting my sister Ottilie and her family for the past decade, giving them money to build an extension and paying for their annual holiday to the Mediterranean. I wanted to pay for my nephews to have a private education, but Ottilie was having none of that. 'If the state sector was good enough for you and me, then it's good enough for them too,' she said. Her husband would have accepted the offer, but there's this simmering resentment between Ottilie and me. The fact that she's still in Stoke while I'm in, as she calls it, Fancy London. The huge difference between our lifestyles. I'm the big sister who got away.

I've always loved property, and with my banking contacts, I reckoned I could set up a real estate business, selling top-end properties in central London. It's been a highly successful venture and three years ago, when Niall approached me about merging his European agency with mine, it seemed like a sensible idea. Hutchinson Brown now has two offices: one in Knightsbridge, London, and the other in Cannes, South of France. Not that Niall restricts himself to selling in the South of France. He's forever jetting off to the Italian Riviera and the Swiss Alps. Between us, we've sold over one hundred million pounds' worth of houses during the past twelve months. Not bad for a boutique business that employs just ten people.

'Let's go back up to the house,' I suggest. 'Drinks are in order.'

'Good to see you relaxing.' Niall laughs, and turns towards Danielle. 'Did you know that my business partner here hasn't taken a proper holiday in three years?'

'Really?' Danielle's eyes widen. She reminds me of Bambi with her long chestnut hair, wide eyes lined with enormous false lashes, and matchstick-thin limbs. She's the typical young trophy wife, and both Lewis and I have been known to tease Niall for his choice of spouse. But she seems like a sweet girl and, unlike many of his previous girlfriends, she had a high-flying career in one of the large management consultancy firms before quitting work when she got engaged to Niall.

'Elodie doesn't believe in holidays,' Lewis says, with no hint of irony. It's not strictly true, it's just that I love my work and there never seems to be a good time to take off more than a couple of days. I was naive to think I'd be working less hard in my own business.

We settle at the big table underneath the pergola. 'It's beautiful here,' Danielle says, as she removes her gauzy dress to reveal a barely-there bikini top.

Lewis appears from the kitchen carrying a tray with four wine glasses, a bottle of rosé and two cold beers. Niall and I talk a bit about the business, particularly about the new holiday house-swap business. Danielle is telling Lewis about her punishing fitness regime.

'I've got at least twenty houses already signed up,' Niall says. 'Ones that rent for high five-figure sums per week. Several here in the South of France, a handful on the Balearics and Sardinia. What have you got in London?'

'It's proving a bit harder to convince landlords to swap rather than rent by the week or month. I'm having to focus directly on home owners. And I wonder if our annual fees might be a bit too high. How are things going with the bank?'

'All good,' Niall says. We're looking to raise some money for the new venture, to employ a few staff, create a top-end website and invest heavily in marketing. Yes, I could just take out a director's loan, but I have chosen not to so as to keep things clean between Hutchinson Brown and myself. 'I'm really excited about it.'

'You guys should stay for supper,' Lewis says. 'We've got enough food, haven't we, Els?'

I'm not sure that we have, but before I can check, Niall says, 'That would be fabulous. What do you think, Danielle?'

She lounges back in her chair, twirling her wine glass in her fingers. 'I love it here. Sure, would be great to stay on.'

'Dani can help you with supper, can't you? Although she's not the greatest of chefs, are you, darling?'

'Niall!' I say, throwing him a filthy look.

Danielle scowls at him, and I lean towards her. 'Me neither. I generally buy in.' I stand up. 'I'll just go into the kitchen and see what we've got.' Danielle follows me.

'It's a little make-shift inside, isn't it?' she says, glancing around the unfitted kitchen. I'm peering inside the fridge when a female voice comes from the main hallway.

'Hello!'

'Goodness, I wasn't expecting any more people.' I smile at Danielle. As I walk towards the kitchen door, Colette appears. What is it with these people just turning up?

'Oh, sorry. You have visitors,' Colette says, her hand rushing up to her face.

'Don't mind me,' Danielle says.

'Colette, meet Danielle. Colette owns the neighbouring vineyard and treated Lewis and me to a fabulous wine tasting.'

'I have another wine I was wondering if you'd like to try,' Colette says, holding up two bottles. 'They go perfectly with fish.'

'We could have fish for supper,' Danielle says. She's still peering in the fridge. 'You've got a couple of sea bass in here.'

'I have a fabulous recipe for sea bass,' Colette says. 'Actually, the fishmonger is in the village this afternoon and he has the most wonderful fresh fish.'

'We could go,' I say with some reluctance, because all I'd really wanted to do was relax by the pool this afternoon, and not spend a couple of hours in the kitchen.

'I would offer to help you cook but we have some important buyers visiting the winery a little later,' Colette says. 'I'll text you the recipe. I can help you add the finishing touches later.'

We all stand there awkwardly and I realise with some dismay that she's angling to join us. 'Would you like to come for supper?' I ask. 'You and Didier?'

She claps her hands together and grins as if that was the only possible outcome of our conversation. 'We'd be delighted to,' she says. 'We would love to hear what you think of the wine and how it goes with the fish. What time would you like us?' She holds out her phone. 'Here, let's swap numbers.'

I DRIVE and Danielle comes with me. Pontarles is a little village just beyond the Moreaus' vineyard that seems to consist of one road, a handful of pretty houses, a church with a towering spire and a boulangerie. The fishmonger has set up a stand underneath a blue and white striped awning in the church carpark, and he's clearly popular as there's a queue of several people. I buy some more sea bass and a handful of vegetables that the fishmonger is selling from a stand of wicker baskets. Back at Chateau Lester, I see that Colette has indeed emailed me a recipe, but it's in French and after a while I give up on Google translate, realising I don't have most of the ingredients anyway. Danielle and I cobble up a few salads and chat amiably as she tells me about her luxurious honeymoon on a super yacht, loaned to them by some of Niall's friends. I'm sure supper won't be up to Colette's standards, but so be it.

An hour later, and they've arrived. I've barely had time to take a shower and get changed, but the atmosphere is convivial and despite my reluctance to be socialising on holiday, I'm feeling surprisingly relaxed and happy. Perhaps it's being in Niall and Danielle's easy company, or the fact the weather is so gorgeous and we're able to lounge around outside.

DIDIER MAKES a beeline straight for Niall and they talk together in rapid French. Then Niall is patting Didier's back. 'We met before,' Niall tells us. 'I'd forgotten. When the chateau was up for sale, the Moreaus put in an offer. The vendors accepted the Lesters' offer as it was higher. No hard feelings though,' he says, winking at Colette.

She smiles tightly. 'No hard feelings,' she confirms.

The food may not be the best, but fortunately no one is impolite enough to mention it. Instead, a lot of wine is drunk. It isn't until we are almost finished with the main course that Danielle lets out a little yelp.

'We've been drinking too much!' she exclaims, bringing her hand up to her forehead. 'There's no way that I can drive now, not after downing several glasses of wine. And you've also drunk too much,' she says to Niall. They look at each other, confusion and embarrassment on both their faces.

'It's not a problem,' I say, thinking of the empty rooms upstairs. 'I'm sure I can find some spare linen and you can stay the night.'

'Really?' Danielle asks. 'I'm so sorry. We've never done this before, have we, Niall? Not checked in with each other.'

Welcome to married life, I think rather meanly.

'It's no problem, really,' I confirm. Not that there's any choice. I know for a fact that there aren't any available hotel rooms in the vicinity.

There's an awkward silence which Colette breaks. 'So, do you know the history of this house?'

We all shake our heads. 'The previous owner was a man called Florian Dupont,' Colette explains. 'He had a wife called Margot, a very shy, quiet woman who never mingled with the neighbours, and they had one son. We were friends with Florian, who used to come and drink wine with us, but never with his wife. There was always an excuse – she wasn't well, or she was busy working, or had to look after their son. I think we only met her once or maybe twice?'

'It was on la Toussaint,' Didier adds. 'When we went to the cemetery to lay flowers on the grave of your grandparents.' I'm surprised how well Didier is speaking English. Previously he only uttered a few words and Colette had implied that his English was poor. Clearly not.

'Ah, yes,' Colette adds. 'So, Fête de la Toussaint is the day when we commemorate the dead in France. It's on 1st November and is a public holiday.'

'It's All Saints Day, isn't it?' Niall asks.

'Yes. A little like your Halloween but more serious. Actually, November 2nd is le jour des morts, officially the day of the dead, but we celebrate it on 1st November. Anyway,

Didier is right. We saw Margot outside the church, and it was shocking. She was as pale as a ghost, and so thin. I wondered if she was sick, but she said she was fine. She was carrying an enormous bouquet of white chrysanthemums and strangely she was dressed all in white too. Almost as if she was a ghostly bride at a wedding.'

'I said hello, asked her if she was alright,' Didier interrupts. 'And she stared at me as if I wasn't there. It was like she'd lost her mind or was on drugs or something.'

'It was horrible,' Colette says. 'Her eyes were blank and her face expressionless. Anyway, then Florian arrived with their son, who must have been in his early teens. Florian explained that it was a difficult day for Margot. Her grandparents had died on la Toussaint thirty years previously. We didn't ask any questions, but just wished them well and left.'

'Later we discovered that Margot's grandparents didn't just die.' Didier turns to Colette. 'How do you say, ils ont été assassinés?'

'They were murdered,' Colette adds. 'Horribly murdered by an axe man when they were asleep in bed.'

Danielle gasps. 'Goodness, that's awful. Was the murderer ever found?'

'Non,' Didier says, shaking his head gravely. 'Margot's parents had died in a car crash when she was young, so she was brought up by her grandparents. Very sad.'

Colette carries on. 'We knew that murders had taken place in the chateau, but not that it had been Margot's parents.'

'Sorry,' Danielle says, fluttering her hands. 'You mean the murders took place here, in this chateau?' She gasps.

'Yes. And ever since, people have said this place is haunted. Of course, I don't believe such nonsense,' Colette says, taking a sip of wine.

'But what about Alain, the postman, and Bruno, the carpenter?' Didier asks. 'They are very rational men.'

Colette shrugs. 'Some people believe in ghosts. Alain says he saw a woman wearing a flowing white dress, running down the drive holding an axe. He refused to deliver the post here ever again. And Bruno came here to do some work for Florian. One day when the place was empty, he heard a terrible scream. Frightened, he ran out of the house. Glancing over his shoulder he saw a man wearing old-fashioned clothes holding an axe. He got into his van and refused to come back.'

This all sounds like nonsense to me – people imagining things that aren't there – but I keep my thoughts to myself.

'But it wasn't the only tragedy to befall this place,' Didier says. He turns to his wife. 'Will you explain?'

Colette takes a large sip of wine and then leans back in her chair. 'A year to the day, again on la Toussaint, we were driving back from the cemetery when we were passed by lots of emergency vehicles, blue lights shining through the low fog and rain. We were terrified something had happened at our vineyard, but the police all turned up this road. Eventually the gendarmes came to our house to say that Margot was missing. There was blood but no body. There was a long investigation. To begin with people suspected Florian, but really he was a very lovely man. Gentle, an old soul, you know. I couldn't imagine him doing anything bad towards his wife. For the first year or so he seemed broken, truly devastated, and soon the police exonerated him. Then people assumed that she had run away to be with her lover, or maybe she had taken her own life by suicide.'

'And was she found?' Danielle asks. She's leaning towards Colette, hanging on her every word.

'No. Their son left home the day he turned sixteen. Said he couldn't bear living with the ghosts of his dead relatives. And Florian, well, he was never the same. People said that he killed Margot and hid her remains somewhere here in the chateau. That Margot had killed her own grandparents and when Florian found out, he used the same axe to kill his wife. They say the axe is still hidden here, probably in the tower. I have to admit that there is a coldness about this villa, and even I have heard the *chop-chop* sound, much like someone rhythmically cutting wood,' Colette says.

'Yes, I've heard it too,' Didier adds. 'But maybe it's the old boiler or a woodpecker, perhaps.' He lifts his shoulders up and lets out a pff.

'I haven't heard it,' Lewis adds. I can tell that my husband is extremely cynical, much like I am. 'Perhaps with all the building works the Lesters are doing, the noise has gone away.'

'Maybe.' Colette stares into the middle distance. 'Anyway, eventually Florian died. He was only sixty-five, and maybe he passed away with a broken heart. And then the Lesters bought this place, as you know.'

'And there have been no traces of Margot ever since?' Danielle asks. Her eyes are wide and glistening in the low light.

'No. Of course, people think they have seen her over the years, but nothing was ever proven one way or another. Nowadays the young people think that her ghost lives right here, along with the ghosts of her grandparents.'

Lewis makes a scoffing noise. I don't believe in ghosts or stories propagated by gossips, but I can see how a strange disappearance like that might become like Chinese whispers, a story morphing with intensity as time passes by.

A few minutes later, I excuse myself to visit the bathroom. It's beginning to get cold outside now that the sun has gone down, and I shiver as I walk through the kitchen into the hall. And then I freeze.

I hear the creak of floorboards overhead. My first thought is Margot, the woman who has disappeared. The ghost. And then I shake myself out of the ridiculous thinking. But it's there again. A footstep. Then another. Everyone is still seated around the table and I can hear the hum of their voices. No one else should be in the house. I recall the break-in. Could it be possible that someone would be so brazen as to enter the house when we're all sitting outside? I swallow but it feels like something is caught in my throat. I hear it again. More creaks, footsteps. There's definitely someone upstairs. Where is Pushkin? Is he still sitting next to the table, hoping for titbits of leftover food? I hurry back outside to where the others are chatting loudly, alcohol having loosened everyone.

'There's someone in the house.' My voice comes out as a

croaky whisper. At first they ignore me, so I repeat myself. Louder this time, shaking Lewis's shoulder. 'There's someone inside the house.'

Everyone looks at me, but it's Niall who jumps up first. 'Darling,' Danielle says, tugging at his sleeve.

'Niall and I will investigate,' Lewis says, as he pushes his chair back and stands up.

'Do you want me to call the police?' I ask. I'm normally good in emergency situations but today my legs feel weak.

'Qu'est-ce que c'est?' Didier asks Colette. She rattles off something in French that I can't follow, and he stands up too. He grabs a knife off the table, which does nothing to ease my nerves, and the three men disappear inside the house.

'They will be safe, won't they?' Danielle asks.

'I'm sure it's nothing,' Colette says. 'You know, we have a lot of burglaries now in Provence, but normally they just run away when they're interrupted. The thieves are looking for passports and cash.'

My heart is hammering. On the one hand I hope that they catch whoever it is who has been hassling us and then we can have an easy week ahead, but the thought of violence numbs me. We sit at the table in silence, listening to the cicadas and the soft sounds of the night, but all I hear is my own heartbeat. It's maybe three minutes later when the silence is broken by the sound of men's laughter and foot-steps returning. Did I imagine the footsteps? Are they laughing at me? Perhaps I've drunk too much, yet again. Maybe I imagined it?

'Look who we found, sneaking around!' Lewis has his hands on Lucille's shoulders. She's wearing black jeans ripped at the knees and a black bomber jacket, an unreadable expression on her face.

'Bah alors! What are you doing?' Colette asks, her cheeks flushing.

'I said I would come and collect you, and Raf asked me to check something in his room,' she says, shrugging her shoulders as if it's completely normal to be creeping around a house without telling anyone you're there.

'No ghost, then!' Danielle exclaims. 'But who is she?'

'Colette and Didier's daughter,' I say.

Lucille crosses her arms over her chest. 'You told me to come,' she says defiantly, 'so you could drink, and it looks like you've been doing plenty of that.' She waves her hand at the several empty wine bottles standing on the end of the table.

'Would you like something to eat?' I ask Lucille, as I pull out a chair for her.

She wrinkles her nose and says, 'No, thanks.' But she does slip into the seat and immediately pulls out her phone, her fingers whizzing over the screen.

The Moreaus stay for another half an hour but Lucille is getting twitchy, yawning without putting her hand in front of her mouth, and eventually her parents get the message. I'm glad because I'm tired too. I start clearing some of the dirty dishes away, piling them up in the kitchen. I listen to the crunching of the Moreaus' car tyres as it disappears down our drive and think of Lucille, who looks nothing like either of her parents and somehow seems distant from them. What was she doing upstairs, anyway? Had Raf really asked her to check something? It seems strange. Why didn't she tell us she was here, and then she could have gone upstairs? Or am I reading too much into it? She wasn't exactly rude this evening, but she didn't go out of her way to be engaging or polite. Perhaps that's just teenage girls. Lewis, Niall and Danielle are still seated at the table outside, laughing and drinking. We got through so many bottles of wine this evening. Not me, as I've been careful not to drink much, but the men have certainly been tipping it back.

I'm scraping some of the leftover scraps from people's plates into the bin when I notice an unpleasant smell. I lean into the bin, expecting the sickly sweet odour of rotting food to be wafting upwards, the bin needing to be taking outside. Except strangely, the bin doesn't really smell. Nevertheless, I tie up the bag and place the rubbish outside in one of the larger dumpster bins before returning to the kitchen. Danielle comes in carrying some glasses.

'If you tell me where the linen is, I can make up our bed, assuming it's not already made up,' she says. She stands still and wrinkles her nose. 'Eugh, what's that smell?'

'I thought it was the remnants of the fish but it's not.' I open the oven door to check we haven't left anything inside. It's empty. The old dishwasher doesn't exactly smell clean and there is a definite stench of fish coming from it, so I slide in a tablet and switch it on. The machine gurgles, makes some thumping noises and then settles down into its normal cycle.

'That's not a fishy smell. More like something else that's rotting. Gross though.' Danielle checks herself and her cheeks flush slightly. 'Sorry, don't mean to be rude. It's probably nothing.'

I smile. I'm not in the slightest bit offended. This isn't my house after all. 'Come on,' I say. 'Let's sort you out for the night.'

As we walk upstairs and into the bedroom corridor, Danielle wrinkles her nose and shivers dramatically.

'You okay?' I ask.

'This place kind of gives me the creeps.'

I laugh, wondering if she's let the history of the chateau fire up her imagination. I'm not surprised she's unimpressed with the interiors though, which undoubtedly aren't up to the standards of the places she and Niall normally stay.

Danielle doesn't say anything further and she attempts to help me make up the bed in the only room that has a spare bed, except she's more than tipsy and is constantly falling over her own feet and stumbling onto the mattress.

'Sit down and I'll do it,' I say eventually. She seems to think that's really funny and dissolves into a fit of giggles. Her drunkenness is rather endearing and I can see why Niall is so fond of her.

'I don't think it's me that's smelling,' she laughs. 'But maybe it is.' She leans back on the bed, her hair splaying on the mattress. 'I find it really hard to sleep in this hot climate, and Niall snores like a pig when he's been drinking. It'll probably be another sleeping pill tonight.'

I'm surprised. She seems too young to be a regular sleeping pill user but I don't say anything.

'Can you tell Niall to come up to bed?' she asks, before kicking off her sandals and bringing her legs up onto the bed.

Downstairs, the rancid smell is stronger but as I walk back into the kitchen, it seems to lessen. Lewis is standing at the sink drinking a glass of water.

'I'm going to bed,' he says, filling the glass up again. 'Will you lock up?'

'Sure.'

He leaves the room without touching me and I let out a sigh as I lean against the kitchen table and look out into the darkness.

'You're looking very wistful,' Niall says, startling me as he appears in the doorway. 'There's half a bottle of Domaine

Coste-Caumartin. It's really good stuff. Come and finish it off with me.'

I follow Niall back outside and he pours me a glass of the red wine. The night is completely still now and the temperature has dipped. I shiver slightly but enjoy the cooler air. Now that everyone has gone, I feel the tension ease from my shoulders, and lean back tipping my head so I can see the myriad of stars twinkling in the sky.

'So, how are things going with work?' I ask.

'I'm returning to London tomorrow and intend to sign off things with the bank. I think we're nearly ready to go. I'm excited for the new house-swap adventure.'

'Me too,' I say. 'We've done our research and there's definitely scope for a new kid on the block to switch up the market. Obviously, we need to look at the agreements. Make sure no one is having work done to their property, and we'll have to organise careful inspections. But beyond that, how are you? You seem really happy,' I say.

He throws me a lazy smile. 'I am. Married life is treating me well.'

'I'm thrilled for you. Danielle is a lovely girl.'

'And I'm very lucky. We're talking about starting a family.'

I raise an eyebrow. I never imagined Niall would settle down, let alone have children, but if he's found the right woman, then I assume that changes things for him.

'What about you? Everything okay between you and Lewis?'

I pause, taken aback by Niall's question. Honestly, I'm surprised he's noticed. Then again, we've known each other for so long, perhaps he can see the miniscule cracks that most people would fail to notice. 'Yes. Why do you ask?' Except

I've allowed a long pause to fill the space between Niall's question and my answer.

He swivels the stem of his wine glass between his fingers before placing it on the table and leaning towards me.

'You don't seem... I don't know, not quite your ebullient self. And Lewis is a bit distracted, kind of ignoring you. I remember the days when he hung on your every word, like some kind of adoring puppy.'

I'm surprised that my eyes well up and I blink hard to stop the tears from overflowing. 'I guess that's what happens after twenty years. You've got all that to come.' I try to make light of it, except I know I've failed.

'How are the gyms doing?' he asks.

Niall is one of the few people who knows the truth; he's completely aware that Lewis is, and for most of our marriage has been, a kept man. We put on a good pretence that Lewis is successful in his own right, that we're this power duo living the luxury life, that we both earn hefty salaries, and sometimes I even kid myself that that is the case. Except Lewis's businesses have never made a profit, and if I didn't inject serious money each year, he would have been bankrupt ages ago. Occasionally when Lewis doesn't pull his weight around the home, or he buys some flashy new clothes, I feel a simmer of resentment, but on the whole I've accepted that's the dynamic of our relationship. He loves his gyms, and what makes him happy makes me happy. At least I thought it did. But Niall is right. Something has shifted recently, yet I can't quite put my finger on it.

CHAPTER ELEVEN

PIERS

Sitting in the darkened theatre, the joviality of the actors, the upbeat storyline and the catchy tunes all pass me by. All I can think about is what Dr Gupta told me. If I'm infertile, then my wife must have cheated on me.

I think back to when Susan was pregnant, how utterly happy we were. Raf was a honeymoon baby. He must have been, because he arrived just under forty weeks from the day of our wedding. We laughed about how lucky we were, how easy it was for Susan to fall pregnant, how fertile we both must be. But then there were no more babies. We tried to conceive for a few years but Susan didn't seem that bothered. We'd give our only son a wonderful life; he wouldn't have to share our affections with a sibling, she told me, and eventually I accepted it. There would be no more children. At one point I wondered whether she was secretly taking birth control because I wouldn't describe Susan as a natural mother, and it crossed my mind that she didn't actually want another child. She's grown into the role the older Raf has become, but in those baby and infant years, she definitely struggled. When he was very young, it was me that Raf called out for in the night when he'd had a nightmare, and me who taught him how to tie his shoelaces and ride a bike.

But if I didn't make Susan pregnant on our honeymoon, who did? Did she sleep with someone else when we were in Italy on the beautiful Amalfi coast, holding hands and so very much in love? Were we even apart during those ten days? It's so long ago, I just can't remember. I think back to before our wedding. Susan and I met at a bar. There was nothing particularly romantic about it – we just happened to be ordering drinks at the same time, each there with a group of our own friends, both of us failing to attract the attention of the barman who was more interested in talking to his mates than serving strangers. We got chatting, didn't return to our respective groups of friends, and had dinner together the following night. I knew almost immediately that she would become my wife. I adored her and asked her to marry me within a month of us meeting. She'd laughed, told me to ask her again when we'd been together a bit longer, and I did. I asked her every month on the anniversary of our first kiss. A total of fifteen times, and to be honest, on the fifteenth occasion, I expected the answer to be the same. 'I love you, Piers, but I'm not quite ready to settle down yet.' Except that wasn't what she said.

I was down on one knee, a ring in my pocket – the same small solitaire diamond ring I'd had in my pocket for the previous fourteen months. We were staying in a country pub somewhere on the South Downs and had returned from a long hike, soaked to the skin by an unexpected downpour. When I asked, 'Will you marry me?' Susan paused before answering and said, 'Yes, I will.' I could hardly believe my ears and asked her to repeat herself. 'Yes!' She had laughed, throwing her arms around me, telling me she would at long last relinquish her flat and her independence, and we should get married as soon as we could. And goodness, when my wife set her mind to something, she was a whirlwind. We were married less than three months later.

But was Susan hiding something back then, and ever since? Did she have a secret lover all of that time? Is that why she didn't want to move into my flat during the months before we were engaged, why she tried to maintain some distance from me even though we were together? She insisted that she have at least three nights a week in her own place to catch up on sleep, so that her heart wasn't completely broken when I eventually split up with her. I didn't understand that and I reassured her that she was the love of my life, and that I'd never end our relationship. I assumed she'd been hurt previously, something she didn't want to talk about. And so I never pushed her for answers.

I try to recall the name of her boyfriend prior to me but now I wonder whether she actually told me. Someone she worked with, I think. A solicitor probably, because back then, Susan was employed as a paralegal in a big London firm. Whoever he was, I never met him. Was this stranger the birth father of our child? Or was he a complete stranger, a one-night stand or a final fling before committing to me for ever? The thought sickens me. I redo the calculations in my head. Raf was definitely born 40 weeks after our wedding, so she either slept with someone else just before our wedding or during our honeymoon. Or did she artificially inseminate herself with someone else's sperm? But why? She chose to marry me; surely she'd want my genes for her child. No, that's a ridiculous thought. She must have had one final fling.

But was it just the once? Has my wife been with someone else for all these years?

I know that I need to ask Susan, but our relationship is as highly strung as a taut rubber band about to snap. The last couple of years have been particularly hard, compounded by our money problems, the issues of living in a country where neither of us is fluent in the language and the locals have certainly not accepted us as one of their own. Can I really ask her? And what about my relationship with Rafael? It will destroy him to know that Susan has misled him his whole life. However strained our relationship might be now, I'm still his dad. And what about me? My body has failed me, lied to me. All this time thinking Raf is my child, carrying my genes for better or worse. Laughing how he has the same eyebrows as me, that annoying trait of always being on time even if he's left it to the final second, or how about his instinctual sense of direction, the same as mine? Is that all learned behaviour? Have I been searching for traits that aren't actually there? Have I been delusional for seventeen years? Or could Dr Gupta be wrong? It's possible, isn't it, because doctors aren't infallible. Perhaps I should seek a second opinion, to be sure that this isn't a newly developed problem. Except I can't forget the look on his kindly face or the test results which are typed up in solid black ink on that official medical report.

It's impossible to enjoy the musical or to concentrate knowing that the boy sitting next to me might not be my biological son and the woman on his other side has lied to me for the whole of our marriage. Raf has put his ear buds in; he thinks I haven't noticed, but I know my boy and actually wish I had some of my own. This fake joviality is wearing. At the interval, which can't come soon enough, Susan leans over towards me.

'Get us some ice-creams, will you, love? Vanilla for me.'

A wave of fury chokes me and I feel like yelling, 'Get your own bloody ice-cream.' Raf nudges me. 'Can I have chocolate, please, Dad?' Raf is the innocent party in all of this and I can't help but think of all the many times we've eaten ice-cream together. On the sea front in Cannes, ice-lollies made with varying degrees of success at home, Cornettos in Brighton, and how we have stacks of photos of Raf with chocolate smeared across his face from when he was a toddler. I get up and ease my way along the row of seats, actually quite glad to be away from my wife.

Throughout the second half of the musical I toy with the different scenarios. Me confronting Susan. How is she likely to react? She might try to deny it, but I could easily demand genetic testing, so that wouldn't work for her. What if she tells me the truth; is that something I actually want to know? Or even worse, what if she's still in touch with Raf's birth father and she takes him to be with this stranger? I could lose my marriage and my son. I think of how Susan is in difficult situations, how combative she can be. She'd have made a great barrister, if only she'd continued with her studies. Somehow Susan has the ability to twist other people's words, to make it seem as if she's in the right, regardless of her culpability. That's why I try to keep the peace in our family. It's not worth the shouting and the tears and the bad feelings. Raf may think I'm weak in that respect but I'm only doing what I think is best for a harmonious relationship. So if I'm not going to confront Susan, I'll need to do some detective work behind her back. If she has any papers showing Raf's true genetic background, they'll be in France. But thinking about our move, our filing cabinet and the little red book that we had when Raf was born, I really don't think there are any papers hidden away. What would be better is to talk to the friends Susan had when we got married. She still gets Christmas cards from a few of them – old work colleagues, college friends and her closest friend, Marianne. In fact Marianne would be my best bet. I'm sure if there was anything Susan wanted to hide, she'd have confided in Marianne.

As the curtain is rising for the third time and the final wave of clapping seems to go on for ever, I have a bright idea. What if I organise a surprise party for Susan here in London? A get-together of her old friends, the people she no longer sees because we've emigrated to France. I'm sure Marianne would help me. A surge of energy rushes through me at the prospect, not only because it might allow me to probe into my wife's past, but also because it gives me something to do over the next few days.

Later, when we're back in the Browns' house, when Susan is once again luxuriating in the roll top bath tub, I rummage in my wife's handbag. There's a sense of guilt, because this isn't something I'd normally do, but I convince myself it's for a good reason. I lift her phone off the bedside table and plug in her pin – the year of Raf's birth. It opens up and I quickly look through her text messages, except nothing jumps out at me. There are no hidden love notes or names of people I don't recognise. Realising I don't have long, I navigate to Marianne's phone number, sharing the contact with my own phone. Then I hurry downstairs to the cinema room in the basement, closing the door behind me, hoping that my voice won't carry through the house. It's nearly 11 p.m., but Marianne answers on the second ring.

'Hello?' There's a concerned inflection in her voice.

'I'm so sorry to be calling you this late. It's Piers Lester.'

'Is everything okay? Is Susan alright?'

'Yes, yes. All's fine.' She lets out an audible breath.

'Good. I'm seeing Sue tomorrow night.' Marianne is the only person who is allowed to call my wife Sue.

'Um, I would like to organise a surprise party for her; a gathering of her old friends, colleagues and the like. Some of the people who came to our wedding but whom we've lost contact with because we've moved to France. I was wondering if you could help me.'

'Well, aren't you the sweetest,' Marianne says. I've never been able to read her well and can't tell if the sentiment is genuine or whether she thinks I'm being saccharine. 'I assume she hasn't told you that a group of us are meeting up tomorrow night? I'm sure I could find a few more people to add to the party.'

I refuse to be side-swiped, so I fib. 'Yes, she mentioned it, but I wasn't sure how many of her old gang would be there. Are you still in touch with any of Susan's colleagues, the ones that have moved on from Root Rothstein Sparrow?' Marianne is a solicitor still working in the firm that Susan left nearly eight years ago.

'Sure,' Marianne says. 'I don't know how many people will be able to make it this last minute but I'm happy to ring around. It'll be fun to surprise Sue.'

Marianne has had a series of long-term boyfriends but has never married or had children. She describes herself as being wedded to her job. She comes to stay on average once a year, and arrives laden with expensive gifts. I try to stay out of the way during her visits, largely because I get the impression she's never thought I was good enough for Susan. Occasionally, I question whether she's right.

'What time and where are you meeting?' I ask, and then regret the question because now it's obvious I didn't know about it.

'The Pink Peony on Sloane Avenue at 7 p.m. Do you know it?'

'No. But then again so much has changed since we lived in London.' I probably wouldn't have known it anyway; Chelsea drinking venues were hardly my scene back then.

'Right. Leave it with me and I'll see what I can do.' She hangs up without saying goodbye.

THE NEXT EVENING, Susan has carefully applied her makeup, and she must have had a blow dry during the afternoon, because her hair is definitely more bouffant than normal. She's wearing a dress with the scarf I got her tied jauntily around her neck.

'Right, I won't be back too late. Although with Marianne around, who knows.' She laughs. 'What are you going to do this evening? You could take Raf to the cinema.'

'I'm coming with you,' I say.

She stops still, a deep line appearing between her eyebrows. 'But Marianne's organising a get-together of our girlfriends. It'll just be the five of us.'

'Actually, it's going to be a party. It's meant to be a surprise, but I've just let the cat out of the bag,' I say, holding my breath in the hope that Susan doesn't react badly.

'A party?'

'I contacted Marianne and she's getting together a bunch of people that you haven't seen in ages. We thought it would be fun for you. I'm sure they'll all want to hear about life in Provence. It'll give you the chance to reconnect with old friends.'

Susan's face softens and I feel a wave of relief. 'Did Marianne do this?' she asks.

'Actually, I asked her to.'

'Okay,' she says slowly. 'I mean, it's a bit weird seeing people I've lost touch with, but I guess the sentiment is nice. Thank you, Piers. But won't it be boring for you?'

I wonder if she doesn't want me there. 'Not at all. It'll be fun to see some of the people who came to our wedding, and it will be nice to reconnect with your old friends. We need to fill up our little black book for when we finish the renovations and start renting out the rooms on Airbnb. It's what you want to do eventually, isn't it? And as your friends are well connected, they could be the perfect guests.' I'm blustering now because we haven't really discussed renting out rooms, and finishing the bedrooms seems so very far off.

Susan bites her lip and then grabs her handbag. 'What about Raf?'

'I've told him that he can spend the evening with Hugo, and I've given him the second key so he can let himself back into the house if he wants to come home before us.' What I don't mention to Susan is that I made Raf promise to not drink more than two beers, and told him if he returned home drunk again, I'd tell his mother, who would most likely ground him, remove his phone and pocket money.

'Well, if we're going, we'd better get a move on,' Susan says, walking towards the door.

THE PINK PEONY is a wine bar with a pale pink front
door and hanging baskets containing faux flowers in pinks
and greens. Inside, the aesthetic is more Scandi than sugary
peony, with wooden slatted walls and green plants hanging
from the ceiling. There are tall pine tables and stools covered
with sheepskins, and wood that curves pleasingly around the
large bar at the back of the room. It's already busy inside,
with a few people milling on the pavement, large glasses of
wine in their hands, dressed smartly in business suits, ties in
pockets and large leather bags slung over shoulders. I feel
immediately out of place in my chinos and casual linen shirt.
Within seconds, Susan is screeching, arms flung around a
woman I don't recognise, more people crowding in towards
her. I stand awkwardly to one side, until Marianne appears.
She's wearing a sharply cut black jacket and cream trousers,
pin-thin, wearing her trademark stiletto heels which make
her slightly taller than me at six feet.

'Hello, stranger,' she says, placing a single kiss on my
cheek. I move in for a second kiss before remembering that
we're in Britain, not France, where kissing is kept to the
minimum. 'We've got a good turnout,' she says, waving
towards the group of people encircling my wife. 'Turns out a
lot of people have missed Sue, or perhaps they just want to
know the truth behind the blog.' Marianne is one of the few
people who knows what's really happened and she's made
no effort to hide her disdain for my lack of success in France,
and our cash-strapped lifestyle. But ultimately she's loyal to
Susan and I very much doubt she's gossiped about our true
situation.

'I'm not sure I know anyone,' I say, glancing around.
'Who's who?'

Marianne reels off a few names, women mainly,

although I make out at least two men in the small crowd. 'That man looks familiar,' I say, although I can't place him.

'Which one?'

'The tall chap with the red hair.' As if he can sense we're talking about him, he turns to look at me and Marianne and nods, but then immediately turns his back on us.

'That's Tim De Withers. He's managing partner of Root Rothstein Sparrow now.'

'Was he at the firm when Susan was still there?' In Susan's day the city solicitor's firm was just called Root Rothstein.

Marianne throws me a strange glance. 'Of course.' There's a subtext here which I'd like to explore, except that a woman in a tightly fitted pale yellow dress strides over and pulls Marianne away from me. I edge through the throng of people and put my arm around Susan's waist.

'What would you like to drink?' I ask in her ear.

'Gin and tonic, please,' she says, but she doesn't introduce me to anyone. I leave her and make my way to the bar, ordering a G&T for Susan and a beer for myself. As I've come to expect, the price is exorbitant. I return and hand Susan her drink, which she takes from me without an acknowledgment. There are more loud squeals as another four join the throng around my wife. I stand awkwardly, as if living in rural France has made me forget my people skills, which is ridiculous because I used to be more socially gregarious than Susan. I turn to a woman standing next to me.

'Hi. I'm Susan's husband, Piers.'

She shakes my extended hand. 'Great to meet you, Piers. I heard a lot about you back in the day.'

I wonder what she means by that. 'And you are?' I ask.

'Suraya Patel. I used to work with Susan. She hasn't

changed at all. Life in France must be suiting you. I follow her blog and occasionally let myself dream, but with three kids, a husband who's a partner in a large accountancy firm, and the fact I was made partner two years ago, it's just a pipe dream.' I cringe inwardly at Suraya Patel's bragging and wonder whether this is what Susan is missing. The ability to brag about me, or herself even. My smile is tight. Suraya pats me on the arm. 'I think you're very brave for following your dreams through. Your chateau looks idyllic.'

I wonder if she would still like our dream if she knew the truth; that we're scrimping and saving for every penny. That Susan's photos are so carefully curated, they're almost fake.

'It's lovely to see such a big turnout from Root Rothstein Sparrow. Susan must have been popular. Who were her best friends back then?'

'Goodness...' Suraya gazes towards the bar. 'There were quite the bunch of us. We all started at the same time and bonded over the photocopier and bitching about the long hours. But then Susan drifted away a bit when she started going out with... But it's really lovely to see her now, settled with you, and I understand you have a son? How old is he?'

'Ah yes, the boyfriend who came before me!' I laugh, trying to sound relaxed but I'm sure it comes out more like a choke. 'The least said about that the better.' I wink at her, trying for the conspiratorial look but by Soraya's reaction, I've clearly failed. 'What was his name?' I glance away and pretend to think.

'Are you talking about Tim?' she asks.

'Yes, of course. Silly me.'

Suraya's eyes are drawn like a magnet to the man with the red hair, and then back to me. She smiles but there's a hardness to her expression now, and gripping her glass tightly, she says, 'It was lovely to meet you, Piers. I hope you have a great time in England. Please excuse me as I need to say my goodbyes and get back to the kids.'

And then she's gone.

I edge nearer to Tim De Withers, but he's always deep in conversation with someone, his eyes never glancing towards me. In fact, he doesn't even talk to Susan. I wonder if that's because they're consciously trying to avoid each other. Someone has bought Susan another drink and she's laughing, her head thrown back, a look of delight on her face, an expression that I haven't seen in such a very long time. I wonder why, if she's that happy here amongst these old friends, she's so determined to live in France, far away from them. I would return if she wanted to. And then Tim De Withers turns around and picks up a raincoat and a black leather briefcase. I see his face in profile now and there's something about his nose, the positioning and shape of his ears that strikes me hard in my gullet. Raf. Raf's nose is shaped like that, slightly rounded and wider at the base, unlike my nose which is long and sharp, like a ski slope. And his ears are neat, as if they're pinned back; perfect ears, also like Raf's. Is he Raf's birth father? Is this the man Susan was dating prior to getting engaged to me? Was he the reason she took so long to accept my engagement? Was it because he rejected her at the last moment, or was he perhaps already committed to someone else and Susan was his bit on the side?

I hurry to Susan and grab her wrist. 'I'm going home, love. Is that alright with you?'

'Sure,' Susan says, almost batting me away as if I'm a nuisance. And perhaps I am.

'I'll see you later, then. Have a lovely time,' I say, but

Susan is already laughing at whatever a broad, stocky man is saying, a man with black skin who I'm sure can't be Raf's father.

Tim De Withers is striding out of the front door and quickly darting between the tables. I follow him. He turns left onto Sloane Avenue and walks with long strides, his leather shoes *clip-clopping* on the pavement. He pauses for a moment, removing his phone from his jacket pocket and holding it to his ear. And then he's off again, talking in a low voice and walking so fast I almost have to jog to keep up with him. I'm relieved that he ignores a taxi that hurtles past, its amber light lit up indicating it's free. Wherever Tim De Withers is going he's walking there. When we reach King's Road, he turns right and I wonder for a moment if he's going out for dinner, meeting his wife perhaps. Should I accost him and ask him whether he's still in touch with my wife, whether he knows my son? No. It's a stupid idea. He'll think I'm crazy, and perhaps I am. And then he's turning right again, onto Markham Square and, halfway up, he climbs a short set of steps and stops at the doorway, fumbling in his briefcase. He turns his head quickly in my direction and I crouch down behind a car, unsure if he's seen me. But by the time I glance upwards again, the door is open and Tim De Withers has stepped inside. Has he simply gone home?

I stand there for a moment, wedged between a shining black Range Rover with a personalised numberplate and a silver Maserati. Is my wife here in London to see this man? Is this why she was so keen to do a house swap in Knightsbridge, because it's just a few streets away from her ex's home? Is that why she bought new clothes, because she knew that she was going to see him tonight? Has she already reconnected with him, or was that the plan for this trip? I feel sick as I walk away, my shoulders slumped. I can never compete with a man like Tim De Withers, who lives in a multi-million-pounds London house and is managing partner of a leading law firm, no doubt earning millions every year. But if this man really is Raf's birth father, why didn't Susan stay with him? He would have been a much better choice for my materialistic wife. Or perhaps he rejected her and I was her rebound. I pass a pub and wander inside, edging towards the busy bar and ordering a pint of beer and a shot of vodka, needing alcohol to calm my manic brain. I sit there for ages, letting the melancholy shroud me, watching strangers, trying to calm my racing thoughts, and drinking. Lots. By the time the bartender rings the bell at 11 p.m. to indicate it's closing time, my head is spinning. I haven't drunk this much in years. Almost falling off the bar stool, I weave my way out of the pub. What am I going to say to Susan? How am I going to save our relationship and our family?

I'm not sure how I get back to the Browns' house, and I've no idea how long it takes me, but when I'm standing on the doorstep, trying to get the key in the lock, I notice that the lights are still on in the house. That's good. Susan and I can talk.

I stumble as I enter the hallway, crashing against the hallway table, saving the flower arrangement from toppling over at the last moment. I'd thought the walk had sobered me up a bit, but perhaps not. And then Susan is there, standing in front of me, her arms crossed over her chest.

'What's going on?' she asks.

'Didn't think you'd be back this early.' My words sound slurred.

'You're drunk.'

I chuckle because she looks so annoyed, giving me the

stare that she normally reserves for Raf when he's done something bad.

'I thought you'd come straight home, would be here to look after Raf, but instead, you've been out drinking! For heaven's sake, Piers. You're not a child. You should have been here to let me in. Instead I had to get Raf to open the door for me.'

'At least I wasn't with my ex,' I mumble.

'What?' She throws me a confused look. 'Ex? What do you mean?'

'I want to talk to you,' I say. 'I thought you'd be grateful that I organised the get-together for your old friends.'

'It wasn't you though, was it? Marianne organised it.'

'Was it nice seeing Tim de whatever his name is?'

Susan climbs up the stairs in stockinged feet and I follow her, grabbing the handrail to keep myself upright.

'I want to talk,' I say.

'Fine. Talk.'

I follow her into our bedroom.

'I want to go home. Back to France,' I say.

Susan swivels around. 'Well, I don't.'

'It's not working, us being here. We're not acting like a family and it's not good for us. You, me...'

'What the hell are you talking about?' Susan glowers at me. 'We're on holiday, having a break from the hassles in France, staying in a beautiful house that we could never afford. Besides, we can't go home. Elodie and Lewis are staying there.'

Here we go again. The money issue. It's always the bloody money with Susan.

'What's really going on, Piers? Why don't you organise

to meet up with your old friends, do stuff that you want to do?'

'I don't have any old girlfriends that I want to see.'

The words hang between us like shards of glass hanging from the ceiling, ready to drop down and shatter into a thousand little pieces, spearing us or not.

'Your male friends.' She spits the words out. 'Who's talking about girlfriends? What's really going on here, Piers? You're acting so strangely.' She takes a step towards me, her arm outstretched, her face softened. I was so close to saying something. So close to asking her the truth about Raf. I've never been the jealous type, never had the need to be. But now, I question my judgement.

'It's nothing,' I say and step backwards.

'For God's sake, Piers! It's obviously not nothing!' She's shouting at me now. How quickly Susan shifts from one emotion to another. It's always impossible to keep up.

There are footsteps behind me. The door swings open. 'What's going on?'

It's Raf, wearing that manky grey T-shirt again and grey joggers.

'Your father wants to go back to France,' Susan says.

'Yeah, me too,' he says.

'Well, we're not going. We're here on holiday in this beautiful house,' Susan snaps.

'It's fine, Raf. Ignore us. Just go to bed,' I say. 'Your mum and I are allowed to argue from time to time.'

'Weirdos,' he mutters and stomps back to his room.

'I'm taking a shower,' Susan says.

'We need to talk,' I say, trying to stand without swaying.

'We'll talk when you're sober,' Susan replies. Then she

strides into the bathroom, and pulls the door shut behind her. I hear her slide the lock across the door.

CHAPTER TWELVE

ELODIE

I wake up, sweat drenching my torso, adrenaline pumping through my veins. I sit up, pushing the thin duvet off me, trying to remember the nightmare that must have caused this physiological reaction. Except my mind is blank and I can't recall anything. Lewis is snoring irregularly, the result of too much alcohol, and an irrational surge of resentment hits me. Here he is, fast asleep without a care in the world, unbothered that he's keeping me awake. I nudge him with my foot but he just grunts more loudly and turns over. I try to settle back on the mattress except then I hear something.

What was it? A footstep? My heart speeds up as I sit up again. And then I remember that Danielle and Niall are here, and one of them is probably stumbling to Raf's bathroom. Probably not Danielle, if she took a sleeping pill. I listen out for Pushkin's deep bark, but there's only silence.

For some reason I can't stop thinking about the story Colette told us, about poor Margot Dupont whose body may or may not be buried at Chateau Lester, about her grandparents who were murdered here. I wonder which room it happened in. Were they asleep at the time, possibly even lying unsuspecting in this very bedroom? I shiver involuntarily, even though the room is warm and Lewis is radiating heat. Are the floorboards underneath the thin, worn carpet soaked with blood? I know my imagination is running away with me and I'm being ridiculous but her anecdote has really affected me. It's not like I believe in ghosts and I certainly have no interest in true crime, except knowing that a horrific crime happened here makes me feel uneasy. I wonder what the Lesters think about it, whether they purchased the chateau at a knock-down price because of its unfortunate history.

Despite the beauty of the setting here, the house has a coldness to it, and it's nothing to do with the crumbling interior. I lie in bed trying but failing to fall asleep. Lewis's irregular snoring is frustrating; it's as if every time I'm about to drop off, he snorts and I'm startled awake again. I prod him in the ribs, but it doesn't make any difference. Eventually, when the clock hits 6 a.m., I give up on sleep and get up, pulling on some old clothes and heading downstairs.

The smell hits me the moment I reach the bottom step. What was an unpleasant odour earlier is now a rancid stench, like something is rotting. I walk towards the kitchen, expecting that the smell might be worse in here, but weirdly it's not. Although I took out the bin last night, I open it anyway to double-check. I also double-check the oven, wondering if we left something inside it, and then remembering that I already looked earlier. But there's nothing suspect and it doesn't smell like fish. Back in the hallway the stench is worse and as I walk into the living room, I feel like gagging. I squeeze my nostrils together and hold my T-shirt up over my mouth. There must be something dead in here.

The smell is equally disgusting in the library but it's not obvious where it's coming from. I open all the windows and shut the doors behind me, returning to the kitchen. I've just turned the kettle on when Niall appears.

'Good morning,' he says jovially. 'What's that awful stink?'

'I don't know. I can't work out what it is or where it's coming from. Not exactly pleasant to be greeted with that first thing in the morning.'

'Could the builders have disturbed something? Opened a sewage drain by mistake, perhaps?'

'Maybe, but they weren't here yesterday and the smell only materialised yesterday evening.'

'Doesn't mean much. It would take a while for the smell to emerge.'

He's probably right, but I think back to how Lucille was creeping around the house last night. Could she have done something? But if so, why? I don't see any reason why Raf's girlfriend should leave a dead something or other in the house, and besides, she was upstairs and I'm positive the revolting smell emanates from somewhere downstairs.

'Would you like a coffee?' I ask Niall. He shuts the kitchen door and settles in a chair at the old wooden kitchen table.

'Sure would. Strong, please. We drank a lot last night, didn't we?'

We chat for a few minutes until Lewis appears.

'Smells like someone's died,' he says, as he strides into the kitchen. 'I've searched through the house and can't work out where it's coming from.'

'I was wondering if the builders disturbed something,' Niall suggests.

I can't help but think of Margot, although if she was buried here, that would have been years ago. It's a ridiculous notion.

'Yeah, good point. We'll need to get them back to investigate.'

I groan inwardly. Just when I thought we were set to have a tranquil rest of the holidays, André and his men will have to return.

Niall and Danielle leave quickly. She seems disinclined to hang around in our rancid house, and frankly, I don't blame her. And just as they're leaving, André's van speeds up the drive, throwing white dust up behind him. That was quick. Lewis goes out to greet him and as I watch through the window I see both men waving their arms around as if they're having an angry discussion. This is unusual for my normally placid husband and I wonder what André has said to upset him.

CHAPTER THIRTEEN

RAFAEL

This is the worst ever holiday. Mum and Dad have been at each other's throats, yet when they're around me, they're pretending all is peachy. Do they really think I'm that stupid? So when Hugo messages and says he and a bunch of his mates are going out for the afternoon, and do I want to join them, I leap at the opportunity. I've wondered why he's being so nice to me, but actually I think he might be lonely. He's an only child like me and his parents are completely overbearing.

His mother, who has had so much work done to her face she looks freakish, only comes home to deliver her shopping. Although she doesn't lower herself to do anything as basic as carrying designer shopping bags; her chauffeur does that for her. And she doesn't cook or clean either; the maids do that. In fact I wonder what she does do all day. I've only met Hugo's dad once, and he threw me such a disdainful look I hope I never meet him again.

Hugo's told me what they expect from him; top grades, studying at Oxford followed by accountancy qualifications

THE HOUSE SWAP   129

and then off to work in his father's investment house, what-ever the hell that is. I feel sorry for him because actually Hugo wants to be an actor. He's had leading roles in loads of his school plays and he showed me a clip from when he was Hamlet. He's seriously good. But apparently his parents don't consider acting to be a proper job. I asked him why he doesn't just do it anyway, go to RADA or wherever, but he looked at me like I was deranged. I can't think of anything worse than going to boarding school, but Hugo says he loves it there. He's surrounded by his friends and has more freedom at school than he does at home. I know Mum and Dad think life is worse when you're poor like us, but honestly Hugo is like a caged animal despite all the wealth. It's sad.

Anyway, I've put on my best shirt and now I'm heading next door. The moment I ring the bell, the door swings open and Hugo is standing there wearing black cargo pants and a pale pink Hollister shirt that I wouldn't be seen dead in.

'Raf, my mate. Meet the gang!' He stands back and I see three girls and two guys. They all look a lot older than me, the girls' faces heavily made up with long fake eyelashes and airbrushed skin. 'Raf here lives in a chateau in France and is staying at the neighbours' for a couple of weeks. We're off to our fav pub. You gonna join us?'

'Sure, thank you,' I say, feeling super awkward. Hugo is speaking with his plummy voice but it's as if he's affecting a common way of speaking and it's all a bit weird. He glances at his phone.

'Right, the cabs are here.'

A moment later, I'm bundled in the back of a black cab with Hugo and two of the girls, one with long, dark brown hair, the other blonde with long fake nails embellished with little diamonds. They're both wearing really short dresses, their tanned legs impossibly long. The blonde, who I soon discover is called Flora, cosies up to Hugo, but I'm fine with that because the dark-haired girl seems nicer.

'I'm Isabella,' she says, smiling at me. I'm surprised that she has a tongue piercing.

'Raf,' I say awkwardly. I'm facing backwards in the cab and I'm trying to stop my knees from bumping up against hers.

'Where are you going to uni?' she asks.

'Um, I'm not sure yet. I live in France, so probably somewhere there.'

'Oh, right. You're taking a year out then?'

I smile because I don't want to outright lie and let them know I'm at least a year younger than them.

'Where are you going to uni?' I ask.

'I'm at Exeter. Second year, Psychology. My family is so screwed up, someone needs to sort them out.'

I laugh, but she looks completely serious, which is embarrassing.

'Hugo says that you live in a chateau. Has it got turrets and a moat?'

'Something like that,' I say.

Isabella leans forwards and squeezes my knee. 'You're cute.' I feel my cheeks flame up. I try not to look at her too much, because she's really pretty, model-like, and her hair is so glossy it's reflecting the streets as we drive past. I have no idea where the taxi is going but when I swivel around to look out of the front of the car, to my dismay, the meter says the fare is already thirty-one pounds. How is that possible? What if I'm expected to pay a quarter? I finger the ten-pound note in my pocket that Dad gave me earlier.

Eventually the taxi pulls up outside a brick building, geranium-filled hanging baskets lining the front. Hugo is the last out of the cab and I wait for him to pay the driver, or ask us to contribute, but he doesn't. He just slings his arms around Flora and strides away.

'Don't we have to pay?' I ask Isabella.

'You really are sweet,' she says. 'It's on account. Hugo's dad takes care of things like that. Come on, let's go and get a drink.'

I follow her inside. The pub is busy with young people, mainly in their early twenties. Hugo seems to know quite a few, and greets the guys with fist bumps and the girls with three cheek kisses. 'Let's get a table outside and then we can order drinks,' Hugo says. I follow him through the pub and only when we're outside do I realise that we're right on the banks of the river Thames. I've no idea which part of London we're in, but it's attractive and bustling. The girls sit down on benches at a large wooden table and I'm about to follow suit when Hugo says, 'Felix, you, me and Raf can get the drinks in. What do you all want?'

Hugo jots down everyone's drinks order on his mobile phone; it's mainly beers and white wines with the occasional Aperol Spritz and gin and tonic thrown in. Everyone is drinking alcohol, which must mean they're all over eighteen. Well, perhaps some of them have fake identities but I don't get the sense they need to. From the way they're talking they have either just left school this term and are waiting for their A Level results, or they're on gap years prior to going to university, or a couple, like Isabella and Felix, are already in their second year of uni. I'm definitely the youngest.

At the bar, Hugo reels off the order and then turns to me. 'What are you having, buddy?'

'Um, a Coke please.'

'That's a bit lame. Have a beer.'

'No, it's fine. I'm good with a Coke.' To be honest, I don't even like the taste of beer. If I was going to have anything, I'd have a glass of red wine. Perhaps I'm more French than I think I am. I only drank beers with Hugo because that's all that was on offer. The total bill comes to just over seventy quid. I'm shocked. Then again, what do I know about London prices? I pull out the tenner and offer it to Hugo. He laughs at me and bats it away.

'This round's on me,' he says, handing the server a shiny black credit card. Hugo and I carry the drinks back on two circular trays. I walk gingerly, worried I'm going to spill something, because I can't afford to replace them. At the table, Isabella pats the empty space next to her and I wedge myself on the end of the bench. I can feel the heat of her as my thigh almost touches hers and it makes me feel guilty, thinking about Lucille.

'What are you drinking?' Flora asks, pointing at my Coke.

'Just a Coke,' I mumble.

'That's so lame. You live in France, don't you? You must know loads about wine, or do you prefer beer?'

'Wine. I mean beer's okay, but we drink more wine in France.'

'So what are you doing drinking Coke?' Flora asks. She flicks her long blonde hair over her right shoulder and fixes her bright blue eyes on mine. I shuffle uncomfortably and then feel a warm hand on my knee. That makes me feel even worse, because I'm sure Isabella is just toying with me. She's way out of my league. Besides, I remind myself I'm in love with Lucille.

'Go and get a proper drink,' Flora says. I glance at Hugo, hoping he'll come to my rescue, but he's deep in conversation with one of the other lads. 'In fact, choose us a couple of bottles of wine. No, make that three. One red, two white. I haven't got a clue what's good wine and what isn't. Do you, Issy? Daddy orders for all of us when we go out.'

'I'm useless at wines, too,' Isabella says. 'But I know a bad wine when I taste it. That's why I normally order spirits when I'm out. Do you remember that acidic pee-like wine we had at Darcy's? I was sick for days afterwards.' The two girls laugh at some shared memory. Flora leans backwards and swipes a menu off an adjacent table. She hands it to me.

'Have a look through and order us something good, Frenchie.'

I grab the menu and get off the bench. What the hell am I going to do? I'm underage and I've got ten quid on me. That's barely going to buy a glass of wine, let alone three bottles. I walk slowly to the bar looking at the menu, unable to swallow when I read the prices of bottles. I'm standing there, the words swimming in and out, when the server leans forwards, propping himself up by his elbows.

'What can I get you?' he asks. 'You're not buying alcohol, are you?'

I open and close my mouth, unable to meet his eyes.

'Can I see your ID?'

I stare at the server and I realise that he's laughing at me, that he knows I'm underage and I haven't got a clue what to do. 'My ID?' I mutter.

And then there's a heavy hand on my shoulder and I see that it's Hugo, and before I know what I'm doing, I let the wine menu drop onto the bar and I've wriggled myself out of Hugo's grip. 'I've got to go,' I mutter as I race between the tables and out the front door of the pub. I run, my trainers pounding on the hard pavement, along the side of the road that edges the river, not once glancing back over my shoulder. I run and run until I'm completely breathless, and only then do I bend over, trying to catch my breath. I glance backwards, towards the direction of the pub, but I don't see Hugo or any faces I recognise. What the hell is he going to think? Stupid tears spring to my eyes. What was I doing, trying to fit in with people like that? Entitled kids with credit cards and fancy dreams. And now, I have no idea where I am or how to get back to the Browns' house. I lean against green railings and call Dad. He's the lesser of the two evils and the least likely to bite my head off for getting lost in London, but he doesn't pick up and I don't leave a message. Reluctantly, I call Mum, but surprisingly she doesn't answer either. I open up Google Maps and plug in the address of the Browns' house (which Dad insisted I write down on my phone, and now I'm glad he did) and then select walk from my location. It will take one hour and fifty-six minutes to walk back. I could take the tube, I suppose, but I've never been on it alone and I don't know if my ten quid will be enough, so walking it is.

I follow my phone and walk along footsteps that edge busy roads, fumes from traffic making me feel nauseous, and all these people... At one point a guy in a black hoodie walks towards me and I'm sure I see the glint of a knife in his hand. I try not to catch his eye but he's staring at me, a vacant, terrifying gaze, and I'm not sure what to do: run across the busy road darting between the red buses and speeding white vans, or turn around and pace back the way I came. I hesitate, my heart pounding hard, trying to watch the guy but at the same time avoiding catching his eye. And then a silver Prius comes to a halt just adjacent to me, a couple tumbling out of the back seat, and the guy with the knife disappears down an alleyway.

I let out a small gulp of relief and walk faster. This place terrifies me. It's too busy, too many people and so much noise. It's not just the traffic, but the intermittent sirens, the chattering of voices, hooting of horns, the rumbling of the ground underneath from the tube trains, and the planes overhead on their descent into Heathrow airport. Everything and everyone is moving so quickly and I find it hard to breathe. My phone is down to 5% battery but at last I turn onto the now familiar street lined with smart houses and an atmosphere that is so rarefied in comparison to many of the places I've just walked through. With relief, I walk up the steps, put my key in the door and turn the handle.

I'm parched, so I walk straight through to the kitchen to pour myself a glass of water from the filtered water tap integrated into the fridge. But the place is a tip. There are dirty plates on the island unit and a glass of wine lying on its side, drops of red wine like blood staining the white marble. Mum isn't the tidiest of people, but this is bad. And we're not even in our own home. If I'd left a mess like that, I'd have my head bitten off.

'Dad!' I shout through the hallway, but there's no answer. I run up the stairs and am about to push open my parents' bedroom door when I hear Mum's voice. She's talking in a low voice, kind of with a revolting sexy edge to it, a bit like the way girls talk on OnlyFans.

'But meeting up with you is the whole reason I organised this trip to London.'

There's silence, and then she says, 'I know. I've missed–'

I take a step nearer to the door but my foot makes the

floorboards squeak and Mum says hurriedly, 'I've got to go. I'll call you back when I'm alone.'

I hurry into my bedroom but not before Mum shouts at me. 'Raf! Where have you been?'

To my disgust she's wearing some silken underwear that shows way too much, and it's gross. I've never seen her in anything like that before, but it's what she was saying that's upset me the most. I slam my bedroom door shut and lean my back up against it.

What did Mum mean talking like that on the phone? It sounds like she's having an illicit affair. And then I think about how Mum and Dad have been arguing, and perhaps she really is having an affair and that's what all the tension has been about. My legs ache and my feet are burning with soreness, so I slip to the ground and hug my knees to my chest. I hate everybody. And I hate myself. I'm never going to be able to see Hugo again now that I ran away like a total idiot. I miss Lucille so much. I haul myself up to my feet and plug my phone in, then I call her via WhatsApp but it rings and rings and eventually stops. It's like I've got no one. I don't fit in anywhere. Here in London I'm not cool enough, not rich enough, not old enough. And in France I'm the foreigner, the kid who still pronounces things just a bit wrong, the stupid Brit who lives in a fake chateau which sounds oh-so-glamorous but in fact sucks. And what if Mum and Dad split up? What about me?

CHAPTER FOURTEEN

ELODIE

André and his colleague are making a total racket, slamming and banging, pulling up floorboards, creating clouds of dust. Meanwhile I'm upstairs stripping the bed that Niall and Danielle slept in, putting the sheets and towels into the washing machine, trying but failing to ignore the dreadful smell that seems to engulf the whole house. I wonder if the builders know about Margot and the suspicions that her body is buried here. And do the Lesters know? I'm not sure I would want to buy a property that had such a history.

And then I hear a yell, and immediately catastrophise. Have they found human remains? Or the axe, perhaps. I hurry downstairs, pinching my nostrils together as I walk into the living room. Lewis is there, a broad smile on his face.

'We found it!' André says. He's holding a dead squirrel by its tail, the stench making me want to vomit.

'Where was it?' Lewis asks.

'Up the chimney, which is strange, because we only worked on the chimney a week ago. But these things happen in old houses.'

Do they, I think.

André puts the dead animal into a black bin bag held open by his colleague, who swiftly ties the top into a knot and carries it outside. The rancid smell decreases quickly.

'Go and buy yourselves a drink as a thank you from us,' Lewis says, handing André some euro notes that he's removed from his trouser pocket.

'Are you sure?' André asks. He looks equally surprised and delighted.

'Of course I'm sure, mate,' Lewis says, patting André on the back.

'WELL, THAT'S A RELIEF,' I say to Lewis as we watch the men leave. 'At last, a day to ourselves.'

'I was thinking I'd go out for a bike ride since the weather is so lovely,' he says.

He must note the look of disappointment on my face. 'We'll have a romantic time when I get back, alright?' Lewis's idea of romance is sex, and not the romantic type that we used to have when we were newly married, but wham-bam-thank-you-Ma'am. It's not what I had in mind. I shrug, because I can't be bothered to get into an argument. At least I'll have a few hours alone.

When Lewis has gone, I wander down to the pool, pull out a sun lounger and lie there for a while, soaking up the sun, feeling completely languid and relaxed. When I get too warm, I slip into the pool and take lazy lengths up and down. This is the holiday I was dreaming of.

And then there's the sound of a crash. I start, sitting upright, trying to work out where the noise came from. Pushkin starts barking from inside the house and I realise that I can't ignore him. Perhaps there's someone at the front door, the opposite side of the building to where I am. I pull on my kaftan and hurry up the path, onto the veranda and around the side of the house. The dog appears, wagging his tail at the sight of me, trotting along at my heels. There is no one there.

'Hello!' I shout, glancing around for a person or a vehicle. But the air is still and the gravel dust-free.

And then I hear a noise again. It sounds like something has fallen to the ground and broken. I swivel around in a full circle, sure I hear footsteps. My heart starts thumping. It's hard to work out where the noise was coming from. Perhaps the tower, or at the side of the chateau.

Pushkin barks as I stride towards the tower. There is scaffolding around the outside and a door that is half open. I haven't paid this section of the chateau any attention, mainly because the builders have been hanging around there. It's a square tower, not particularly tall, but extending above the roofline of the main house, turrets at the top. I walk quickly around the side, where there are raised vegetable beds, empty of any fresh produce, the soil dry and flaky, the grass around them overgrown but burned from the hot sun. There's an old, rusting lawn mower lying abandoned up against the wall. Perhaps there's a gardener or a pool maintenance person here to do some work, but no. They would arrive in a vehicle.

'Hello!' I shout again. I'm met with silence. Perhaps I imagined the noise, overtired from a late night and red wine. I walk back to the entrance to the tower. The door is old, with paint peeling, but standing ajar, as if inviting me inside. I push at the door, but Pushkin is at my feet, nudging his wet nose into my bare legs, as if he's trying to tell me something.

'What is it, boy?' I ask, rubbing the top of his smooth, velvet-like head.

'Hello?' I shout again, but my voice echoes, bouncing around the inside. It's dark inside the tower but my eyes adjust quickly, and I can see there's a spiral wooden staircase rising to the top. I'm sure the view must be beautiful from the turret. There's silence now and I wonder if an animal caused a tile to tumble to the ground, but didn't I hear footsteps? The turret's interior walls are made from exposed bricks, many of which are crumbling, but the staircase looks solid enough. Pushkin nudges me again, but I tell him he's a good boy.

Then I notice it. A wet droplet on the first rung of the staircase. What caused that? It's so dry here. I bend down and peer at it, but it looks like water. Wondering if it's sensible, but doing it anyway, I use the pad of my index finger to wipe the drop and bring my finger up to my nose, inhaling deeply. It smells of nothing. Why is there moisture here? Or could it have come from Pushkin when he shook his head at me? I reckon I'm overthinking, so I put my right foot on the first rung of the staircase.

'Anyone up there?' I ask, but I'm pretty sure no one is here. The air feels cooler inside and very still. As I step further up I jump as a cobweb wraps itself around my neck. My heart is beating a bit faster now and I hesitate. Is this a good idea? Telling myself that I'm being ridiculous, I walk upwards more resolutely, my flip-flops making smacking noises with each step. I wonder if I can see the sea from the top of the tower. The wood feels a bit soft under my foot, spongey, as if it's been wettened. But there are no further droplets of moisture up here and I reckon the droplet on the bottom must have come from the dog. I grip the handrail tightly and gingerly put my left foot on the next step. I glance upwards, my neck cricking, and catch sight of something that's glinting from the light coming in at the top of the tower. I take another step upwards, my eyes trying to make out what it is.

I gasp. It looks like an axe, the metal catching the glimmer of the sunbeams, the old wooden handle gnarled with age and use, just lying discarded on the top step. I blink a few times to be sure it's what I'm seeing. Is this *the* axe? Quickly, I come to my senses. Of course it isn't. This will be one of André's tools. There are plenty lying around the property. Besides, the police would have searched every inch of this place after Margot disappeared, and goodness knows how many people have been in here in the intervening years. Telling myself I'm being ridiculous I take another step upwards.

I hear it first. A loud crack, as if someone has brought the axe down on wood. And then I feel it. My foot goes straight downwards. The wooden step has just disappeared and I'm trying desperately to hold onto something. Anything. The handrail seems to have vanished and I'm tumbling downwards. Backwards.

I scream.

My hands are speared by splinters of wood, except that initially I feel nothing. Just the air that is racing around my face, the dust in my eyes, the cracking and crumbling of the staircase. Wood that should have been secure breaking up into jagged particles. And me. Plummeting to the ground. The hard, stone-covered floor.

The second seems so very long as I wonder whether this is it. Whether this is the end.

Am I about to die in an old tower, in a fake chateau in the South of France?

IT COULD BE a couple of seconds, or even a minute, but the shock blanks my brain. And then Pushkin is whimpering, nudging me, licking my cheek.

I try to raise myself up but my shoulder screams with pain. I'm not dead, at least. I rotate my feet and one ankle hurts, but it's definitely not broken. The same with my wrists. I look at the palm of my left hand. It's scratched and bleeding, full of wooden splinters. And then I try to do the same with my right arm and there's a searing pain when I try to lift it, radiating across my neck and shoulder. I'm such an idiot. What was I thinking, climbing up a derelict staircase? I try to sit up, edging myself backwards so I can lean against the brick wall, but tears spring to my eyes, and I know I've done something major to my shoulder. I cough as dust thickens the air and settles all around me. Pushkin nudges his head against me once again, and I'm so thankful that the dog is here. Taking a deep breath I wriggle backwards so at least I'm supported by the wall. I glance at my watch. Goodness knows when Lewis will be back, and will he even hear me, stuck out here in this brick tower?

TIME PASSES SO SLOWLY and at some point, despite the pain, I must doze off. When I awake, the shadows are much longer. The air in here feels dank and unpleasant, whereas earlier it was just hot and dry. I try to move and cry out in pain. I call out for Pushkin, but he's no longer here and my voice just echoes around the tower. Lewis should be back by now, and surely he'll come looking for me. Or will my independence play against me? I've never been one of those needy wives who clings to her husband the moment he returns from work. Lewis and I do our own things, leading increasingly independent lives, and perhaps he'll think I've taken myself off for a walk, or popped over to Colette's winery. My phone. I fumble around, feeling for pockets, but I'm only wearing my kaftan with no pockets. Where did I leave my phone? On the sun lounger or upstairs in the bedroom? Lewis will find it, surely, and then he'll wonder why I've left it behind. But will he? I'm not even sure how Lewis thinks these days. Perhaps he won't care. Perhaps he'll just pour himself a beer and settle in front of his iPad watching cycling races. Perhaps he won't bother to call my phone, let alone look for me. That loneliness pierces deep within and I stifle a little self-pitying sob. I could be here for hours.

Despite the pain, I'm going to have to get myself out of here. I move very gingerly, biting my lip so hard I taste metallic blood, and with my left arm, clutch my right shoulder. Whereas before my whole body was screaming, now the pain seems more localised. I'm sure that something is broken; my shoulder or arm perhaps? A rib or two maybe? Every so often I have to take slow, deep breaths to calm myself, to stop the nausea. But my legs are working, even if they're sore and bleeding. I hobble so slowly and then, as if fate is now on my side, Lewis comes cycling up the driveway.

'I'm hurt,' I say, before sinking back to the ground.

'Bloody hell,' Lewis says, securing the bike and then hurrying towards me. 'What's happened?'

'I fell through a rotten staircase in the tower.'

'What were you doing up there?' He scowls at me.

'I heard something and went to investigate.' I don't mention that I'm sure I heard footsteps because now I'm wondering if I imagined them. After all, the story of Margot is still reverberating in my head. And Pushkin barked, and the dog wouldn't have barked for no reason. I don't mention the axe lying abandoned on that top step.

'We'd better get you to a hospital,' Lewis says. Somehow, he bundles me into the rental car, supporting my shoulder and arm with multiple cushions, and I squeeze my eyes shut to try to stop some of the pain. He returns with a bottle of water and my handbag, then starts the car engine before turning to me. 'Where am I going?'

'I don't know!' I yelp. 'You're the one who's been exploring on your bike. Work it out.'

He opens his mouth as if he's about to argue with me but then seems to think better of it. After fiddling with his phone, which seems to take an age, he plugs in the Sat Nav and we're off.

It turns out that there's a small cottage hospital on the outskirts of Sainte-Chouette although to me, it looks more like a doctor's surgery.

'Stay in the car and I'll get someone to come and help you,' Lewis says. A few minutes later and I'm in a wheel-chair, being pushed into a darkened room with an X-ray machine. I'm impressed. This wouldn't be happening if I was in the UK. I'd likely be left on a hospital trolley for hours until I could be seen. A female doctor wearing a white coat operates the machine. She is gentle with me but she doesn't speak any English and my French seems to have deserted me in the haze of pain. But we make do with pointing and facial gestures. She wheels me back into a small waiting room

where Lewis is the only person waiting, pacing up and
down, his jaw clenched tightly.

'Why are you so uptight?' I ask.

'This shouldn't have happened! I'm worried about you.'

I smile gingerly because this is Lewis being sweet. He's
normally so brusque and it is heartwarming to know that
deep down he really cares.

And then I'm taken in to see another doctor and Lewis
insists on accompanying me.

'So, Mrs Brown.' This doctor speaks flawless English.
'You have fractured your collarbone and have bruises on
your shoulder and arm. You do not need an operation.'

I breathe out with relief.

'We will put your arm in a sling and you will need lots of
ice. Apply ice to the shoulder every thirty minutes for the
next three days to reduce the swelling and I will give you a
prescription for painkillers. You will need to keep your arm
in the sling for at least two weeks and then you need to see a
physio to start exercises until it is fully recovered.'

'That's good news,' Lewis says. I suppose the fact I don't
need an operation is good news, but it's going to be very frustrating keeping my arm in a sling. Just as well I'm lefthanded.
And it also means I won't be able to swim in the pool or do
all the things I'd planned on doing during this holiday.

'And please do not take an airplane for at least forty-eight
hours and ideally several days. You need to rest,' the doctor says.

Back in the car, laden with boxes of painkillers and my
arm strapped up, Lewis mutters, 'I don't know what you
were doing up there. If it was dangerous they should have
put a barrier up, told us that it wasn't safe.'

'Who's they?' I snap.

'Bloody André. In fact I'm going to call him.' Before I can stop Lewis, he's dialled André, whose voice comes blaring out of the car's loudspeakers.

'Oui,' he says.

'André, it's Lewis Brown. My wife has just had a nasty accident when the staircase in the tower gave way.'

'The tower?' His voice is uncomprehending.

'At the Lesters' place.'

'But you should not have gone in the tower. There is a barrier to stop people from entering.'

'There isn't,' I say, staring at Lewis's jawline where a nerve is pinging.

'It was there two days ago,' André says. 'A panneau d'interdiction. Do you understand?'

'No,' Lewis says.

'It's a sign with a red circle and a black hand in the middle with the words *Entrée interdite*. You know what that means?'

'Yes,' I say. 'No entry. But it wasn't there.'

'And there was tape across the doorway too. I don't understand why it wasn't there. For sure it was there yesterday or the day before.' There's concern in André's voice. I wonder if he's thinking about liability.

There's a long pause and I can sense that both men are wondering whether perhaps I ignored the sign and went in anyway, except I didn't. I'm not that stupid.

'Well, someone has screwed up,' Lewis says. I'm relieved he's on my side. 'Did you know the staircase was dangerous?'

'Of course. That is why we put the sign there. The staircase needs replacing.'

'Someone has put our lives in danger by removing the sign,' Lewis says.

'But no one would do that on purpose.' André sounds indignant. 'My workmen are good guys. They are not stupid.'

'We're at the hospital and I need to get Elodie home,' Lewis says.

'I am very sorry you are hurt,' André adds. Lewis cuts the call.

On the way back to the Chateau Lester, Lewis seems agitated, much more annoyed than I am. 'I'm going to sue the Lesters. This whole holiday has been a shit show and there they are, swanning around in our lovely home. And now you're incapacitated. I mean, you won't even be able to make a meal or pack the suitcase. Hardly a holiday for me, is it?'

I grit my teeth. For one moment I'd hoped that Lewis was thinking of me first. Clearly not. He glances at me and must notice my expression.

'Sorry, love,' he says. 'It's just it's disappointing for both of us. You won't be able to do the things you want to do and I won't be able to take any long bike rides because you'll need me around.'

'These things happen,' I mutter. 'We'll have a few days of rest and then we can go home.' Not a day too soon.

CHAPTER FIFTEEN

PIERS

The email I receive from Lewis is vitriolic and angry. Apparently Elodie climbed the staircase in the tower and fell, breaking her collarbone. What the hell she was doing going up that knackered staircase, I've no idea. And now Lewis is threatening to sue us, saying that we and our builders were negligent.

'What's the matter?' Susan asks. I show her the email.

She snorts. 'They won't sue. It's all bluster.'

'How do you know? Lewis is obviously the combative type, and let's face it. They've got plenty of money to sue us. They'll use the very best solicitors and we'll be completely shafted.'

'Stop catastrophizing,' Susan says dismissively. She is standing at the bathroom mirror, applying her makeup. She seems to be spending ages over it, carefully edging eyeliner along her lower lashes, pouting at herself. And then she sighs, and removes all the makeup with cotton wool pads before starting all over again.

'But we don't even have public indemnity insurance because you said –'

'I know what I said,' Susan cuts me off, and then chucks a cotton wool pad towards the bin. She misses. We had quite an argument over insurance. I'm the type who prefers to over-insure everything whereas Susan is happy to take risks. I was worried, and still am, that if anything happens with the builders or the scaffolding, we'll be held personally liable. Susan said it was an unnecessary expense and as a lawyer, she knew best. I called her a pseudo-lawyer. That didn't go down well.

'Just send Lewis a message to apologise and wish Elodie a speedy recovery,' Susan says, licking her teeth as she peers at herself in the mirror.

'But that's akin to admitting responsibility,' I say.

'For God's sake, Piers. Why do you always think the worst of everything and everyone?'

I pause for a moment, because she's right. I do have a tendency to do that. It's ironic, really, considering it's Susan who had the legal training. But then again, this is coming from the woman who has lied to me for the past eighteen years, and who is probably still lying.

'Can you do something with Raf today?' Susan asks.

Raf hasn't come out of his bedroom and when I asked him, through the closed door, if he wanted any breakfast, he just grunted no. I'm not sure what happened yesterday, because he came home exhausted and then hid away in his room refusing to talk to either of us.

'I'll try. I wonder if he's had a falling out with Hugo, because he's refusing to talk.'

'Mm,' Susan says, putting lipstick on and then patting her lips with a tissue. She seems really distracted and it's weird because her tendency is to micromanage what Raf is up to, not be this laissez-faire. This combination of carefully applied makeup and disinterest in Raf is making me highly suspicious.

'Are you not joining us today?' I ask.

'Um, no.'

It's like getting blood out of a stone and I'm riled. 'What are you doing?' My words come out a bit harshly and she glances up at me through the mirror.

'Just having a last-minute lunch with a girlfriend.'

'Which girlfriend?' I ask, hackles rising further because I don't believe a word my wife is saying.

'Rose. She was there last night.'

I've no idea who Rose is and clearly my wife must think I'm an idiot watching her applying her makeup with extra care, two dresses laid out on the bed as if she can't decide which one to wear. I don't believe a word she's saying. Susan would never get dressed up like this just to go for lunch with a girlfriend.

I sit on the edge of the bed pretending to read something on my phone and watch as she selects the royal blue dress and slides into it, patting it down over her hips, putting on the necklace that I bought her a few years ago along with the matching earrings. She looks way too dressed up for a lunch.

'Right, I need to get a move on. I'll message you later.'

'I'll walk you to the restaurant. I could do with some fresh air,' I say, getting to my feet. 'I'll pick up some food so Raf and I can have some lunch.'

'No need to come with me,' she says hastily, unable to meet my eyes and fumbling in her handbag. 'I'll take a taxi.'

I want to retort that taxis are expensive, that she's said herself that we need to watch the pennies, but something holds me back from starting another argument. Instead, I wish her a good time. She walks down the stairs and I hear the front door opening, and then I hurry to the window and I watch her emerging onto the street below. A second later, as she's adjusting her raincoat, a taxi passes with its light lit up indicating that it's free, and I can see my wife is looking right at the vehicle. Yet she doesn't raise her hand to hail it, but starts walking along the pavement in the direction of Knightsbridge. Another lie.

Before I know what I'm doing, I'm racing down the stairs, grabbing my jacket off the hook, and I'm outside, also turning briskly to the right, following my wife. I catch a glimpse of her just as she turns left at the bottom of the street. She's walking with purpose, but carefully, and I see that she's wearing the same high heels she was wearing last night. I know Susan, and this is not a woman on her way to a casual lunch with a girlfriend. It's easy enough to follow her. I keep at a fair distance, but I know my wife's gait, recognise the back of her head, and I follow as she walks onto the Brompton Road. For a moment I'm worried that she's going to take the tube, but no. She walks straight past the entrance. And then she turns left onto Beauchamp Place, a street lined with designer dresses and numerous restaurants serving up different cuisines. She stops outside a restaurant and glances up at the sign, before walking up the steps, opening the door, and disappearing inside. I stand on the opposite side of the road and wait. She mustn't see me, and now I'm not sure what to do. Except then a black cab pulls up outside the restaurant and a suited man climbs out. It's handsome, successful Tim De Withers. Exactly whom I feared it might be.

My feet feel like they're glued to the pavement. I'm

jostled by annoyed shoppers, yet I can't seem to move. Is Susan having an affair with Tim De Withers? Is he Raf's birth father? It's as if an invisible string is pulling me forwards, compelling me to watch even though I don't want to see. I hurry across the road, eliciting the hoot of a horn from a car which only just avoids hitting me. But I'm in time to see through the restaurant window as Tim De Withers places a kiss on my wife's cheek, his hands proprietorially on both of her shoulders, her face ever so slightly flushed as she looks up at him. Nausea rushes into my throat. This is why we're in London. This is why Susan has been acting coldly towards me. I shiver as I realise that it's this man who will be taking my wife and my child and destroying my life. Yet I have one little advantage. I know what's going on, and I know where he works and where he lives. But what am I going to do with that information?

I stand on the pavement staring in through the window. They sit down and the waiter hands them both menus, then walks away. Tim De Withers says something and Susan roars with laughter, her head thrown back exposing her milky white throat. My stomach clenches. And then Tim turns towards the window and I see him frown. Has he seen me? I dart backwards, away from the window, standing in the shop door adjacent to the restaurant, doubled over, with my hands on my knees.

I simply don't know what to do.

CHAPTER SIXTEEN

ELODIE

Piers calls me and he's deeply apologetic, saying that the tower was out of bounds and that André's men are to blame. Honestly, accidents happen and I should never have gone up there. I can tell he feels really bad, and fortunately Lewis's initial idea of suing both the Lesters and André seems to have been ignored.

'Has André put the barrier back?' Piers asks.

'Yes, he has. But he and the other builders aren't on site.'

'Do you need anything?' Piers asks. 'I could ask a friend to come over, help you with shopping and stuff like that.'

'It's kind of you, but Lewis is out doing a grocery shop and I'm sure we'll be just fine. You have lovely neighbours. Colette has been so kind, inviting us to a wine tasting at their vineyard, and she and Didier joined us for supper here. You're lucky to have them.'

There's a long pause at the other end of the phone and for a moment I wonder if we've been cut off.

'Piers?' I ask.

'They're not our friends,' he says eventually. 'In fact our

relationship with them is extremely strained and I'm shocked that they are ingratiating themselves with you.'

'Oh,' I say, stunned that the previously mild-mannered Piers seems to dislike the Moreaus so much.

'I'd really appreciate if you didn't invite them into our home.'

I'm tongue-tied for a moment. And then Piers sighs.

'The thing is we had a real problem with them shortly after we moved in, and things have only gotten worse since. When we first moved into the chateau, they seemed friendly enough. In fact Didier offered to be the foreman when we shared our renovation plans with them. We'd appointed a firm of local builders but none of them spoke English and our French was pretty much non-existent at that time.'

As Piers pauses for breath, that strikes me as strange because I recall how Colette said Didier's English wasn't great. He didn't talk much at the wine tasting but he was happy to interject during the telling of the Margot tale. His English is certainly a lot better than my French.

'Anyway, on the first day the builders started working for us, we returned home to discover that one of the panelled walls in the library had been completely ripped out. As you know, it's the most beautiful room in the house and the wooden panels are a couple of centuries old. There's no way we would have authorised that. Didier claimed that I'd said I wanted them removed but when I protested he said it was a breakdown in communication. Honestly, none of that made sense. I'm afraid our relation-ship fell apart after that and I had to fire the builders who refused to listen to me and only listened to Didier. We've tried to reach out to Didier and Colette over the years, but they've rebuffed us. And we know for sure that they've been badmouthing us in the local community, spreading gossip about us, telling people that we're poor payers, that we can't keep a workforce, that we're decimating the chateau.'

'How awkward,' I say, as Piers stops talking for a moment. 'And now?'

'Well, as you know, Lucille is dating Rafael so we rather hoped that relationships would improve between our two families. We invited Colette and Didier over for drinks at Christmas but they never responded. So you see how weird it is that the Moreaus are befriending you when they shun us.'

'Yes, that is strange,' I concur.

'So you'll avoid them going forwards?' he asks. 'I mean, I don't expect you to be rude. It's just awkward to have them in our house.'

'Don't worry, I completely understand,' I reassure Piers. And yes, it is bizarre that the Moreaus have been so friendly with us. I guess their dislike for the Lesters is very personal.

TWENTY MINUTES later and there's a familiar voice on the terrace. 'Elodie!'

I'm walking cautiously now, with my arm in a sling, so by the time I reach the kitchen door, Colette is already standing there, rapping on the glass. For a moment, I wonder if she somehow overheard my conversation with Piers, but then I dismiss the thought as ridiculous. I really feel like I'm losing the plot out here in the hot sun. Perhaps it's the painkillers mixed with the heat.

'Mon dieu!' she exclaims, as I open the door. 'I heard that you had a very bad accident. I brought you some goodies.'

She holds up a basket full of fruit and fresh vegetables along with another bottle of wine.

'Oh, um, yes,' I stumble over my words, recalling what Piers told me only a few minutes ago. 'How did you know?'

She laughs. 'This is a small town. My sister is a nurse in the local hospital, so she told me. What can I do to help?'

She moves as if she wants to step inside the kitchen, but I block her, awkwardly leaning my good shoulder on the doorframe and extending my left leg across the open doorway. 'This is so kind of you but really not necessary,' I say, gesturing to the basket she's holding.

'So what can I do to help?' Colette asks. 'Can I put this inside, prepare a meal for you, perhaps?'

'That's very kind,' I say hastily, 'but Lewis is doing a shop and he's quite capable of cooking. We really don't need all of those lovely things.' I glance at the full basket.

Colette's face falls, and I feel terrible for being so ungrateful, but Piers's words echo in my head. 'You don't want me to put this inside?' She frowns. 'Surely you can't carry anything heavy.'

'It's really generous of you, but please don't worry. Lewis will be back soon.'

She stares at me again, a puzzled look on her face, and she opens her mouth as if she's about to ask me something. But then at the last minute, she shrugs her shoulders and places the basket on the ground. 'Okay then,' she says. 'Call me if you need anything.'

'Thank you, Colette,' I say, but she's already striding away around the terrace, and a few moments later, I hear the engine of her car start up.

I feel terrible. Colette has been nothing but lovely towards us, and just because the Moreaus and the Lesters have a problem with each other, it shouldn't affect us. I'm very tempted to pick up the phone to Colette and apologise for my rudeness, explain it off due to the pain I'm in, but realising I don't have a mobile number for her, I walk back into the kitchen and, with great difficulty, make myself a strong coffee.

IT'S the middle of the night and I'm jolted awake by a noise, my heart already racing and adrenaline pumping through my veins, as if a nightmare has filtered through to my consciousness. The noise comes again but it's short and I can't place it. Once again, it sounds like someone is in the house.

'Wake up!' I nudge Lewis, who is snoring gently. I glance at my alarm clock. It's 2.43 a.m.

'What is it?' he asks groggily.

And then we both hear it. Something is banging outside. 'Not again!' I whisper, my fingers clutching the edge of the light duvet.

Lewis is up and off the bed, the light switched on, pulling on some clothes, but I don't want to be left alone. 'I'm coming too,' I say, wrapping a shawl around my thin night-dress, cursing my useless arm.

'Best if you stay here.'

But I ignore Lewis and follow him to the door. 'Who's there?' he shouts into the darkness of the house. Another thud. Lewis switches the hall light on and I peer over his shoulder. The place looks empty but there was definitely noise. I follow Lewis downstairs and hover in the hallway whilst he looks in the kitchen. He returns holding a large knife and my stomach clenches.

I follow him through into the living room and then into the library.

'Here,' he says. A window is wide open and a shutter is banging gently in the wind. Lewis climbs onto a chair that quivers precariously with his weight and steps out of the window onto the scaffolding. He shines the phone on his torch out towards the front of the house.

'They've gone,' he says. 'Did you leave the window open?'

'Of course not. It's not like I could have reached to open it with my arm in a sling.'

'Well, I certainly didn't. Haven't even been in this room.' He peers around. 'Looks like some idiots climbed the scaffolding again, but heavens knows why. Not sure how they got the window open from the outside because it doesn't seem broken.' He clambers back inside.

I think back to what Piers told me earlier, and his falling out with the Moreaus, how Colette was here but I sent her scuttling. I've been preoccupied with my shoulder, popping painkillers for the last twenty-four hours, so it is possible that the window wasn't secured properly and neither Lewis nor I noticed it. But then I chastise myself. Why am I always taking responsibility for everything? This is not my fault.

And suddenly it hits me. Pushkin. 'Where is the dog?' I ask Lewis.

A heavy silence falls between the two of us as we stare at each other. The last time there was an intruder Pushkin barked and scared them away. So why hasn't he barked tonight?

'No!' I mutter, swivelling around and hurrying back to the kitchen, then through the open door into the wide utility room, switching the lights on and blinking rapidly. I quickly make out the black form of a dog lying in his basket.

'Pushkin!' I say, rushing towards him. He doesn't move and I feel a sickness in my stomach. 'Pushkin!' I shout louder this time. I bend down, my slinged arm a frustration. I pause before placing my good hand on his coat, terrified what I might find. When I stroke him, his coat feels warm but his eyes are firmly closed. I place the palm of my hand in front of his nose and his breathing is so gentle it's barely noticeable. 'Wake up, boy,' I say, stroking him a little more vigorously this time, but he doesn't stir.

'Lewis!' I shout. My husband is right behind me. 'There's something the matter with Pushkin. I can't wake him.'

Lewis kneels down next to me and places his hand on the dog's chest. 'His heart is beating steadily but his breathing is shallow. We need to get him to the vet. Can't take any risk with someone else's dog.'

'He was fine earlier,' I say, recalling how greedily he ate his supper and how he bounded around the garden sticking his nose into bushes. 'Do you think he might have eaten something he shouldn't have done?'

'Like what?' Lewis asks. 'Has Susan left details of the vet anywhere?'

I hurry to the kitchen and pull out the address book, flicking through until I find Clinique Vétérinaire. I telephone the number but in my panic, I don't understand what the message says. I call again, getting the same message. Something about in emergencies come to the clinic, I think. I take a photo of the address and rush back to the utility room.

'We'll have to take him there. I'll go and get dressed.'

TEN MINUTES LATER, we're both haphazardly dressed. Lewis has lifted Pushkin, who is still lying in his bed, onto the back seat of our rental car and we're heading down the lane, the headlights illuminating the white clouds of dust. As best I can with my strapped-up shoulder, I stroke the velvety soft head of the dog and murmur platitudes. I can't but think of Muffin, who I hope is being well cared for at home. The Sat Nav on Lewis's phone gets us to the clinic which is on the edge of the town, a modern building that looks more commercial than residential. I just hope someone is there.

Lewis hurries to the door and presses the buzzer, keeping his hand on it for what seems like an inordinately long time. Eventually, a light comes on in one of the upper windows. A bare-chested man opens the curtains, unlatches the window and leans out.

'J'arrive! J'arrive!' he says.

Five minutes later and we're inside the veterinary clinic, Pushkin still seemingly asleep in his basket. The vet is decidedly grumpy and even more so when he discovers we're English and can barely understand a word he's saying. But he's gentle with the dog and carefully examines him.

'The dog is okay. His heart is strong and his breathing is too slow but alright. He's just asleep, very deeply asleep. Did you give him something?'

'What do you mean?' Lewis sounds affronted.

'Some sleeping pill, something to make him this – how do you say – drowsy?'

'Of course not,' Lewis replies.

'Maybe he found something, something that you dropped. I see you have an injury, Madame. Perhaps some medication for your arm, maybe?'

'Absolutely not,' I reiterate Lewis's statement.

'But this is not your dog, no?' He glances at the computer screen behind him. 'He belongs to Susan and Piers Lester.'

'Yes, but we're dog lovers. We have our own dog and know how to look after them. There is no way that we would endanger his life by giving him human medication,' Lewis says, crossing his arms in front of his chest.

The vet harrumphs and I can tell that he doesn't believe us, that he thinks we've deliberately or unintentionally harmed Pushkin. The big black dog may not be mine, but I've come to love him and I would do anything to protect a pet.

'Is he going to be alright?' I ask, noticing a weakness in my knees and stepping backwards to lean against the wall.

'Yes, Pushkin will be fine, but I will keep him in the clinic for a few hours for observation. We need to be sure. If he worsens, I will pump his stomach and carry out tests.'

I feel completely sick. How could we let something bad happen to this beautiful animal? What will we tell the Lesters?

The vet waves his hand at us, as if he's shovelling us out of his clinic. 'Call the clinic at 9 tomorrow morning and I will give you an update.' We're dismissed.

BACK IN THE CAR, I slump into my seat. 'Do you think the person who broke in poisoned Pushkin so he wouldn't wake us?' I ask.

Lewis starts the ignition but I can see the tension in his shoulders. 'It's weird, that's for sure.'

Back at the chateau, we're both too wired to sleep. Despite the warm night, I shiver when I walk inside, pacing restlessly around the kitchen.

'Do you want a hot chocolate?' Lewis asks.

I stop and actually look at my husband, this big, bulky, soft-hearted man, and feel an unusual surge of love.

'Sure,' I reply, sitting heavily in one of the uncomfortable wooden chairs. 'Not been much of a holiday,' I say, accepting a mug of steaming hot chocolate. Lewis sits down next to me.

'I had some good bike rides and it was fun seeing Danielle and Niall.' He blows at his drink. 'Bugger that you hurt yourself, though. How's the pain?'

'Honestly, I'm more worried about Pushkin.'

'Me too,' Lewis admits.

'It's like failing to care for someone else's child. Such a responsibility. We're not so good at that, are we? Caring for each other?' I muse.

Lewis frowns. 'Where's this coming from, Els?'

'We've drifted apart of late. Don't you think? You're always off doing your own thing, I'm doing mine, and there doesn't seem to be much middle ground.'

'But this holiday is good.'

'Other than the weird things that have been happening. The break-ins, Pushkin, me falling...' I let my voice trail off.

'Are you saying I should be taking better care of you? Because you know you make that hard. You're so independent, Els. It's tough for me too.'

'I know. But let's try harder, shall we?'

Lewis glances at me and I see a moroseness in his eyes, as if we've lost something, but I'm not sure what. And I don't think being here in France is helping.

'I want to go home,' I say. 'What do you think?'

He blows out a stream of air. 'We need to see how the dog is, and once he's alright we can ask the Lesters to come back. Deal?'

I nod.

'Right. Let's get some sleep.'

What I want in this moment is for Lewis to hold out his hand, to put his arm around me and help me up the stairs. To hold me as I lie in bed and drift off to sleep. Except he doesn't. He takes both our mugs and places them in the sink and then he bounds up the stairs, leaving me to switch off the lights and lock up. I hear him in the bathroom but by the time I'm back in our bed, my husband is fast asleep, his snores regular and immensely frustrating. I turn away from him and cry silently into my pillow, tears for whom or what, I'm not really sure. I hope that a quiet sob might make me feel better, but it doesn't, and the only thing I feel is utter exhaustion.

CHAPTER SEVENTEEN

RAFAEL

I want a glass of juice but Mum and Dad are shouting at each other in the kitchen. I hang back in the corridor for a bit, wondering why they can't just be nice.

'But if André leaves now, you know he'll never come back,' Mum says.

'We can't expect the Browns to put up with their noise.' Dad's voice is quieter and calmer than Mum's. 'We'll just have to take the risk. I mean, they've had two break-ins, the noise from the builders, and now Elodie has hurt herself because some idiot removed the no entrance sign to the tower. It's a wonder they haven't demanded to swap right back.'

'It's hardly my fault,' Mum retorts.

'I'm not saying it is, but this holiday... Well, it's hardly a holiday, is it, Susan? You're off doing your own thing all the time, and who is it that you're so busily meeting?'

'Oh for God's sake, Piers. Grow up. You're the one behaving like a child, returning pissed last night.'

I can't stand this anymore, so I stomp into the room and

both of them turn to look at me, guilt on their faces. I think of Mum in her slinky nightdress and talking in that creepy hushed whisper. Does Dad also think she's having an affair? Should I tell him?

'I'll see you both later,' Mum says, shifting her handbag onto her shoulder. Dad's right about one thing, and that's that Mum is hardly here.

'Who are you meeting?' Dad asks.

'Marianne. She's got a few hours off work.'

Mum doesn't hang around to ask what I'm doing, or suggest we do something together. I'm relieved about that. We both listen to her stride to the door and bang it shut behind her.

'What would you like to do today?' Dad asks me, after a while.

I shrug. 'Thought I'd spend the morning with Hugo,' I lie. I can never show my face around Hugo's again but Dad doesn't need to know that. He looks disappointed.

'I'd like to go to the Tate Modern,' Dad says. 'What to join me?'

'Nah. I'll be here with Hugo.'

WHEN THEY'VE BOTH GONE, it's a relief to be in the house alone. I kind of feel sorry for Dad, who seems so dejected, pathetic even. If Mum really is having an affair, I wonder what will happen to us all. I go upstairs to their bedroom. The white bedcover is pulled up tightly over the duvet and pillows and Mum's suitcase is lying on the floor next to a dressing table. I open it up and rifle through her stuff, but all I find are clothes. There are no papers, no hidden phone, nothing to suggest whom she might have been talking to last night. I open the chest of drawers and rifle through the things, but I don't recognise any of the jumpers or scarves, which must belong to Elodie Brown. The same goes for the walk-in wardrobe where there are enough clothes to set up a shop. Nothing here belongs to Mum. I run my hands underneath the bed linen, under the mattress and then I go into the bathroom and rifle through her wash bag. I find nothing.

The thing is, I'm not really sure what I'm looking for. There's another smaller bag next to Mum's, which I unzip, and flip the upper half flat onto the carpet. It's Dad's bag, full of neatly folded shirts and boxer shorts. I'm about to zip it back up, but when I lift the upper section, a white envelope slips out of the pocket of the case. Strangely, there's no name on the front of it. I take out the envelope and remove two pieces of paper. The address at the top says Dr Gupta at Harley Street. It takes me a moment to realise that these are medical results for Dad. I skim through the letter but don't understand the medical terms. And then I read the word *infertile*. What the hell? There's a word called *varicocele*. I grab my phone and put the word into Google search.

*A varicocele is an enlarged vein within the scrotum —
the bag of skin that holds the testicles. In many men,
varicoceles develop on the left side during puberty. If
left untreated, varicocele can decrease sperm quality
and production, which can lead to infertility.*

I read the letter through again and it's written there in black and white. Dad is infertile and it's a genetic condition. My first thought is Lucille. We might be young, but she's told me she wants a family with four kids, ideally. If I'm infertile, then what will that mean for our future? And then it hits me. It's not me that's infertile. This letter from Dr Gupta spells it out so clearly. It's Dad who is infertile, and it says right here that he's had the condition since birth.

I sink onto the soft carpet and lean against the side of the bed. Dad is infertile, and he's always been. That means that he's not my real father. No. That can't be right. Mum and Dad have always talked as if they're my real parents, my birth parents. I think back over the years when we've laughed about the features I've inherited from both of them, and not just their features but their annoying habits, the way Dad talks and walks, his tall lean frame, his punctuality. But if this letter is correct, that's all been a lie. Dad – Piers – cannot be my dad. I recall the thick photograph album full of my baby photos, that very first photo of me as a newborn lying in Mum's arms, Dad grinning like an idiot as he sits next to the hospital bed. And then there was that photo of Mum with her huge, distended stomach, with Dad's arms around her, proudly displaying their pregnancy bump. The pregnancy was real. Mum definitely gave birth to me, but who was my dad? Did they use a sperm donor, perhaps? Or did Mum cheat on Dad? Has he always known that he's not my real father, and if so, why have they both lied? And if he's not my real father, who the hell is? I stagger up, shove the letter back into Dad's suitcase and hurry out of the room.

I want to scream. No, I need Lucille. I need someone who will help me make sense of this. The lies that my parents have told me for the whole of my life. And I don't want to be here a single second longer. I need to get out of this place, get away from them. If I never see them again, then I just don't care. They're liars and cheats, the both of them, and I hope they suffer.

CHAPTER EIGHTEEN

ELODIE

The tears dry up but I don't sleep. All I can think about is that poor dog, the way it was impossible for him to open his eyes, and how it might all be our fault. Could I have dropped some of my medication by mistake? It's possible. What if I kill him? What will we say to the Lesters? They'll be heart-broken and I'm not sure that I'd ever be able to forgive myself. And I'm missing my little Muffin so much. I want to wrap my arms around her soft, warm body, bury my face into her white fluffy fur, and not care if she licks my face.

Shortly after 8 a.m. Lewis's phone rings. He grabs it and I feel an overwhelming sense of relief as I see his face break into a smile. He hangs up.

'The vet. Pushkin is fine, he's had breakfast, and we can pick him up after 10 a.m.'

'Thank heavens,' I say, relaxing back onto my pillows. 'But I think the time has come for us to go home. The last few days have been anything but relaxing.'

'Look, I know I said we could go home last night, but thinking about it, why rush back? Pushkin is fine, the weather is glorious, and besides, we can't go home when the Lesters are in our house. And didn't the doctor say you shouldn't travel for a while? Let's chill here and properly recuperate,' Lewis suggests.

'The doctor said I could travel in a couple of days. We just have to ask the Lesters to
leave.'

'Come on, Elodie. This whole holiday experiment thing is meant to be a proof of concept for your new house-swap division. If we bring it to a premature end, then we're as good as saying it's a failure.'

I feel a surge of annoyance. Here is another example of Lewis trying to minimise conflict. Just because the holiday swap hasn't worked for us, doesn't mean the whole idea is dead in the water. It just goes to show that we need much more stringent checks on the properties we allow onto our books, and it's something I need to discuss with Niall.

'Well, I want to go home.' I realise I sound petulant but frankly, I don't care.

'Let's say we do return to the UK. What about Pushkin? Haven't we caused the poor dog enough grief? We can't just leave him here alone. We'd have to find someone to dog sit, or the Lesters would have to come home first.'

I groan. He's right, of course.

'We could leave him with the Moreaus, I suppose,' Lewis says eventually, no doubt realising that my silence is indicative of my disapproval. I realise I haven't shared the conversation I had with Piers with my husband. How adamant Piers was that we should have nothing to do with the Moreaus, that there is bad blood between them.

'No,' I say. 'But a compromise could be for us to move to a hotel and Pushkin could come with us.'

'Really?' Lewis sounds doubtful. 'We'd have to get the Lesters permission for that. How would you like it if they took Muffin to a strange place?'

'Let's see if I can find somewhere for us to go and then we'll cross that bridge.'

LEWIS DISAPPEARS off for a swim while I make myself a strong coffee and heat up a croissant. Then I go online to search for hotels. Again. I create a spreadsheet with all hotels within an hour of here, choosing only those that accept dogs. I make phone call after phone call, except all the four- and five-star hotels are either booked or not inclined to accept a Labrador as a guest. There is literally nothing available for the next week in this vicinity. Some of the establishments have a list for cancellations and I add our details, but I'm not hopeful. I try holiday cottages too, except once again, I hit a brick wall. It's hardly surprising that everything is booked. This is one of the most popular regions of France for holidays and it is peak holiday season. Feeling extremely frustrated, I telephone Niall. As he knows the Lesters, I'm hoping that he might be able to broker a deal which allows us to go home early. If needs be, and they can find someone to look after Pushkin, Lewis and I could stay in a hotel in London until they leave our home. That's how desperate I'm feeling. Except unusually, Niall doesn't answer his phone. I leave a message asking him to call me back. By the time Lewis has returned from his swim, the frustration is threatening to overwhelm me. I'm not sure why I feel so very out of control; it's a bizarre and unusual sensation for me. An irrational feeling that despite the beautiful scenery and the gorgeous warm weather, I don't want to be here any longer.

'Lewis,' I say as he strides upstairs, no doubt to change into his cycling shorts. 'I'm going to call Susan and tell her that the house swap is off.'

He pauses for a long moment, his back to me, but I can see the tension in his neck, the way he's trying to process how best to react towards me. Slowly, he turns around.

'Look, love. You're too upset about everything that's happened. Leave it to me. I'll give Piers a call, have a chat man to man, and I'll tell them they need to come home. I'm sure he'll understand.'

'Really?' I ask. This is quite the surprise. Normally the difficult conversations are left to me to handle.

'Yes. You're overtired, in pain, and it's all caught up with you. Leave it to me.'

A few minutes later, Lewis is back downstairs, as I expected dressed in his cycling gear. 'I had a quick chat with Piers and he asked for another couple of days in London. I agreed to that, so we can go home on Thursday. It'll give us time to check that Pushkin is alright.'

'Did you mention anything about the dog?'

'No, because he's fine now, and I didn't want to worry him unnecessarily.'

I'm not sure that was the right decision, because we don't know exactly that Pushkin is fine, but I'm just relieved to know that in three days' time I'll be back in my own home, in my own comfortable bed.

On the dot of 10 a.m. we're back at the vets. We're led through to the vet's practice room and Pushkin is brought in. He bounds towards us, his tail wagging vigorously, his backside swinging from side to side. There's such joy in his reaction I can't help but smile.

'Hey, boy,' I say, stroking him with my good arm. 'I'm happy to see you too. You gave us quite the fright.'

'So we ran some blood tests,' the vet says, his face serious. 'And we found traces of Donormyl. Is this something you use?'

'I don't know what it is,' I say, frowning at Lewis.

'It's a French sleeping pill used for periodic use.'

'Neither of us uses sleeping pills.'

'You weren't given anything for your arm?' the vet asks, screwing his eyes up as if he doesn't believe me.

'Absolutely not.'

'And where you are staying? Could someone else have dropped a pill perhaps?'

I still for a moment, thinking of Danielle. She mentioned taking sleeping pills. Could she have accidentally dropped a pill? She was very drunk, and accidents do happen.

'I don't think so,' I say. But now I'm unsure. I can never tell her. Danielle seems such a sweet woman; she'd be devastated to think she'd accidentally poisoned the dog. But at least it explains the situation and for the first time since we've been in France, I feel a sense of relief that there's a logical explanation for one of the bad things that have happened.

CHAPTER NINETEEN

PIERS

After strolling around the Tate Modern and then mooching along the South Bank, I head home. The Knightsbridge house is quiet so I take advantage of being alone and switch on the cinema-like television in the Browns' basement. I try to distract myself by flicking through the sports channels but find it impossible to concentrate. The front door chimes, and I hope it's Raf. It's not. Susan is standing there, but the second the door is ajar, she scoots past me so quickly, we don't even touch.

'Good day?' I ask.

'Yes, good. Fun to catch up with so many old friends.' She has her back to me as she hangs up her raincoat in the hall cupboard.

I can't stop thinking about Tim De Withers. Was she back with him?

'I'm going to have a quick bath and then I'll make supper. Where's Raf?'

'I assume still with Hugo. I'll message him.'

Is Susan having a bath because she's spent a steamy hour or so with Tim De Withers?

An hour later, she's in the kitchen making a mess which I'll have to clear up, and Raf hasn't responded to my message. In fact, worryingly, he hasn't even looked at it. The two ticks are still grey. I wonder if they don't have good reception down in the basement. I telephone him, but his phone goes straight to voicemail. That isn't unusual but it's annoying. I hope he hasn't drunk too much again.

I wait another few minutes, but consistently get no response. 'Raf isn't answering,' I tell Susan.

'Well, he needs to be back here for supper. I'm not slaving over the stove on holiday for nothing. Go and get him.'

I sigh, accepting that that's probably the best solution. I slip on my shoes and walk down the steps and up the steps of number 32 next door. I ring the gold doorbell and also note the cameras that seem to point at every angle, covering the whole of the front of the house and likely much of the pavement too. Initially there's no answer and a bubble of annoyance catches in my throat. I press the buzzer again, for longer this time. And then I see a shadow at the door.

A small woman opens it, trying to attach a black apron around her waist. 'I'm so sorry, sir. It's my day off so I was downstairs in my room.'

'Oh,' I say, a bit startled to realise that this lady must be the neighbours' housekeeper. 'Apologies for disturbing you. I was wondering if my son was here with Hugo? We want him back for supper.'

'I don't think so,' she says with a heavily accented voice. 'Mister Hugo is in the cinema room. Let me go and check. Would you like to come in?'

I walk past her into the grandiose hallway, which is twice the size of the Browns' and features the largest glistening glass chandelier that I've ever seen in a private home. I stand in front of the mirror, but turn my back to it. My hair needs a cut and my face is pasty.

'I won't be long,' she says, and then bustles through a door. A minute or so later she's back, accompanied by Hugo.

'Hello, Raf's dad,' he says, grinning at me, his hands in the pockets of his chinos.

'I was wondering if Raf was here with you?' I say.

'Nope.' Hugo shakes his head. 'Haven't seen him since he did a runner out of the pub yesterday.'

'A runner?' I ask, fearful that Raf might have not paid for something.

'Don't worry. He didn't nick anything, but something happened and he took off like a hare. He hasn't answered my messages.'

'Oh,' I say, because this is all news to me. 'I'm sorry if he was rude.'

Hugo shrugs his shoulders. 'No worries. Hope you find him.' And then he turns away from me and I'm left standing in this grand hallway, unsure what to do. Eventually I turn, and close the front door behind me.

Back in the Browns' kitchen, I repeat my conversation with Hugo to Susan. 'So where the hell is he?' she asks, grabbing her phone off the island and tapping away.

She pales. 'He's switched off the tracking on his phone. I can't see it.'

'Do you think he's lost his phone or had it stolen?' I ask.

'I can't tell.' She tries calling him, but it goes straight to voicemail yet again. Susan leaves a message. 'Raf, this is Mum. Call me back immediately.'

Susan and I stare at each other. 'When did you last see or speak to him?' I ask.

'This morning, just before I left. And you?'

'Same,' I say. 'He just slouched off to his room, said he'd spend the day with Hugo. Except he didn't.'

'Do you think he's done something stupid, like tried to go home?'

As soon as Susan says that, it clicks. Of course. He's been missing Lucille and he didn't want to come to London in the first place. And if something happened yesterday when he was out with Hugo, the person he'd most want to seek consolation with is his girlfriend. I race up the stairs and into his bedroom and stand in the middle of the room, looking all around. His duvet is a heap on the bed and his pillow retains the imprint of his head. The black suitcase he used is lying on the floor so I flip it open. There are clothes inside but did he bring more? I run into the ensuite shower room and see that his wash bag is still perched on the edge of the sink. Opening it up, I glance inside. There's nothing much in there except some shampoo, a shower gel and a hair gel. And then it hits me. His toothbrush and toothpaste have gone. Back in his bedroom, I pull open the wardrobe door, looking for his Nike rucksack. As I'm tipping the room upside down, Susan appears in the doorway.

'Did Raf give you his passport back?' I ask.

'Yes, I think so. I'll check.'

Five minutes later and we realise that Raf's passport is missing, as are his phone charger, laptop and his favourite pair of shorts, which he may well be wearing.

I sink onto his bed. 'He's done this on purpose,' I say. 'Our son has run away in one of the biggest, most dangerous cities in the world.'

'Come on, London isn't any more dangerous than Paris.'

'It is for a seventeen-year-old who doesn't know his way around, who isn't used to navigating capital cities. Raf is naive for his age, and besides, he doesn't have any money. If he's gone back to France, how will he get there?'

'Hitch-hiking?' Susan says in a whisper. I shiver. 'What are we going to do?' She starts crying then, big tears that fall silently down her cheeks.

'We need to call the police.'

'Can you check that you haven't got his passport?' Susan asks, but it's a futile request because we both know that Susan is the keeper of passports. I head back into our bedroom and open my bedside table where I've put an envelope with cash and the keys to the chateau. As soon as I open the drawer I swallow hard. The envelope was thick with notes but now it's slender. I take it out and pull out the cash, the money that I intended to keep for emergencies. Raf has stolen most of our holiday money. Our son has planned this. And then I see the white envelope lying on the floor, next to my suitcase. Quickly, I pick it up and pull out the two sheets of paper, the letter from Dr Gupta. They're creased, shoved back haphazardly into the envelope. With a sinking heart I realise that Raf must know. Raf must have been looking in my suitcase and found the letter that I'd stuffed into the zipper compartment. And he's read it. Because I'm positive those pieces of paper weren't creased, and I'm equally positive that I left the envelope inside my case, hidden from Susan.

Hearing Susan's footsteps, I shove the letter under my pillow. She stands in the doorway looking at me, her hand over her mouth, her eyes red.

'Can you call the police,' I ask. 'I'll call Lucille and the Browns, let them know to be on the lookout for Raf.'

Susan nods and retreats into the corridor.

I don't have Lucille's telephone number. It seemed weird to be asking Raf for her number, and despite pretending that I was relaxed about the relationship, I haven't been. And it's not just because of our falling out with her parents but because Lucille is older and so much more mature than Raf. I didn't want him to get hurt – I still don't. Susan, in her typical way, was much more vocal about it. She wanted to forbid them from seeing each other and I had to work hard to convince her that the more we put pressure on Raf to step away from Lucille, the more likely we were going to propel them into each other's arms. But there's something about the girl that I don't completely trust, and it's not just that she's a Moreau. I'm going to have to swallow my pride and call the vineyard.

As I feared, Colette Moreau answers the phone.

'Hello, Colette,' I say croakily. 'This is Piers Lester. Sorry to be disturbing you–'

'Yes, you are,' she says abruptly, cutting me off. For a horrible moment I think she's hung up, except then I hear a background noise.

'I'm sorry, it's just I need to speak to Lucille. Raf has disappeared and we're really worried about him.'

Colette snorts and I squeeze the phone so tightly I'm worried I might inadvertently break it. I force myself to release my grip.

'He's an adult,' she says.

I take a deep breath to stop myself from retorting that he's not, that he's only seventeen. 'Please, would it be possible to talk to Lucille?'

'She's busy,' Colette replies, too quickly.

'Please. I would really appreciate it.'

Colette sighs loudly and then there's a clatter as if she's dropped the phone on a table. I wait for a long time, wondering whether she's hung up on me. But eventually I hear footsteps and breathing.

'This is Lucille.'

'Oh, Lucille, I'm so glad to talk to you. Raf has gone missing in London and I'm wondering if you've heard from him.'

There's an intake of breath. 'Missing?'

'We think he left this morning, took his passport and some money and is probably trying to return to France. If you know anything about this, I beg you to tell us. He's only seventeen and although he thinks he's an adult, he's out of his depth here in London.'

'But I haven't heard from him,' she says.

'When was the last time you spoke?'

She pauses for a moment. 'Maybe two days ago. He left me a message but I didn't get around to returning it.' There's a regretful tone to her voice and I wonder if they had an argument.

'Will you call me if you hear from him? He's not in trouble. We're just really concerned about his safety.'

'Yes, I'll call you,' she promises as I give her my telephone number, and then she ends the call.

I can hear Susan on her phone in the hallway. After a moment, she comes into the bedroom tugging at her hair. 'The police aren't taking this seriously. It's crazy. They say he's not vulnerable and he's probably gone to stay with friends, except he doesn't have any friends in England.'

'That we know about,' I add. 'He might have reconnected with some of his old school mates, like you've reconnected with your old work colleagues.' My words come out harshly and Susan frowns at me.

'I asked them to put alerts at the borders – the train stations and the airports – and the guy was so mocking, saying a runaway seventeen-year-old is not a matter for Interpol. So what are we going to do? Shall I go back to France and organise a search over there while you stay here?' Susan's voice sounds shrill and panicked.

'You've got more friends in London than me,' I say, trying not to think about Tim De Withers. 'Look, Raf might just be trying to give us a fright.'

If he's read Dr Gupta's letter, then our son will be angry and confused, perhaps wanting to punish us for hiding the truth about his parentage. It makes sense that he's run away. He'll need time to calm down and then when he's had enough of hanging out around London, he'll return to us.

'Why would he want to give us a fright?' Susan asks.

Except I can't answer her. I can't tell her that Raf has probably read the letter saying I'm infertile. And I don't tell her that Raf has stolen our money.

'Angry teenage boy stuff.' I shrug. 'Look, in the very unlikely event he hasn't tipped up by tomorrow, I'll go back to France and you can stay here.'

She nods. 'We need to call Elodie and Lewis and warn them that Raf might turn up at the chateau.'

'Sure, I'll do that,' I say.

Susan glances at her bare feet. 'There's something I didn't tell you.'

My heart stops from a moment. Is now the moment she's going to share the truth and tell me that I'm not really Raf's father?

'I took a call from Lewis this morning. He asked if we could end the house swap early.'

'What?' I exclaim. 'Why?'

'What with Elodie's accident and the break-in, she wants to come home. I said I'd discuss it with you and perhaps we could return to our respective homes in a couple of days' time.'

'None of that matters now,' I say, running my fingers through my hair. 'We just need to find our son. Even if he took a flight, he would only be arriving in France around now. I'll call the Browns.'

CHAPTER TWENTY

ELODIE

I am shocked by Piers's phone call. He sounds utterly distraught and even more so when I confirm that I haven't seen Raf since they all left together. I promise to call him if their son turns up. And I'm also relieved that I didn't push for us to end the house swap prematurely, or tell him about Pushkin's poisoning. That would have been too much.

Lewis returns from a bike ride, red-faced and sweating.

'Raf has gone missing in London,' I say.

'Missing? How is that possible?' He pales and leans against the table. 'Don't they keep an eye on him, for heaven's sake? He's still a kid.'

'Hey!' I say, putting a hand on Lewis's broad arm, surprised by his judgmental reaction. 'It's terrible, but it's not for us to get worked up over.'

'Still a shock though.' Lewis peels off his T-shirt and pours himself a glass of water. After drinking noisily he says, 'This house swap has lurched from one disaster to the next. I don't think it's been a relaxing holiday for any of us. Perhaps you were right in wanting to go home.'

I don't say anything, because Lewis has had a relaxing few days. He's taken long bike rides every day, and until I broke my shoulder, he hadn't done any cooking or house-work. Even since, he's shopped once and begrudgingly helped me cut up vegetables.

'I'll take a shower and then fire up the BBQ,' Lewis says.

Half an hour later, and Lewis is outside. The scent of paraffin rises up through the open bedroom window so I shut it. With some difficulty, I'm stripping off, aiming to have a shower, when there's the ping of an incoming text on a phone. I pick up my phone but there are no new messages. The ping comes again, from somewhere here in the bedroom. I rummage around the room, pulling the sheets off the bed, looking under the pillows, and then lift up some of Lewis's discarded clothes on the chair in the corner. Under-neath a pair of cotton shorts, I find Lewis's phone. I pick it up and glance at the screen. It's a message from Susan Lester. Normally I would never open Lewis's phone, but right now I'm undressed, Lewis is outside, and this message is obviously about their missing son. I tap in Lewis's passcode and the phone unlocks.

> Have you told E you're leaving her yet?

I read the message twice. Three times. The words swim in my eyes until the screen goes dark and I'm logged out. What the hell!

Have you told E you're leaving her yet?

The words turn around and around in my head and I let the phone tumble from my fingers onto the bed. I sit down heavily, shock making me dizzy. E is me, I presume. Elodie. Is Lewis leaving me? And what has Susan got to do with it?

It's as if my brain has slowed right down as it tries to make sense of those simple seven words. Susan is asking Lewis if he's told me he's leaving me. Which means Susan and Lewis... Are they together? I wasn't aware they knew each other. Do they? What has Lewis been keeping from me? And this house swap. Did they set this up together? But if so, why? We're in each other's houses. It's not like we've run into each other on holiday – we are in different countries. Niall organised this house swap, didn't he? Or was he just a convenient pawn in Susan and Lewis's game, whatever that might be?

My head is swimming. I stand up, using the furniture to support me as I weave into the bathroom, Lewis's phone in my hand. I lock the door behind me, sinking to the black and white tiled floor, like I did the night I drank too much. I think back through the unpleasant things that have happened since we've been here – the scary break-ins, the barrier that was removed, the drugged dog. Was Lewis or Susan behind all of these events? No, that's ridiculous. Why would anyone do those things on purpose? But perhaps they were trying to scare me, to hurt me even? But this is Lewis we're talking about. My big, burly, pussycat husband. The man who has been by my side for so many years, who has never given any indication that he's unhappy. I think back to any missed signs that he might have been having an affair and realise with dismay that I've given him so many opportunities. All of those nights that I worked late; the weekends away evaluating properties; the meetings with Niall. So much time for him to go off and meet other women. And then there are his gym clients. The scantily clad, Botoxed women that fawn all over him. We've laughed about them so many times, but have

I been naive in my confidence that Lewis only has eyes for me? I know I've put on weight recently, let myself go a bit, but that's normal, isn't it? I'm aware that Lewis's gyms have struggled the last couple of years, with the increased competition and the fact that so many people are now working from home and going to their local gyms rather than the ones near their workplaces. But he knows I'll bail him out if necessary; after all, it was me who put up the money in the first place.

And this week. Yes, he's been spending a lot of time on bike rides, but that's Lewis. It's what he does. He's never been one for lounging by a pool, and I can't remember the last time he read a book.

But is he leaving me, and for Susan, or has he met someone else? Or is Susan just a confidante? This doesn't make any sense. Or perhaps it does. Perhaps Lewis really does want to leave me. It would explain our lack of intimacy. I let out a sob as I realise I'm going to have to confront Lewis. But then there's another ping and it's as if the phone is on fire. I drop it and it clatters on the tiled floor. Worried I might have cracked the screen, I pick it up again, quickly. The screen is fine and there's another message from Susan. My hand is shaking as I press the screen and open it up once again.

> Sorry, darling. Meant to send this to your other phone. So stressed about Raf. Need to see you. Please delete this message. Sxx

Susan is calling my husband darling. This is incontrovertible proof that they are having an affair. I let out a whimper and then read the message again. *Your other phone.*

Lewis has a second phone that he's been using to communi-
cate with his lover. The bastard. I've been so trusting, so
very, very stupid. Anger courses through me as I swing the
bathroom door open and stride towards Lewis's side of the
bed. I tip his suitcase upside down on the bed and rifle
through everything, including unzipping the fabric base of
the case and searching inside. I look through his bedside
table, under the bed, inside the wardrobe and the chest of
drawers that are still full of the Lesters' belongings. I fling
everything onto the bed haphazardly. Yet I find nothing.
Now what?

Reluctantly, I return to the bathroom and remove my
underwear, ready to step into the shower, intending to sob
under the weak stream of water. But then my eyes settle
on Lewis's wash bag. It's one of those bags that is full of
pockets, that you can hang on a hook on the back of a door.
It's dangling there, packed full of his lotions and potions. I
lift it off the hook and sit down on the floor again. I take
every single item out of the pockets; random strips of pills,
an empty toothpaste tube, a razor. And then I run my
fingers along the bottom of each pocket and remove a
single condom. When was the last time we used those? A
decade ago, probably. The packet looks old, so it might just
be a legacy from years ago. It isn't until I'm sure every
pocket is empty that I realise there's still something hard
and small wedged at the bottom. My fingers clasp the cool
plastic and I remove a very small, black telephone. It's tiny,
less than 5 cm in height, and for a moment I wonder if it's
a toy. I've never seen a phone this small and am unsure it
is even real. But then I press a button and the screen lights
up. I input his normal passcode except nothing happens. I
try our birthdays, wedding anniversary, various combina-

tions of his gym phone number. Not a single combination works.

All I have is proof that my husband has a burner phone, but I've no way of accessing it. I search through his normal phone, my eyes seeking out more messages from Susan, from other women too. Anything that might suggest that Lewis has been unfaithful. I find nothing. But of course I don't. All the illicit information is on this stupid little burner phone. I'm tempted to crush it on the hard floor, except that wouldn't be in my interest. I need to think strategically now, work out what's really going on, what Lewis and Susan are planning. And the only way I'm going to do that is pretend I don't know the truth. If I confront him now, Lewis will disappear off in a huff or turn things around so as to make his digression my fault. No, I need to play the long game. I'm good at logic and strategy. I need to work out what's really going on and then bide my time. Strike when I have all the facts, because I'm the one with the power. Money talks, and I know that Lewis loves my money. I'll try to act as normally as possible this evening. Can I actually do that? Am I strong enough to pretend to my husband that all is rosy? I think back to all those years ago when I first started out in that American investment bank, how I quite literally faked it until I made it. The strategy worked then, but this is different. This is the man I love, who promised to be there to support me through sickness and health. This is the man whom I thought I knew. I'm veering manically between explosive anger and deepest sorrow, but I know I need to calm myself.

I stand up and turn on the shower, standing underneath the warm water, letting the tears flow. At the end, I turn the hot tap to cold and force myself to be resolute. I will play the long game. I will eat my supper with dignity, but Lewis and I will not be sleeping in the same bed. I'll play on his hypochondriac tendencies and say I feel like I'm coming down with something. Lewis can sleep in the guest room whilst I work out what my next move will be. Because information is power.

CHAPTER TWENTY-ONE

PIERS

We're both too stressed to eat. I toast a couple of pieces of bread but they taste like cardboard. I feel like we should be out there, pounding the streets, looking for our boy. And so I tell Susan that I'm going out. There's desperation and fear in her eyes, the first time I've ever seen her look so terrified and vulnerable, and for one moment, I'm actually glad. Does that make me a horrible person? But I want Susan to feel the pain, to know what she's putting us all through with her lies and deception.

So I leave her. I walk to South Kensington tube station and hold my phone out in front of everyone I pass, displaying a photo of Raf, asking them if they've seen my boy. I choose the picture I took when we were standing in the queue to collect our tickets for the musical. Raf is scowling and I realise to my dismay that I haven't taken a single photograph of my son during the past five months. What was I thinking, letting all of that time pass by without capturing any of the special moments we've shared together? I feel utterly sick at the thought that this photo might be the last one I took of my son.

I step inside every shop and show my phone to all the local shopkeepers, to every barista and server, to the train guards and the staff at the only manned ticket booth. They all shake their heads. Some tell me that they see a thousand young men like him pass through here every day. I ask a guard if it's possible to view their CCTV and he looks at me as if I'm completely crazy.

'You need to speak to the police if you've got requests like that,' he says, before turning his back on me.

I pound the streets, shoving my phone into the faces of everyone in the vain hope that someone will say, 'Yes. I saw him. He walked that way.' But after three hours of making no progress I decide to go to the police station. The nearest is on Earls Court Road, an uninspiring red brick building with a blue door. Inside there is a uniformed officer sitting behind a plexiglass screen and several people milling around the reception area, mostly drug addicts, exuding pungent smells of alcohol and sweat. After waiting to be seen, I explain that we telephoned earlier but I wanted to talk to someone directly as I felt our concerns weren't being taking seriously. The officer sighs.

'Look, even if I do issue a missing person's alert, the chances that any action will be taken is slim. Does your son have any learning disabilities? Physical disabilities perhaps?'

I shake my head.

'Has he got a record? Got in with any dodgy kids?'

I think of Hugo and want to laugh. I don't think our poshly spoken, privately educated neighbour could be described as dodgy.

'Most of them turn up. Come back tomorrow if he hasn't

made contact and try not to worry. You'd be shocked at the number of parents who are in here worried about their errant kids. They like to push boundaries at that age. Got one of my own.'

I'm getting increasingly frustrated, so I curtly thank him and leave.

AS I HEAD BACK to Knightsbridge, I try Raf's phone yet again. I'm not sure I've ever felt so dejected. Our poor boy must be so confused and angry after reading Dr Gupta's letter. It's no surprise he's run away. But my fury is directed towards Susan, and by the time I'm back at the house, I know that we need to have the conversation. It's time for her to tell me the truth.

I storm in through the front door, my heart pounding, trying not to think of what I'm going to say.

'Susan?' I shout. 'Any news?'

She appears at the top of the stairs, barefoot, wearing jeans and a T-shirt. Her face is makeup free and her complexion is blotchy, as if she's been crying.

'No, nothing,' she says. 'And you? Any luck?'

'No.' I stride up the stairs, my trainers squelching on the glass treads, not caring if I'm bringing in London dirt. 'We need to talk.'

Susan raises an eyebrow, but she steps backwards as I stomp past her into the doorway of our bedroom. 'What's the matter?' she asks. 'You're scaring me.'

'Oh, I'm scaring you?' I say, my voice heavy with sarcasm. 'I know the truth, Susan. How you've lied to me.'

She pales. 'What do you mean?'

I cross my arms. I can't stand still so I pace out the room

again and along the corridor, passing the slim console table on the left with the fancy carriage clock and photos of the Browns' wedding. Susan is standing in the doorway to the bedroom so I swivel to face her. 'Were you ever going to tell me? Were you just hoping that your secret would stay hidden until we died? That Raf would never ever find out?'

'What are you talking about?' she asks, crossing her arms over her chest, except I think I see a widening of her eyes, the narrowing of her lips.

I push past her, shoving her out of the way, realising that this is the first sign of physical aggression I've ever shown towards my wife during the whole of our relationship. It sickens me, knowing what I might be capable of. Striding towards my side of the bed, I pull the white envelope out from under my pillow with a flourish.

'Do you know what's inside this?' I ask.

She shakes her head, but her eyes are very wide now.

'It's the results of my sperm test. It says that I'm infertile. That I've always been infertile.'

'That's not possible,' Susan whispers.

'Oh really? You're saying that by some miracle my zero sperm count roared to life on our honeymoon and that Raf was conceived via a sort of immaculate conception, and that the medics are wrong? Is that what you're saying, Susan?' I'm shouting at her now, but I can't help myself. I slam my palm onto the top of the chest of drawers. 'Stop with all the lies! Stop playing with other people's lives!'

Susan drops down into her haunches, clasping her knees with her arms. 'I didn't want you to get hurt,' she says, in a voice that is barely audible.

'You didn't want me to get hurt?' I scoff. 'What did you think was going to happen, Susan? That you'd take this horrible secret with you to the grave? You've lied for eighteen years. Our whole marriage has been a sham!'

'No, it's not like that,' she says. She's rocking backwards and forwards now, unable to look at me.

'And what about Raf? You've been playing with his life.'

'This is nothing to do with Raf,' she says. I cannot believe my ears. This is everything to do with Raf. For a moment I'm speechless, my jaw open, unable to look at this woman whom I've loved for so very long. Did I ever really know her?

'We can't help who we fall in love with,' Susan says quietly. The rocking has stopped and she's standing up now, staring at me with watery eyes, her fingers twizzling her wedding ring around and around.

'You're still in love with him?' I knew it. I saw the way she looked at Tim De Withers. Of course she would prefer him over me. The rich, debonair senior partner who lives in a stunning London town house versus me. 'Have you been cheating on me for the past eighteen years?'

'No, of course not. We only reconnected at Niall's wedding.'

'Niall's wedding? What has Tim De Withers got to do with Niall?'

Susan stares at me and then lets out a laugh that sounds more like a bark. And here, just a few seconds later, I'm seeing yet another side of my wife. The fearful, quivering, rueful persona has melted away and back comes confident Susan. 'I'm not in love with Tim De Withers,' she says. 'I met up with Tim De Withers to discuss my options. It's Lewis. Lewis Brown.' She steps backwards into the corridor.

'You're having an affair with Lewis Brown?' It takes several long seconds to absorb this. I cringe and stride quickly towards the door, into the corridor where Susan is standing, her arms still crossed, her legs planted apart as if assuming a defensive position. Lewis Brown. I can't bear to think that I've been sleeping in the bed of my wife's lover. Has she slept there before, lying in his arms? And the past few nights. Has she been wishing that he was there besides her rather than me?

'So you've been having affairs the whole of our marriage,' I say as a statement, because now the words slip off my tongue it is completely obvious that must be the case.

'No, of course not!' she exclaims, her voice shrill.

'Stop with the lying!' I shout. 'I know that I'm not Raf's birth father. I know that you've lied to me for so many years, and not just me. You've lied to our son and now he's found out. That's why he's run away, Susan. It's because of your terrible lies.'

She closes her eyes briefly and bends forwards, placing her hands on her knees. 'Raf has found out.' She speaks more to herself than to me.

'Who is it? Who is Raf's birth father?' She remains silent, not looking at me. 'Look at me, Susan!' I'm really yelling now, but I can't help it. I've never shouted at my wife like this, but the anger is so overwhelming. I clench my fingers into tight fists and keep them behind my back to stop myself from hitting something.

She stands up now and holds my gaze. 'It's Lewis. I had a fling with Lewis just before our wedding. It wasn't really a fling, more of a goodbye, because we'd had a relationship before I met you, before Lewis met Elodie. And now. I'm sorry, Piers, but we're in love.'

'In love! Do you even know the meaning of the word? You've been playing with Raf's life, with my life and Elodie's. You're utterly selfish.'

'Maybe, but at least my feelings are real. I have a passion with Lewis; he makes me feel so alive! And you? You're just passive and pathetic, Piers. How can I respect you when you just drift through life with no spark or ambition?'

'Do not blame me for this.' We're both shouting now. Susan's face is getting redder, blotches blooming on her neck and cleavage. 'You're the liar. You're the one who is destroying our son's life. He doesn't deserve you as a mother.'

'Well, that's who he's got. And at least his birth father has a backbone, unlike you. You saw the way that Raf was in awe of Lewis. When he gets to know him properly, there'll be no going back. I should have left you years ago. In fact, I should never have married you. You're nothing to Raf. He has no respect for you, and neither do I.'

Furious tears are pricking at my eyes now. I knew Susan could be spiteful, of course I did. But she's never turned her venom on me. Never accused me of being a bad father. Never been so very hurtful. I know that if I don't leave this instant, I might hit her. I can feel the tiny impulses coursing down my arm to my fingers. I turn my back on my wife and take a couple of steps towards the staircase.

'Oh no you don't!' she yells. 'You always walk away when the going gets tough, don't you, Piers? You can never stand up for yourself.'

I turn to look at her, this woman whom I thought I knew so well, her eyes narrowed, her lips a thin straight line, and I wonder where all the love went. I take a step backwards again, but Susan has reached for something. In that moment, I see a flash of gold. The squat, square carriage clock with its white face and gold numbers. Susan lifts it above her head and hurls it at me. And I realise that my wife, who I thought was poor at hand-eye coordination, isn't at all. The side of the clock hits my head and for a split second it feels as if my head has been torn open, and then I'm stumbling, my limbs desperately grabbing for anything, gasping only air. The world goes black.

Except not for long. My eyes flicker open and I see the grotesque features of my wife, tugging me, pulling my ankles.

'What?' I mutter but I'm not sure the word comes out.

My head feels as if it's been split open with a hammer and as it bounces along the carpet, the pain becomes so overwhelming. I've never felt anything like it. My whole body is in my skull, and in that final moment of lucidity, I'm positive that my brains are spilling out of my head and will leave snail-like traces along the carpet. And then I'm tumbling, once again. This time, when my world turns black, it stays that way.

CHAPTER TWENTY-TWO

RAFAEL

I didn't take much. Just a small rucksack which I packed with my laptop, phone and charger, one change of clothes, my toothpaste and toothbrush and the wad of notes Dad had stuffed into an envelope in his bedside drawer. I found my passport in the pocket of Mum's suitcase. She hadn't even bothered to hide our most valuable documents properly. I felt guilty about taking so much money, but as Dad always laughingly says, 'What's mine is yours and what's yours is mine, even if we haven't got a euro to our names'. I could have tried to hitchhike back to France but I know Mum and Dad would have had a complete fit if I did that, so better I took the money and be safe.

I left the house hurriedly, worried for a moment that Hugo might spot me. But he didn't and I made it to the tube station and then got the underground to St Pancras station. I hadn't realised how expensive the Eurostar train was going to be, and for a moment I wondered if it would be cheaper to get back to France another way. Except I was already at the Eurostar terminal, and I just wanted to get back home, the quickest way possible. So I paid the exorbitant ticket price, got on the train and sat there for just over two hours as the train sped through the English countryside, then plunged into the darkness of the tunnel under the sea and out again into the bright sunlight in France. I kept my phone turned off because I knew once Mum and Dad realised I'd gone, the shit would hit the fan. I also had the presence of mind to switch off any location settings on my phone so they couldn't track me if I turned the phone back on.

I have to admit to feeling a bit nervous in Paris. I've only been there a couple of times – once on a school trip and once with Dad – but I reminded myself that it's probably a safer city than London and I speak the language fluently. I took the metro and made it without any problems from Gare du Nord to Gare du Lyons. Then I bought myself a one-way ticket to Aix-en-Provence. No one took a second look at me; no one cared about my age or where I was going. So when I was installed on the French train, I fired off an email to Lucille asking if she could pick me up from the station and telling her something awful had happened in London. I then switched my phone on, super briefly, and sent her a Whats-App, asking her to check her email. I expected to find loads of missed calls and messages from my parents, except there was nothing. Absolutely nothing. At first I felt really winded, as if they couldn't give a toss about me, but after a few moments I realised they probably thought I was still with Hugo. Even so, it made me mega angry. Because the truth is they don't give a flying fuck about me. Not really. If they cared they'd have taken me on holiday somewhere by the sea or let me go travelling with Lucille. Instead, off they were, gallivanting around London, doing their own thing, not in the slightest bit interested in their only son. I hoped it would hurt them when they discovered I'd gone. Once I'd hit send to Lucille, I switched the phone off again and dropped it into my rucksack.

The train journey from Paris to Aix was just over three hours and I slept for a lot of it. It's weird how I felt so knackered. I had horrible, warped dreams that left me with a sensation of dread when I woke up, yet I couldn't actually recall what the dreams were about. I checked my emails but there was nothing from Lucille, so I turned my phone on again. This time my phone vibrated with ping after ping and the woman opposite me frowned as she fixed me with an evil glare. I turned the sound off on my phone. Loads of messages from Mum and Dad all saying the same – where are you? Call as soon as you get this. We're worried about you. Please call to let us know you're safe. In amongst all their messages was a single-letter message from Lucille.

'K.' I took that to mean she'd be there to pick me up.

My heart was thumping when I got off the train at Aix-en-Provence and emerged out of the station to the road where all the cars and taxis were waiting. I'd used pretty much all the cash on my train journeys and had less than fifty euros in my French bank account, so there was a knot in my throat at the thought of what I'd do if Lucille wasn't there. I'd be sleeping on a bench or calling one of my mates from school, spinning them some story about why I'd hurried back to France alone.

But Lucille was there, the engine in her bright yellow Renault whining as she kept the car running so she could use the air con. I have never ever been so happy to see someone in my entire life and literally danced across the road to her car.

After chucking my rucksack onto the rear seat, I threw

myself into the passenger seat and grabbed her face with both hands, pulling her towards me for a kiss.

'Thank you, thank you, merci,' I murmured against her soft lips, trying hard to stop the tears from welling up in my eyes.

'Alors, what is the emergency?' she asked, pulling away from me. 'We need to go, otherwise I'll get a ticket.' She pulled on her seat belt and steered the car away from the kerb.

I had planned to be all cool around Lucille, to not blurt how much I'd missed her, except when I was sitting there in the car, I couldn't stop myself from grinning and the words just spurted out. 'I've missed you so much.'

She turned to look at me briefly, a smile edging at her lips. 'And I've missed you too.'

I don't think I've ever felt so happy. I didn't ask her what she meant when she said she'd been too busy to speak to me and I didn't question her as to whether she was going off me. I couldn't allow my brain to consider that for one millisecond. Lucille and I loved each other, we missed each other, and although we were young, our relationship was way stronger than that of my parents.

'I had to get away,' I said. 'London was horrible. I met all these pompous idiots and then I discovered something awful. Mum is having an affair.'

Lucille laughed. She actually laughed, and that feeling I'd had of love and security just moments earlier hiccupped and bounced, and doubt crept into my head.

'Why are you laughing?' I asked, eventually. We were on the motorway now, driving too fast for the little car.

'Because that's what people do. They have affairs. But

I'm sorry it has hurt you so badly,' she says, softening her tone.

I had intended on telling her about Dad not being my birth father, about that letter which says he's infertile, except I decided not to. I needed more time to process that alone, and then perhaps I would tell Lucille everything.

'Do you want me to take you home?' she asked.

'No,' I said a little too vehemently. 'The Browns are still there and the moment they see me they'll tell Mum and Dad.'

'But you can't stay with me. You know what my parents think of you and your family.'

I was silent for a while, wondering whether perhaps it was a mistake to come here, to ask Lucille to help me out. But she broke the silence.

'There's a place I know where we can go. Somewhere in the middle of nowhere. We can camp there.'

'Really?' I asked, because all I heard her say was *we*, and I dared to hope that Lucille might stay by my side.

CHAPTER TWENTY-THREE

PIERS

'Hello, Mr Lester.'

I don't recognise the female voice. I'm trying to force my eyelids open except they don't want to work. It's as if they've been taped shut and all I can see is blackness. Strange noises drift in and out and I find it hard to make sense of them. Beeps. Distant voices. Other sounds that I can't distinguish. It's so confusing, as if my brain can't grab onto anything for long enough to process things. And I'm so tired, just wanting to drift back to sleep. Something jolts me. A movement, the touch of skin on my arm. A searing bright light.

'Piers, are you awake?' This time it's a male voice. Darkness has given way to a painful white light. My eyelids flutter open and a young man is staring at me, his face just a foot or so away from mine.

'Water,' I gasp. My mouth feels completely dry and my throat painfully sore.

I feel a plastic straw being placed between my lips and I gulp in agonising sucks of water. 'Who are you?' I mumble.

'My name is Doctor Nicholas Murray. How are you feeling?'

'Everything hurts.'

'We'll up the morphine then.'

'What's happened?' It feels like I'm in a fog of confusion, viscous-like and impossible to make my way through. I squeeze my eyelids closed and force them open again. More comes into focus this time and I'm staring at a white ceiling made up of square panels.

'You're in hospital, Piers. You had an accident and we sedated you to let your brain heal.'

'My brain?' I move my hand and try to lift my arm up to feel my head, except there are tubes in it and there's a sharp pain when I move it. I give in and sink back into the hard mattress. 'What happened?' I ask.

'You fell down the stairs. Your wife found you and called the emergency services. Do you remember any of that?'

'No,' I murmur, trying so hard to grasp any memory. But my mind is blank. 'You speak good English,' I say.

There's a pause and when I look at the doctor, he's frowning. 'Where do you think you are, Piers?' he asks.

'In hospital. Are we in Cannes or Nice or somewhere else?'

'You're in London, at Chelsea Westminster hospital in Fulham. Why do you think you're in France?'

'Because we live there. When did I come to London?' I feel an edge of panic now. This doesn't make sense. We do live in France, don't we? Or have I imagined it? In my mind's eye I can see the house where we live, the pale stone, the scaffolding around the side, the beautiful swimming pool surrounded by lavender. Or is that a false memory, a picture that I saw in a magazine perhaps or a hotel where we once stayed?

The doctor is holding a clipboard now, glancing through some papers. 'You're right, Piers. Your home address is in Provence. It's good that you remember important things such as that.'

'I don't know why I'm here. Where's Susan?'

'Susan?' he asks.

'My wife. And Raf, my son.'

'I believe your wife was here earlier. I'll ask your nurse to call her, to tell her you've woken up. I'm sure she'll be very relieved. I'm just going to shine a bright light into your eyes and check your blood pressure. You've had a nasty gouge to your head and you're on strong painkillers which will make you feel drowsy. But now you're awake, we'll slowly reduce the drugs.'

'Will my memory come back?' I ask, trying so hard to work out why I'm in London and which stairs I fell down. Were we staying with friends perhaps? Yet everything is a blank.

'It's hard to say with traumatic brain injuries. Your memory might come back slowly or there might be a permanent gap in your recall. What can you remember?'

I swallow hard but my throat is dry and scratchy. My voice sounds distant, as if it's coming from someplace else. 'Being at home. The house in France. The builders. André. Working in the heat in my clients' gardens. But nothing else. Nothing about coming to London. I don't even know why I'm here.'

'I'm sure your wife will fill you in when she gets here.' The doctor smiles at me reassuringly. But I don't feel reassured. There's a horrible sensation in my chest of impending doom. I suppose something terrible has happened. I fell. I hit my head. I've been sedated, and my brain is quite literally hurt. Yet it feels greater than that. As if there's something that's constantly out of reach. A memory that floats away every time my mind seems to get within touching distance. It creates a panic, a horrible racing of my heart, and when the doctor glances at the machine next to me, he frowns slightly. Can he see that my heart is pounding? The breath catches in my throat and I start coughing, which sends waves of pain through my skull and my chest. The doctor fiddles with something on the drip stand next to the bed.

'You'll feel better soon,' he promises me before he opens the blue paper curtains and walks away. Right now, that feels like an empty promise which rationally doesn't make sense because of course I'll be getting better. That's why I'm in hospital after all.

I must sleep again because when I awake, there is a nauseating smell of food and the clatter of cutlery against crockery. I turn my head away from the direction of the noise and force my eyes open. Susan is sitting on a blue plastic chair, her head lowered, her fingers racing over the face of her phone. The blue curtain is behind her and I can hear someone speaking in low tones, probably in the adjacent bed. Susan doesn't notice that I'm awake and it gives me the chance to study my wife. She looks awful, her face pale, bags under her eyes and her hair unusually lank and unwashed. My accident must have terrified her and it's showing on her face and in her sloped shoulders. I hate to think of the worry I've put her through, the worry that Raf must be feeling, and although I'm pining to see our son, I'm glad he's not here, seeing me in this state.

Susan glances upwards and her eyes meet mine. I smile

at her, waiting for her to leap to the side of the bed, to take my hand in hers, to kiss me gently on the lips. Except she doesn't do any of that. I see a fear in her eyes and for a horrible moment I wonder if I've got it wrong; whether this woman staring at me isn't my wife after all. Is my injured brain playing tricks on me?

'Susan?' I whisper, my voice still hoarse.

'Yes,' she replies.

I feel a frisson of relief. So I have recognised my wife.

'How long have you been awake?' she asks, placing her mobile phone into her handbag.

'Just now.'

'And how are you feeling?' She still doesn't get up and I wonder if perhaps I smell, or my injuries are so terrible that she can't bring herself to touch me. I lift my hand and gingerly run my fingers over my face. I feel the roughness of stubble. My lips, although they're painfully dry, don't feel swollen, and my nose seems fine. I touch gently around my eyes and up to my forehead. Nothing hurts and there are no bandages.

'Is something wrong with my face?' I ask.

'No,' she replies. 'You have a bandage on your head but that's all. And you've got some broken ribs.'

That explains the searing pain when I lift my arms. So why is she looking at me as if I'm a stranger? And where is Raf?

'What happened?' I ask.

'You fell down the stairs.' She glances up at the door. I wait for her to elaborate except she doesn't.

'Which stairs? And what are we doing in London?' I ask.

Her eyes flick towards my face and there's a fleeting

expression in her eyes which I can't decipher. It's as if my brain is coated in sticky honey and can't make the proper synapses.

'We're on holiday, doing a house swap with Elodie and Lewis Brown.' The names mean nothing to me. 'Don't you remember?'

I shake my head and then grimace as the movement sends spasms of pain through my head.

'What's the last thing you do remember?' She edges closer to me but still doesn't reach out.

'I don't know. Talking to André at the chateau. Driving to work. Taking Raf to school to sit his exams. But I don't know when all of that was.'

'About three weeks ago,' she says quietly. 'So you don't remember flying to London, and you don't remember the beautiful house we're staying in in Knightsbridge?'

'No, nothing.' A knot of panic enlarges in my gut. I try to force my brain to remember something. Anything. But there's just a black void and it's scary. 'Is Raf alright? Can you bring him to see me?'

'I'm not sure a hospital is the best place for him to come to. He'll be completely freaked out seeing you like this.'

I open my mouth to say but he's seventeen, he's old enough, surely? But I'm so very tired and the exertion of this conversation is taking too much out of me. I let my eyes close and sink further into the uncomfortable bed, the noises just beyond the blue curtains fading into the background. As I drift off, I wonder why Susan is being so cold. Have we had an argument that I don't recall?

When I awake again, the blue curtain is pulled on the right side of my bed but open to the left and I can see slatted blinds are pulled across an internal window, the door to the room open. It's only the beeping noises that remind me that I'm still in hospital. It takes a few seconds to register, but I'm in a ward with at least one other person, who at this moment lies hidden behind the paper curtain, completely silent. I hear footsteps and turn my head towards the door, expecting to see my wife. Except it isn't Susan. It's a woman, probably mid-fifties, who has let her hair go grey. She's wearing a taupe raincoat and carrying a wicker basket full of fruit, all wrapped in a clear cellophane. I expect her to walk past me towards the hidden person in another bed. Except she doesn't.

'Hello, Mr Lester,' she says coyly. I don't recognise her and I hear my heartbeat in my ears as I try to recall if I should know this woman. There is absolutely nothing familiar about her. Not her look, or the way she moves, or the faint East End accent. And why is she calling me mister?

'Shall I put these on the table over here?' she asks. There's a narrow table at the end of my bed that I recognise as being one of those tray-type tables on wheels.

'Thanks,' I say. 'This is a bit awkward...'

'Oh don't worry,' the woman says. 'The nurse said you might not remember who I am, and we only met the once.' Her face flushes slightly as she stands awkwardly at the end of my bed, interweaving her fingers. 'I'm Teresa, the Browns' housekeeper. I pop in three times a week to clean the place and change the bed linen.'

I stare at her blankly. I don't know who the Browns are.

'Anyway, when Elodie heard what happened, she asked me to pick up a hamper from Harrods and bring it over to you. I don't know if you feel like eating anything, but it'll be nicer stuff than the hospital will serve, at least. And they don't allow flowers in hospitals these days, which is such a shame, don't you think?'

'Thank you,' I say, wondering who Elodie is, wondering what house she's referring to. These names mean absolutely nothing to me. 'I'm sorry that my memory has gone,' I say. 'Hopefully only temporarily. When did we meet?'

'Goodness,' she says, shuffling from one foot to another. I'm not sure who feels more awkward, this Teresa or me. 'I arrived literally seconds after you fell. Your poor wife was completely hysterical, so I helped her call the emergency services and stayed with you both until you were whisked off to hospital. There was a lot of blood, but being glass and stone it was easy enough to clean up. Honestly, I thought you were dead when I saw you there, lying all motionless. You gave us both quite the fright.'

'Oh,' I reply, because I recall none of this. 'I'm sorry you had to clean up after me.'

She chuckles. 'It's my job, so no worries. Anyway, Elodie will be happy to learn that you're awake and I hope that you recover very quickly. Perhaps I'll see you back at the house.'

'Thank you,' I repeat. A nurse arrives wheeling a trolley full of equipment.

'Well, I'll be off now,' Teresa says, and before I can thank her again, she's gone.

'How are you feeling?' the nurse asks. Her name badge says Shireen and I give myself the mental exercise of trying to remember it.

'My head is sore, but I'm feeling a bit better,' I say, although honestly that's a lie, because I can't remember how I was feeling before.

'Are you up to eating a little supper? They'll be around with some soup and bread shortly.'

'I'll try,' I say. 'Where's Susan? Has she left?'

'Your wife?' she asks.

I nod.

'Yes, she left a couple of hours ago. She's very keen to get you out of the hospital. A strong woman, your wife is, isn't she? I gather you live in France.' Shireen is wrapping my arm with the blood pressure monitor, which squeezes unpleasantly. 'She said you'd be better off back home, rehabilitating there. Our Doctor Murray was having none of that.'

'What do you mean?' I ask.

'You've had a very nasty concussion. You were sedated for many hours. I'm afraid it'll be a while before you're fit to travel. But don't worry, we'll make your stay here as comfortable as possible. You're in the best place for a quick recovery.'

Shireen then aims a thermometer in my ear and jots down my vitals on the paper attached to the clipboard at the end of my bed.

'And Raf?' I ask. 'Has my son been to see me?'

Shireen looks up from the clipboard. 'How old is your son, love?'

'Seventeen.'

'Oh, so nearly all grown up. No, I don't think he's been in yet. But you know teenagers. Probably has some phobia about hospitals.'

Except Raf doesn't have any phobia about hospitals. We even mooted the possibility of him training to be a doctor because he's fascinated by the workings of the human body. There's something not right, except I can't put my finger on it. Susan was acting coldly, and why does she want to move me back to France so quickly? And why hasn't Raf been to see me? I try to figure all of this out but the man in the adjacent bed, the faceless man behind the blue curtain, presses his emergency buzzer and there's a commotion as a bunch of medics rush in and attend to him. I press my knuckles into my eye sockets and after a couple of noisy minutes, the sounds start to fade and I drift back into a welcome sleep.

CHAPTER TWENTY-FOUR

RAFAEL

About forty minutes later and we were deep in the countryside, an area I didn't recognise.

'Your father called the vineyard earlier. He was worried about you.'

I experienced a jolt of panic. 'Did you say anything?'

'No, of course not. I said I hadn't heard from you.' I exhaled with relief, leaning my head back against the uncomfortable car seat.

'They're worried about you. They said you're not in trouble but they're concerned about your safety.'

'Of course I'm in trouble,' I said.

'Ah, mon petit chou,' Lucille muttered. Such an old-fashioned endearment, I thought. My little cabbage. 'Don't worry. You're safe with me.'

A few minutes later and Lucille indicated to the left and we bounced along a farm track. At the bottom was a tiny stone building, weeds growing up its sides, a wooden door and a window with a broken panel of glass.

'What is this place?' I asked.

'It belongs to my uncle. He was going to turn it into a gîte but when he divorced my aunt, that was forgotten. I used to come here with my cousins when I was younger. We camped here sometimes. There's running water and there used to be a couple of camp beds, but it's been a while since I visited.' She turned the engine off and we hopped out of the car.

It was getting dark, the sun had slipped behind the horizon, and I shivered at the sudden cold. I followed Lucille up the path and watched as she picked up a flower pot and produced a key. I wondered why they bothered locking the place, because with the broken window, it would be easy enough to scramble inside.

The interior was dank and unwelcoming. I was sure I heard the scurry of little feet, a mouse perhaps. But at the same time, the place felt so secluded and very romantic. The thought of hiding away here with Lucille gave me a permanent smile.

'Get the stuff out of the car,' she said, so I doubled back and, in the boot of the car, found a bin liner stuffed with a duvet, sheets, pillows and towels and a crate with camping gear, plastic plates and cups. I couldn't wipe the grin from my face.

A DAY LATER, and it is every bit as romantic as I anticipated. Yesterday evening, after leaving me at the little brick barn, Lucille drove to the nearest supermarket and returned with food and candles and a disposable BBQ. We cooked on the fire and snuggled up on the camp bed, making love as the candles flickered. Today, Lucille returned to the vineyard, having promised her parents she would work there, and she's told them that she's staying with a girlfriend who is going through a horrible breakup. She has a freedom that I can only dream of. Her parents are so relaxed in comparison to mine, yet you'd think they would be stricter, with her being a girl. Right now, the sun is setting and we're sitting in front of a little fire, my arm around her shoulders, her head leaning on my chest. I feel like I'm going to explode with happiness.

'I've got something to tell you,' she says, her body stiffening.

I brace myself. Is she going to ruin this dream? I sit up a little straighter and she edges away from me.

'Okay,' I say slowly, but really I wish that she wouldn't say anything at all.

'I need to tell you why my parents hate yours.'

I let out a little puff of air and reach for my bottle of beer. Honestly, I don't really care.

'Maman was the carer for Florian Dupont, the owner of your house before you moved there. After his wife disappeared and his son left, he was all alone.'

'Aw, poor Monsieur Dupont,' I say, placing little kisses on Lucille's neck. I would much rather make out with her than listen to this story.

'Are you listening?' Lucille prods me with a finger in my ribs.

'Yes. His wife disappeared, and his son left. Is this some prophecy for my family?'

'Stop being silly, Raf. They thought Florian's wife, Margot, might have been murdered or perhaps she took her own life because her blood was found in the chateau.'

'Ooo, spooky,' I say, wrapping my arms more tightly around her.

'Maman felt sorry for Florian, so she used to go over

there regularly, making him meals, delivering his shopping and stuff. He'd come over for Christmas and birthdays and was a bit like a second grandfather to me. Anyway, he told Maman that he was going to rewrite his will and was going to leave the house to her.'

'What, your mum was going to inherit our chateau? But she didn't, right?'

'Obviously not, as your parents wouldn't own it.'

I nibble at Lucille's ear, but she pushes me away.

'Come on, Raf. This is serious. I need to tell you stuff.'

'Okay.' I sigh, taking a swig from my bottle of beer.

'Florian had a son, but the son never came to visit him and he said his son didn't deserve the legacy. Maman didn't ask for the chateau and honestly she was rather embarrassed at the time. But then one day Florian produced a new will and he got the gardener to witness it. He told Maman that the house would be hers and he'd leave the new will hidden behind the boiserie in the library.'

'The boiserie?' I ask. I'm fluent in French but that's not a word I know.

'The wood panelling in the library. So when Florian died my parents expected that all their money worries would be over. You know, it's tough running a vineyard. Really tough. We've struggled all of my life.'

'I bet your parents don't argue about money as much as mine do,' I mutter. Lucille ignores me.

'The next thing we know is Florian's estranged son is putting the villa up for sale.'

'You mean Chateau Lester,' I say, using my fingers to create air quotes around the name.

'Yeah, Chateau Lester,' Lucille repeats with sarcasm. 'My parents went to see the attorney but the only will he had was the one Florian had lodged with him five years previously. Maman explained that there was another will in the library but by then Florian's son had the keys and was temporarily living there. They could never find it, never prove that the will was there.'

'So you're saying that our house should belong to your parents?'

'Yes and no. It makes my parents seem greedy, but they became completely obsessed with it, saying that it was the greatest injustice, and that the villa should be theirs. I never agreed. Not really. Because Maman was kind to Florian, didn't mean that she should get the whole villa.'

'Why are you telling me this?' I ask, genuinely confused. I poke the fire with a stick and sparks fly up into the still night air.

'Because they're still looking and it's destroying our family. When you first moved into the chateau, Papa offered to be the foreman to your dad's builders. He wanted to get access to the library to remove the panels, except it all went horribly wrong, didn't it? Your dad came home and lost his shit and fired Papa. And now our parents loathe each other and haven't spoken since.'

'And?'

'They've been using me to get access to the chateau, to look for this ridiculous will which probably doesn't exist anyway.' Lucille hunches her shoulder and stares into the flames of the fire. It takes me a couple of minutes to realise what she's not saying to me, and when it hits me, I jump up.

'Did your parents ask you to go out with me? Was this' – I gesture between her and me – 'all a set-up?'

Lucille also jumps up and tries to grab my hand, except I pull it away from her. 'Originally they just wanted me to be friends with you and to begin with, yes, I was doing what they wanted. They went on and on about how it would be my legacy, that my brother and I wouldn't inherit their debts, that our lives would be so much easier, and sure, I fell for it. But then I got to know you and I promise that I really fell for you. I wouldn't be sleeping with you if I didn't love you, Raf. I'm not some common tart.'

I can't look at Lucille. My chest feels like it's been ripped open with betrayal. First my parents lie to me, all of my life. And now my girlfriend. Whom can I really trust? I stride away, walking so fast I'm almost jogging, through the field, sharp spikes of the crop scratching my bare shins, the sun so low I can barely see where I'm going. Tears prick at my eyes and I swipe them away, angry with myself, angry with the world.

'Raf!' Lucille's shout is somewhere behind me, but I don't turn around.

CHAPTER TWENTY-FIVE

ELODIE

When I awake, it's pitch dark in the bedroom. I hear the hoot of an owl in the distance and as my eyes grow used to the night, I make out the faint hint of the moon, it's pale glow visible through the thin voile curtains. I turn towards Lewis's side of the bed, reaching out for the reassuring warmth of his body, but he's not there. And with a start, that's when I remember. I found messages from Susan Lester calling my husband darling, messages asking whether he's told me that he's leaving me yet. My throat chokes up and it feels like a knife has wedged itself in my chest. Lewis has been lying to me.

Last night I told him that I had a migraine and asked him to sleep in the spare room. He pretended to fawn over me, asking if I needed a cold flannel or medication, which he could buy in the local town. I said I just needed to be alone and to sleep. He seemed to accept that, which is strange in itself, because I've never actually had a migraine. And then with a sinking heart I realised that he doesn't care. It's all one big pretence.

I try to think through the implications of Lewis leaving me. I hold the purse strings in our marriage. I've always been the higher earner, and occasionally wondered whether Lewis loved my money more than me, but I was always adept at banishing that intrusive thought. We were solid, or at least I thought we were. If he divorces me, he won't get much. The prenup saw to that, so the only incentive for him to leave is love. Is love enough? I think of this fake chateau, which undoubtedly is a money pit, and based on what the locals have mentioned, the Lesters are struggling to pay their builders. If Piers and Susan divorce, surely they would have to sell this property, and then what? Lewis's business is failing; it has been for years, only propped up by my generosity. But maybe love is enough. Perhaps Susan and Lewis think they'll be happy without financial security. No. We're talking about Lewis. He likes the good things in life; his designer clothes and fancy cars; flying business class and living in chichi Knightsbridge. Surely I know my husband well enough to realise he would wither and die without money. He's avaricious but masks it with a bumbling generosity, buying me beautiful jewellery and fabulous art. With the money from our joint account, of course. My money.

Perhaps he's hoping he can have the best of both worlds. An exciting affair with Susan on the side whilst still living the life of luxury with me. Maybe he's been stringing Susan along, having an affair with her while intending to stay married to me. I suppress a sob. This was not how our holiday was meant to pan out. Not how the rest of my life was meant to pan out.

Sleep is elusive now. I switch on my kindle, desperate to still my whirring brain, but I'm not sure why I bother. The words jumble on the screen, my mind too wired to read. Instead I decide to get up. I switch on the bedside table light, pull on my robe, shove my feet inside my trainers and walk quietly towards the door. Lewis and I need to talk. My initial idea of taking time to uncover the truth is ridiculous. This is our marriage. I don't care that it's 2 a.m. Lewis needs to tell me what's going on, how long he's been lying to me for. My veins are fired with anger. I turn the doorknob and pause in the dark corridor, a strange sensation prickling at my skin, as if I should be scared of the dark. For a moment I think I see a shadow and my heart beats faster. It's my mind playing tricks on me. Straining my ears for any sound, I tiptoe along the corridor to the spare room, surprised that the door is already ajar. I push it open further and step inside. The room is lit up by the moon and the bed is empty, the lightweight duvet crumpled on the end of the bed, a dip in the pillow where Lewis's head must have lain. Did Lewis's creeping around the house wake me? I strain my ears to listen. Perhaps he's in the bathroom. I try to still my rapidly beating heart by reminding myself that the dog is silent, so there can't be anything to be scared of.

I edge out of the bedroom and tiptoe to both the bathrooms, glancing inside. But they're empty. So I walk silently along the upstairs corridor towards the staircase, my eyes now fully adjusted to the low light in the house, my skin covered with goosebumps because it's surprisingly cold in here at this hour.

I yelp.

A dark figure appears at the far end of the corridor, outside the rooms that are not in use. I open my mouth to speak Lewis's name, except the figure disappears into one of the rooms. What the hell is he playing at? And then the most horrible thought hits me. Perhaps Lewis wants me to die. That way he'll be a rich man and he and Susan can live a life of luxury wherever they wish. Is that why the no entry sign on the tower was removed? Did he hope that I might have fallen to my death rather than just breaking a collarbone? But no. Surely I'm letting my imagination run away with me. Lewis is my husband. Even if he doesn't want to be with me anymore, he wouldn't want me dead, would he?

'Lewis?' I shout out, waiting for him to emerge from one of the rooms. Except he doesn't. I retreat backwards and hurry down the stairs, throwing nervous glances over my shoulder. I want to be with Pushkin. The dog will protect me. At the bottom of the stairs I edge around the corner, my back up against the wall, trying to control my breathing. I'm being ridiculous. This is crazy. But then I hear the creak of footsteps above me and I peer around the corner, at the staircase. A large figure is walking down the stairs, slowly. A man dressed all in black, and then I have to shove my fist into my mouth. He's wearing a balaclava. A black balaclava designed to cover his face. And he's holding something that looks like a baton or a stick.

In that terrible moment, I realise that I was right. My husband is trying to kill me. I open my mouth to scream his name but something stops me. What if it's not Lewis? What if he's hired a hitman instead? There is no way that I'll be able to defend myself against the bulk of that person stepping closer and closer to me. I have to run.

I dart down the corridor, my feet pounding against the stone tiles, into the library and then through to the living room, crouching behind the sofa. I can hear his footsteps and now I wonder why the hell I ran in this direction. There's a patio door but is it open? Did he lock it and remove the key?

My heart is so loud, the pumping of blood in my ears almost deafening. I race towards the door, the lightness of outside drawing me towards it like a moth. If I can get out, then I might be able to get away. Not that I have the car keys, but at least I'll be able to hide more easily. Perhaps I can run onto the road and flag down a passing car, assuming there are any in this quiet place. I careen towards the door and pull on it as with all my might. It's closed. I fumble to see if the key is in the lock but find nothing. There's a heavy pewter jug on the side table and without thinking, I pick it up and hurl it at the glass panel. The glass shatters instantly, the noise deafening in the quiet of the night. And then I'm shoving my hand through the opening, turning the handle and I'm outside, running along the patio. I stumble as I misjudge one of the steps towards the pool, my leg sending spasms of pain up my body, my ribs, shoulder and arm screaming in agony. I let out an involuntary groan as I realise I'm going the wrong way. I turn and race back around the side of the house towards the tower and the scaffolding. I slam straight into a person.

'What the fuck?' he says, as he rights himself. We're both still; in silent shock as we stare at each other. He speaks first.

'Elodie? What's happened? What have you got on your face?'

I put my hand up to my forehead and it comes away sticky. Blood, I suppose.

It takes a moment to realise that this is Rafael. The Lesters' son. What is he doing here, creeping around in the dark? And it takes me a little longer to register that this slim, lanky boy is not the man who has been chasing me. This lad is wearing jeans and a grey T-shirt, an expression of shock on his pale face.

'What are you doing?' he asks again.

I wipe the palm of my hand on my leg and place it over his face, grabbing his arm. 'We're in danger,' I whisper. 'Come. And don't speak.'

He stares at me, his eyes glistening in the low light, but I drag him with me.

'Please come!' I whisper urgently. We race towards the tower, the place where I fell, yet despite that I sense the tower is where we'll be the safest. I'm constantly glancing back over my shoulders, looking for the balaclava man, but all I see are shadows. But now it's not just me who is in danger, it's Rafael too, and he's only a boy. I need to protect him, to forget that my body is screaming with pain, and concentrate on making sure that Rafael is safe.

'In the tower,' I whisper, shoving him in front of me. I pull the barrier away, and we're both inside, our breaths too loud.

'What's going on?' he whispers. His eyes seem almost luminous in this low light, his pupils enormous with fear.

'Lewis is trying to kill me.' My voice is barely audible. 'My husband wants me dead.'

CHAPTER TWENTY-SIX

PIERS

It's the middle of the night, except it's never peaceful in a hospital. The man in the adjacent bed is snoring, which at least means he's still alive. With the earlier commotion, I wondered if he was facing his final hours. I can't sleep. My mind is racing, desperately trying to grab strands of memory that are just beyond my reach. I try to sit up in bed, but I must pull on something I shouldn't because it sets off an alarm. My nurse, Shireen, hurries in and checks the cannula in my hand, double-checks if I'm all right.

'Do I have any belongings here?' I ask, wondering if my wallet and phone might be stashed away somewhere. And where are the clothes I arrived in?

'Sure,' Shireen says in a low voice. 'There's a locker inside the bedside cabinet. Do you want me to get something for you?'

'Yes. I'd like to know if my phone is in there.'

She kneels down and pulls open the drawer, extracting a pile of neatly folded clothes.

'I normally keep my phone and wallet in my trouser pockets, but they might have fallen out.'

'Let's have a look,' she says, holding the trousers up and extracting both from the rear pockets. 'Here you go,' Shireen says, handing me the phone and wallet. I hand the wallet back to her. It's just the phone I want for now. I switch it on, hoping that there's still some battery. To my relief, there's 45% left.

'Do you need anything else?' she asks, frowning as she watches me looking at the phone.

'No, thanks,' I say.

'You really should try to sleep,' she instructs me. 'It's the quickest route to recovery.'

'I will,' I promise. But first I need to look at my phone. I open my messages and emails but I don't have anything other than spam. So then I look at my photos in the hope that the images might trigger some memories. There's a photo of Susan, Raf and me standing outside a theatre on Shaftesbury Avenue. I vaguely recall sitting in the dark in a theatre but I've no idea when that was, or what play or musical we saw. I check the date of the photo. Just four days ago, yet it could be forty years by the vagueness of the memory. I scroll through my photos and see one of a smart town house with a black front door and railings. And then a thought pops into my head; we were doing a house swap. It's a relief that little fragments of memory are returning, and when I look through more of the photos, the London town house looks increasingly familiar. Yet I still can't remember anything of my fall. I gaze at the photo I took of the staircase, the floating glass steps rising up to the first floor. But I simply can't place myself on them – neither at the top nor bottom. I go through each photo slowly, studying them one by one, when I'm startled by my phone ringing. The phone slips through my fingers onto the white sheet but I quickly pick it up again. To my joy, Raf's name comes up.

'Hey! What are you doing calling me in the middle of the night?'

'Dad!' Raf whispers. 'There's a man trying to kill Elodie.'

For a moment I wonder if I'm still in a dream, or rather a nightmare. Raf's words don't make any sense.

'Who's Elodie?'

'Elodie Brown.' Raf's voice is impatient.

'I'm sorry but I don't know what you mean.' Panic gnaws at my chest as I realise my memory is failing me, that there's something vital that I need to recall.

'Dad!' Raf's voice is quiet but there's an edge of what sounds like fear. 'Listen. I came back to the chateau to get some of my stuff. I didn't want to be seen so Lucille dropped me off at the bottom of the drive and I crept inside but then a man in a balaclava appeared and he is trying to kill Elodie. She thinks it's Lewis.'

Elodie? Lewis? Whom is Raf talking about? Why can't I remember anything? I'm completely confused now. What does he mean, he ran away? Why is Raf in France? Wasn't he with us here in London? Did Susan let him go home while I was in the hospital or did he go earlier?

'Where are you, Raf?'

'At the chateau, in France. Dad, what the hell's going on?' His whisper is more urgent now and I hear a terrifying quiver in his voice. 'Dad, can you call the police? Just call the police!' And then the line goes dead. I stare at my phone in horror, then try to call Raf back but his phone goes straight to voicemail. What the hell is going on? My heart rate goes through the roof and it sets off another alarm but I haven't got time to worry about my health. I need to call the French police. Now. At least that emergency number pings into my head. I dial 112.

'Which service do you need? Police, ambulance or fire?' the operator asks.

No, no. This isn't right. They should be answering in French, not English. 'I need the police in France. Can you help me?'

There's a long pause on the phone and I can tell immediately that the answer is no. I hang up. What now? I'm stuck in a hospital bed, hooked up to machines, and my son is in danger. Shireen appears.

'Piers, it's not good for you to get agitated. We need to think about your blood pressure and heart rate. Why don't you give me your phone?'

I can't let her take my phone away. It's a dire emergency so I push her away.

'I've got to do this,' I exclaim. 'My son is in danger.'

She slants her head to one side, peering at me as if I'm delusional.

'Please,' I say. 'I have to do this.'

Shireen huffs and I feel bad for being short with her because she's only trying to do her job.

'Right, but try to keep it quick,' she says, and then leaves the room.

With trembling fingers I go onto Google and search for the police station in Provence. I can sense the minutes slipping past as I desperately seek a contact number. Eventually I find a twenty-four-hour telephone number for the police in France and I call them. In faltering French, I explain that my son is in danger and give them my address, but my grasp of the French language is poor at the best of times and now I can barely get the words out. I just hope by stressing emergency and repeatedly giving the address of the chateau that they'll take me seriously and dispatch the gendarmes. At least I remember our address. At least that. All I can do is pray that Raf is safe, that the people he was talking about... And then suddenly, as if a rubber band has pinged in my head, I do remember. When Susan was here earlier, she talked about Elodie and Lewis Brown. They were the people whose house we were staying in.

I try to settle back down under the sheets, leaving my phone on the bedside table with the sound turned up high. I will Raf to call me back, but my phone just lies there silent in the dark. Except something has changed inside of me. Little trickles of memory return. I'm standing at the top of the stairs in the London townhouse and Susan is there. We're yelling at each other. I can't remember what the argument is about, but then I gasp. I'm on the floor, pain ricocheting through my bones and Susan is standing above me, her face puce, her eyes narrowed in fury. There's a look of utter disdain on her face. No, it's worse than that. It's hatred. In that horrible nugget of a memory, my wife hates me. And then she leans down and she grabs my ankles and tugs. The exertion makes the sinews on her neck stand out in relief and there's sweat on her brow. But she pulls and then she pushes and the next thing I recall is a sensation of falling. Down. Down. Down. Until there's a terrifying darkness.

I blink rapidly and swallow hard, reaching for the beaker of water on the tray table. My hand is shaking. Susan was trying to kill me. Susan pushed me down those stairs in the hope that I'd crash my skull open on the sharp glass treads. But why? Why was my wife trying to get rid of me? And then the connections are made and I let out an involuntary whimper.

Lewis.

Susan told me that she was in love with Lewis. That Lewis was Raf's birth father. And then we fought and she threw something at me. When I came to, she pushed me down the stairs. I let out a moan as I realise what really happened. My wife was trying to get rid of me. And now, in France, Lewis is trying to get rid of Elodie. The horror is too much to comprehend. Lewis and Susan intend to murder Elodie and me so that they can be together. Does my wife really hate me that much? I don't understand why she isn't just asking for divorce like most people would do. Of course, I'd be devastated, but we would come to some sort of solution.

It's hard to think straight, to fully grasp what has happened, what is happening. I hear a commotion outside in the corridor; the running of feet, low, urgent voices and then silence. As I'm lying there, trying to make sense of the swirling thoughts in my brain, I sense that someone has come into the room. There is a low light coming from the corridor, and as I turn my head to the door, a silhouette of a person is standing there.

'What are you doing here in the middle of the night?' I ask, shrinking back into the unyielding mattress.

She steps towards me and I flinch, but short of ripping the tubes from my arms and forcing my broken body out of the bed, there's nowhere for me to go. Susan reaches for the chair and pulls it close to the bed and then she pulls the curtains around my bed so we're no longer visible through the door.

'I want you to leave,' I say, a little too loudly. She frowns at me and crosses her arms over her chest.

'Keep your voice down. You'll wake up the chap in the next bed.'

'Why are you here in the middle of the night? It's not visiting hours.'

'I wanted to see you, to check up on how you are.'

'Why didn't you come earlier?'

I look at this woman whom I have spent the last two decades with; the woman whom I thought I knew, who shared my bed and my life. And I realise I don't know her at all. She has been lying to me all of this time and it feels like a sword has been turned in my heart. And how did she even get in here, in the middle of the night?

'I need to sleep, Susan. It's best you go and come back tomorrow during visiting hours.'

'Oh come on, darling,' she says, reaching for my hand. I pull it away from her, shifting to the edge of the bed.

She stares at me for a long moment, her eyes unblinking and cold. How come I never considered Susan's cool blue eyes as cold? But now I can barely bring myself to look at them.

'Please,' I say quietly. 'I need to sleep.'

'Raf is missing,' she says.

'What?'

'Raf has been gone for two days. He disappeared from London with his passport and he stole your money.'

I'm silent, because Raf isn't missing. He is in France, in danger. But I still don't understand why he's there and not here in London with us. And it's clear that Susan doesn't know either, otherwise why would she say he was missing?

There is a long pause interrupted only by a beep coming from one of the machines.

'You've got your memory back, haven't you?' Susan says, taking a step closer to the bed.

'Susan, you need to leave. Now. I have to sleep. We can discuss everything tomorrow.'

'No, Piers. We're going to talk now, while it's quiet. That's why I'm here, so we can talk in private.'

Is the man in the other bed awake? Please let him be awake, listening to our conversation, because then I might be saved. Except I know he isn't. I can hear his snoring, the deep vibrations that are depressingly regular.

'Susan, if you don't leave, I'm going to press the emergency buzzer.'

A sly smile creeps across the face of the woman I thought I loved. She steps around the bed and slides into the blue plastic chair, before bringing her face very close to mine.

She whispers, 'Oh no, you're not.'

CHAPTER TWENTY-SEVEN

ELODIE

'Stay completely still and silent,' I whisper to Rafael. I wish the boy wasn't in danger too, except that so long as he's creeping around here in the dark, he's likely in as much danger as I am. There's little I can do to protect him now. Whether he likes it or not, he's involved. And not just because he's physically here. It's his mother who my husband is running off with. My heart bleeds for this young man and I feel an overwhelming need to hug him tight. I don't though.

As my eyes grow accustomed to the low light in the tower, I see a pile of builders' equipment. Was this here the day I went up the stairs? The broken wood has been cleared away and the remnants of the staircase hang impossibly from the high ceiling. A box of nails spills open onto the stone floor next to a hefty commercial yellow and grey nail gun. I grab it. The nail gun feels heavy in my hand and I'm not exactly sure how to use it, but at least I have some kind of weapon.

'I need you to stay here,' I say.

'What's going on, Elodie? This doesn't make any sense.'

'You have to trust me, Raf. Lewis wants me dead and for your own safety, you need to stay hidden.'

'But –'

'Be completely still and silent. If you're sure there's no one around, then call for help. The police, ideally.'

'I'll call Dad,' he whispers.

I edge out of the building into the shadows, praying that Raf won't do anything stupid. I'm going to confront Lewis. I know him well and I'm hopeful I can talk him around without resorting to violence. He'll find us here sooner or later so I need to be proactive. My thoughts belie my true feelings but it's my job to keep Rafael safe. In reality I'm utterly terrified. A sharp knot sits in my sternum and I pray that Rafael's phone call to his father means the police will arrive soon.

I creep outside, trying to stop my trainer-clad feet from making a crunching noise on the gravel. I stay close to the building, moving as stealthily as I can in the shadows, trying to ignore the searing pain in my shoulder. Except I've never done anything like this before, and my arm in a sling makes it hard to move quietly. Surely Lewis won't actually kill me. Perhaps he just wanted to scare me, except why would he dress up all in black with a balaclava over his face? That doesn't make any sense at all. I see a light bobbing around through the windows of the villa, possibly in the kitchen, although my sheer panic is stopping my brain from working properly. I edge forwards again, the nail gun pulling on my left shoulder, my right shoulder still out of action. The scaffolding comes to an end here, so I duck backwards, wedging myself between the end of it and the stone wall. And then, to my horror, a huge shadow appears from the front door. As he

steps forwards, he is lit up by the low light of the moon and I
see that he's holding a long metal bar, much like a sawn-off
piece of scaffolding pipe. I swallow a whimper. Any doubt
that he isn't trying to harm me vanishes. Why else would he
be holding that, skulking around in the dark, very obviously
looking for me? The whites of his eyes are faintly visible and
I can see his face darting from side to side. I have no idea
where to go. I could make a run for it, hurtle down the
driveway towards the road, except the track is long and
Lewis's stride is far greater than mine. He would catch me in
an instant. My only hope is to talk him out of this nonsense.
To try to get him to see reason.

But before I can plan my next move, his head turns
towards me. He's seen me. With two long strides he's within
striking distance, the metal bar raised. In that millisecond, I
realise that my husband doesn't care. He's going to kill me
and when he finds Rafael, he'll likely kill the boy too. How
could I have misjudged this man so very much? Is that what
new love has done to him? Made him mad, brought out the
very worst in him?

'No, Lewis!' I screech. 'We need to talk.'

And then another figure emerges from the front door.
What the hell? Are there two of them? It takes me a long
moment to realise that I've got it all wrong.

Lewis isn't the masked man. My husband, wearing just
his pyjama bottoms, is racing towards the figure in front
of me.

I gasp, my eyes wide, my right hand painfully racing up
to cover my mouth, my left hand holding the nail gun like a
weapon. The masked man turns around and sees my
husband. Lewis, who was once such a brilliant boxer, throws

a punch, but the masked man ducks and Lewis misses. My husband stumbles. The masked man laughs.

'You're not the boxer you used to be, are you, Lewis Brown?'

I freeze. Do I know that voice? Why the familiarity? But it's like my brain has closed down, unable to make sense of this.

Lewis turns and runs, no doubt realising faster than me that this man wants to kill both of us, terrified by that metal pipe. But the masked man is quick and he races after Lewis, swiping the pipe at the back of Lewis's knees. My husband falls to the ground, his face smashed into the gravel drive. But I'm running too and quickly catch up with them. I jam the nail gun into the stranger's shoulder and neck, and press it repeatedly. It judders as the nails slam into his flesh and he lets out a bloodcurdling scream. Except now I'm not sure which of the men is yelling the loudest. Lewis is writhing on the ground, his arm around his leg. My husband, who is meant to be the macho fighter, is actually crying.

'I'm going to die!' he says repeatedly. 'I don't want to die.'

The intruder is crawling away from me now and I know I need to bring the nail gun down hard on the back of his head, except I'm not sure I've got it in me to kill a man. Can I hit him hard enough to knock him out, but not too hard so he isn't fatally wounded? He's certainly hurt, groaning as he crawls more and more slowly.

And then there are running footsteps and another figure looms out of the darkness. This time I know exactly who he is. Rafael heads straight towards Lewis. His fists are clenched and he is just about to pummel my husband when I shout at him.

'No, Raf! It's the other man we need to restrain. Not my husband.'

We both turn to see the man in black crawling along the gravel drive away from us. Lewis must have hurt him because his leg is dragging behind him. Rafael grabs the nail gun from me and hurtles towards him. 'Stop!' he yells, except the stranger doesn't. Instead he hauls himself to his feet, the metal pole still in his hands. He's wavering as he stands there, trying to keep his balance as he hurls it towards Rafael. Except the lad is quicker and nimbler. The metal bar crashes to the ground, its metallic noise ringing out in the still night air. Then Raf hits the masked man on the side of the head with the nail gun, and the bigger man's knees give way as he concertinas to the ground.

'Oh my God, I think I've killed him!' Raf paces backwards and forwards, his palms jammed in his eye sockets, the nail gun at his feet. 'I think I've killed him.'

I hurry towards Raf, pulling him in for a quick, tight hug. 'You saved us,' I say. 'You saved us.' Then I crouch down over the still body. We're bathed in light now, caught in the beam of the motion sensor exterior light. The man is lying with his face upwards, the balaclava rumpled. I tug it upwards, pulling it off his head as quickly as if I'm removing a plaster.

And then I gasp.

'No!' I exclaim.

'Who is he?' Raf is by my side and I realise that I'm holding his hand.

'It's Niall. Niall Hutchinson.'

'Who?'

'My business partner and friend.' My voice quivers. 'He sold your parents this house.'

From behind us, Lewis moans. 'Can you go and look after my husband? Get him some water perhaps?'

I lean down and press my fingers to Niall's neck.

He's unconscious but there's still a pulse.

'You haven't killed him.' Raf is still standing next to me and his face collapses. He's so pale I fear he might faint. I feel the same way, except I have to keep it together here. I turn towards Lewis, who is still grimacing and moaning on the ground.

'Why?' I ask him. 'Why are you and Niall trying to kill me? What have I done to make you both do this?' My voice catches as I realise that the two men I trusted the most have turned on me in the most horrific way.

Lewis is sobbing pathetically, fat tears glistening in the low light, heavy cries making his voice sound unnaturally high-pitched.

'I don't want you dead,' he says. 'I love you. I don't know why Niall is here.'

I stare at my husband as he writhes on the ground. Raf is standing by my side, quivering. I put my arm around him and pull him towards me.

'Don't lie to me, Lewis. I know you've been having an affair. I saw her text messages.'

He sobs even harder now and all respect I had for this man vanishes. 'I'm so sorry,' he croaks. 'It was a huge mistake. I want to stay with you. I love you, Els.'

None of this makes any sense.

'I should never have reconnected with Susan.'

Raf stiffens and jolts away from me. I realise with dismay that we're talking about his mother. The boy doesn't need to hear this.

'Susan, as in Mum?' he croaks.

'Go into the house, Raf,' I tell him. 'Call the police again, and an ambulance.'

Except he doesn't move.

The word that Lewis just said takes a moment to filter into my consciousness. 'Reconnected?' I ask as I turn back towards Lewis. 'Did you say reconnected?'

Lewis is sobbing so hard now, it's hard to decipher what he's saying. Realisation flows through me that this is much bigger than I had appreciated. Yet how Lewis got Niall to do his dirty work for him is beyond any comprehension.

I realise Lewis is trying to push himself upright except the strength in his arms seems to have dissipated. He's not looking at me anymore, but his gaze is fixed on Rafael. He wipes his eyes with the back of his hand and blood glistens on his skin.

'I'm your dad,' he says. 'I'm your dad, Raf.'

There's complete silence for a long beat. Not a clicking sound from a sole cicada, nor the rustle of the wind, or even a whimper from one of the men. Just stillness. And then Raf speaks.

'No you're not,' he scoffs as he kicks at the gravel, sending a spray of stones in Lewis's direction. It's taking me a while to catch up here, yet there's something in the way that Rafael is speaking to suggest that he's ahead of me. That this revelation isn't the shock that it is to me. 'You might be my biological father but my dad's twice the man that you are.'

'Please, Els.' Lewis is begging now. 'I didn't mean for all of this to happen. It was a mistake.'

'I saw the texts from Susan,' I say, surprised at how cold and calm my voice sounds. 'She asked you when you were going to tell me that you were leaving me. When were you going to tell me, Lewis?'

'I wasn't, because I don't want to leave you. I was going to tell Susan that it was all a mistake.'

'Except it can't be that much of a mistake because you were with Susan eighteen years ago, if it's true that you're really Rafael's birth father. Have you been cheating on me for all of this time?'

'No, not at all. We reconnected at Niall's wedding. It was just a physical thing, an overwhelming physical attraction. It didn't mean anything.'

'Just shut up!' Rafael yells. 'Shut your mouth!'

'So why is Niall here?' I ask, completely confused. I glance over at Niall, who is lying completely still, his leg at a strange angle. I wonder if he's even still alive or whether his life has drifted away while we've been standing here. My brain is telling me that I should go to him, check his pulse, put him into the recovery position, except I never completed any first-aid courses and I haven't got any idea what to do. And my heart is telling me that is the right thing. Niall tried to kill me. He tried to kill Rafael. He doesn't deserve our help. Leave that to the emergency services, who no doubt will arrive shortly.

'Did you ask Niall to try to kill me? Is that why he's here, doing your dirty work?'

'No, of course not. I've no idea what he's doing here. All I knew was I had to try to save you from the masked man. I haven't got a clue what he's playing at.'

Except I don't believe my husband and judging from the look on Rafael's face, he doesn't either.

CHAPTER TWENTY-EIGHT

PIERS

I can feel Susan's knees against the side of the bed, her breath on my face. On some level I know it's ridiculous to feel such fear of my wife, yet I can't believe her intentions are good. Why has she crept in here during the middle of the night? She could have waited until visiting hours tomorrow or even telephoned me. We could have had a civilised conversation on the phone, surely. Except a memory pings like a violent rubber band in my head, over and over, creating more pain with the firing of each synapse. Susan hit me on the head with some object and then she pulled me to the top of the stairs and shoved me down them. Try as I might, I can't see any reason for doing that other than wanting to severely incapacitate me or kill me. Unless, of course, I'm mistaken. Unless she was trying to stop me from falling down the stairs and somehow misjudged.

'Do you remember?' she asks. I can smell her perfume combined with sweat. Susan is careful with her hygiene so this is an unpleasant, unfamiliar scent.

'Yes,' I say. 'And now you've come back to finish off the

job. The thing I don't understand, Susan, is why you want me dead.'

She lets out a quiet bark. 'I don't want you dead, Piers. I'm not worried that you'll go to the police and report me because you have no proof. It was fortuitous that Teresa arrived when she did, finding you in a crumpled heap at the bottom of the stairs and me completely hysterical. Because I genuinely was.' She leans backwards and flutters her hand. 'I want you to go away, but now, frankly, I couldn't care if you were dead or alive.'

I flinch. I would prefer hatred from my wife because at least that's a true emotion, and don't they say that love is just a small step from hate, whereas indifference is the most cutting of all. If she simply doesn't care about me, then our relationship is truly over.

'Why did you try to kill me?'

She shrugs, as if it's of no importance. 'I know you'll never go to the police. You're too weak for that, Piers. You hate rocking the boat and you'd never do anything to hurt Raf, or make yourself look less in his eyes. So no. I'm safe in that respect. Your word against mine. You had a severe concussion and were heavily sedated with a traumatic brain injury. No, they'll just think it's a false memory.'

I swallow hard. She's right in some respects because yes, I think I have been a weak man. I've chosen the path of least resistance, except where has that got me? To the brink of death. And Raf is no longer a child. He's a young man with an extraordinary strength of character. He'll want me to do what is right even if it hurts all of us. And right now, all I can pray is that he is safe; that the Provencal police have turned up to sort out whatever horror he's involved in at the chateau.

'I want a divorce and I want you to give me full ownership of the chateau.' Susan clasps her hands neatly together and tilts her head as if this is the most reasonable of requests. 'I've taken advice from Tim De Withers.'

It hits me then that Susan wasn't meeting De Withers to rekindle an affair but to get help from him as to how best to fleece me in a divorce.

'Where does Lewis fit into all of this?' I ask, the memories flooding into my head as if a sluice-gate has just been opened. I can even see the man in my mind's eye now; a big, bulky man with a many-times broken nose and an annoying swagger.

'We want to be together. Lewis will move to France to be with me.'

'And what about Raf? How does he fit into this plan of yours?' I'm trembling now, but keep my arms underneath the sheets so Susan can't see.

'Raf is nothing to do with you anymore. He's not your son.'

'Don't be ridiculous,' I exclaim. 'Who are you kidding? I brought the boy up. I was with him when he took his first steps. His first word was Dada. I was there to collect him from his first day of nursery school and primary school. I was the one who turned him into the bright, capable young man that he is today. Any emotional maturity he has comes from me, not you.'

'Don't get so worked up,' Susan says. She squeezes my wrist through the sheets, painfully catching the cannula in the back of my hand. I grit my teeth and don't say anything.

'Lewis is a murderer.' I spit out the words.

She rolls her eyes at me and squeezes my wrist even harder. I can feel her sharp fingernails digging into my flesh.

'Don't be stupid. Petty jealousy makes you look even more pathetic.'

I wrench my wrist away from her grasp, an unfamiliar fury lending me a surge of energy.

'You think you know it all, don't you, Susan? Except you have no idea what is really going on. You haven't even mentioned Raf. Do you know where he is? Do you even care?'

'What are you talking about?' A brief look of confusion crosses her face, as if she's realising that perhaps she doesn't hold every piece of the jigsaw. The man in the adjacent bed coughs. I'm not sure if it's in his sleep or whether he's awake now and listening to the horror show of our conversation, a bystander to the disintegration of our marriage.

'Our son is in danger and you don't even care!'

'Where is Raf? What aren't you telling me?'

'You think you know me so well, don't you?' I hiss at her. 'Except you're in for a shock, Susan. I won't just grant you a divorce and I won't give you custody of our son, not that that's even relevant now he's nearly eighteen. I want half of what is legally mine and if it means selling the damn chateau, then so be it. And if you think I will just roll over and forget what you tried to do to me, you're in for another shock. I can remember everything and I'm going to tell the police that my wife tried to murder me.'

Susan jumps up from her chair, which clatters to the ground. If the man in the other bed wasn't awake before, I'm sure he will be now.

'Don't be so foolish, Piers,' she hisses, spittle hitting my cheek.

'You are not going to get away with this.' I move my arm rapidly trying to reach for the emergency buzzer, except

Susan is quicker than me. Her face is puce, even in the low light, and there's a fury in her eyes that I've never seen before. She's clenching and unclenching her fingers and her lips move as if in a parody.

'You'll have to finish me off first, Susan, because I will never let you get away with this. You lied to me and Raf for the whole of his life; you've been having an affair with Lewis and now you just expect me to leave you, handing you over all my money, all my assets and worst of all, our son.'

'He's not your son,' she hisses. I ignore her.

'As if that wasn't bad enough, you tried to kill me. You pushed me down those stairs, and now what? You expect me just to walk away? Expect me not to say a word to the police?'

She raises her hand up and slaps me across the face.

I try to push her away, but Susan is much stronger than me and she has the advantage, standing over my bed. Before I can fully grasp what is happening, her hands are around my neck and she's squeezing. Squeezing. I flail around, my hands desperately seeking the small round buzzer attached to the cord. The room fades in front of my eyes as I try but fail to gasp for breath. I kick out, but my legs are caught in the bed sheets and I can feel the air being tugged out of my body. My wife is killing me, right here in the hospital. I try so hard to prise her hands away with my own, but I know the oxygen is leaving my already exhausted body and my right elbow slips backwards and connects with something hard, plastic-like. I press down with all my might just as I hear a man's voice shouting, 'Help!'

There's a commotion. Running feet, loud voices, lights so bright they're piercing my retinas, and the air – it all comes flooding back, causing me to gasp and cough and gulp.

'It's alright, Piers. You're going to be alright.' I recognise my nurse, Shireen's voice, and I'm so relieved that she's here.

I try to focus and see that the curtains have been swept back and that there's a person on the ground, three, maybe four nurses restraining her. My wife. They've restrained my wife.

I turn to look at the man in the other bed. He is ghostly pale, his grey hair standing up on end, tubes coming out of his neck and both arms.

'You alright, mate?' he asks.

I nod painfully.

'A complete psycho, that one,' he adds.

'Yes,' I murmur. 'Yes.'

HALF AN HOUR later and Susan has been taken away. I don't ask where they've taken her and no one tells me.

'How are you doing?' Shireen asks, gently lifting up my hand and taking my blood pressure.

'It's a shock. Such a shock.'

'The police will be arriving soon to take a statement,' Shireen says.

I nod. I've no idea what I should tell them.

'Does your wife have a history of mental health problems?' Shireen asks gently.

'No.' I shake my head, because no, she doesn't. Lying and cheating and attempted manslaughter are not health issues. Susan was of stable mind and there are no mitigating factors as to why she decided I had to die. It's almost impossible to make sense of her actions, and frankly now isn't the time to rationalise anything. All I'm concerned about is Raf. Is my boy safe? I try calling him back repeatedly, but the phone goes straight to voicemail. All I can do is pray.

'You'll have some bruising around the neck but you're going to be okay, Piers,' Shireen reassures me. 'Why don't you try and get some rest before the police arrive?'

I nod, but there is no way I will be sleeping. Not until I know that Raf is safe.

When the phone eventually rings, I press answer immediately.

'Dad?' Tears of relief spring to my eyes.

'Are you alright, Raf?'

'Just calling to say I'm safe. The police are here.'

'You're not hurt?' I ask.

'No, I'm really fine.'

'Oh thank heavens, Raf,' I say, letting my head loll back on the pillow, relief making me completely weak.

'And Dad?' Raf adds. 'I just wanted to say that I love you.'

CHAPTER TWENTY-NINE

RAFAEL – A YEAR LATER

'Dad, food will be ready in ten minutes.'

'I think I can hear Elodie's car now, so it's perfect timing,' Dad says. His voice fades as he walks to the front of the villa.

I open the oven door to the waft of scrumptious smells. It's one of the many strange things that has happened over the past year. I've gotten into cooking, big time. So much so that I might train to be a chef. Dad's really supportive of the idea, and I don't think it's just because he would starve if I wasn't around to cook for him.

'Oo, something smells good.' I smile at Lucille who has arrived holding two bottles of wine from her vineyard. 'Can I help?'

'You could lay the table. We'll sit outside.' We always sit outside, even when the weather isn't great. Dad has jazzed the place up with planters full of flowers and now the scaffolding has gone, the villa is looking beautiful. We don't call it Chateau Lester anymore. That was Mum's idea and as Dad says, pretension was always her thing and never his.

Instead, we've returned it to its original name. Villa Espigarié – translated as the villa where lavender grows. Sometimes I wonder whether it should be Villa Tragédie. We will probably leave here sometime soon, just not yet.

'Hello, Raf.' Elodie walks in and hands me a gift wrapped in navy and gold paper. 'Gosh, something smells good.'

I rip the paper off the gift. Elodie has given me a recipe book, a recently published tome by one of my favourite Italian chefs. I smile broadly. 'Thanks for this,' I say. 'An awesome present.'

'You're quite easy to buy for.' Elodie laughs.

'You should see the size of his recipe book collection.' Dad laughs. 'It fills up half the library.'

'Dad, can you do the wine? Why don't you all go and sit outside, and I'll bring the food out,' I suggest.

'Yes, sir!' Dad toffs an imaginary hat at me and I grin.

Lucille steps back into the kitchen and gives Dad and Elodie kisses on both cheeks. It's such a relief that Dad has accepted her.

There's an easy banter between the four of us whilst we dig into my salmon en croute, made with homemade pastry, of course, along with buttery potatoes and various salads. When we've finished eating, Elodie takes a long sip of water and leans back in her chair. She looks different these days. Younger somehow, wearing trendier clothes.

'I have news on Niall.'

The air seems to chill a little. The birds sing a little softer. At least that's what it feels like whenever we talk about *that* night. Dad reaches out and squeezes my hand but he doesn't need to.

'The police have confirmed the details of my keyman insurance. It's as we thought. Niall had been living so far beyond his means.' Elodie's voice cracks a little and I look at her with concern. I know how broken she has been by everything. The betrayal not just of her husband but her best friend and business partner too. 'He had a big gambling habit, for years apparently. And it only got worse when he married Danielle, who of course likes the finer things in life. Poor Danielle.' She pauses and takes a sip of wine this time. 'Anyway, now the forensic accountant has submitted his findings and it's as we assumed. Niall had been syphoning money from Hutchinson Brown. Huge amounts of money which he used to fund his gambling. He may have gotten away with it for longer other than the bank was closing in. Setting up the house-swapping arm of the business and me requesting a business loan meant that the accounts would be scrutinised. Niall knew that his dodgy accounting would come to light and he had no way of paying back the company to cover things up. Instead, he intended to use the keyman insurance on me.'

'Keyman insurance?' Lucille asks. 'What's that?'

'It's an insurance policy that pays out on the death of a key company executive. In our case, if I died, Hutchinson Brown would have been paid three million pounds. That would have been more than enough for Niall to pay off his debts and take over the whole business.'

'And could he have gotten away with it?' I ask.

Elodie shrugs her shoulders. 'Fortunately, we'll never find that out.'

'I can't believe that your oldest friend tried to kill you for money,' Lucille says, shaking her head.

'It was all very well thought through. He recommended André to you, Piers, in the knowledge that André had a criminal record. He was convicted for a string of petty burglaries when he was a teenager, but still that would have been enough for the police to pursue him. And then he staged the various break-ins and intended to frame André. Except, of course, it never came to that.'

'What will happen to Niall?' Lucille asks.

'He's currently in prison on remand. The trial is scheduled for three months' time and he'll be tried for first-degree murder and fraud. I saw Danielle last week. She's bearing up, just about. The poor girl is living back with her parents, having paid off as many of Niall's debts as she can, although she's working again and reckons she'll be back on her feet in a few months.'

'She's not still married to Niall, is she?' Lucille asks.

'No. The divorce has come through.'

We're all silent, because hers isn't the only divorce. Dad has divorced Mum and Elodie has divorced Lewis. It's such a mess. Mum is also in prison awaiting trial. I try not to think about it.

'And Lewis? How is he?' Dad asks Elodie.

She rolls her eyes. 'On the verge of bankruptcy. He's closed down all of the gyms with the exception of the one where he's living.'

'He's living in a gym?' I ask, surprised.

Elodie laughs. 'Not in it. There's a studio flat above it and he's living there. He said he wrote to you. Did you get the letter?'

I nod. Lewis has sent me ten letters. Dad and I read the first handful together and honestly Lewis is delusional. He seems to think that as my 'birth dad' he has some rights over me. He simply hasn't grasped that he'll never be my father in any shape or form. We might share some DNA but that means nothing to me. Dad is the man who has supported me through the past year from hell. He's the man who was there for me every time I fell over or got sick or was grumpy, and he'll be the man I go to, to share all the ups and downs of my life.

'I'm surprised you still see him,' Dad says.

Elodie shrugs. 'I don't love him and I don't respect him, but I'll always care for him just a little,' she says. 'He was just weak and stupid but he didn't try to kill me.'

The words hang heavily between us because that's the fundamental difference between Lewis and Mum. Mum tried to kill Dad. That's the thing I'll never understand. Never.

Pushkin stands up and trots over to me, his amber eyes fixed on mine, silently begging me for some leftover food. 'Okay, okay,' I say, rubbing his soft head. 'I'll clear this lot up and maybe, if you're a really good boy, you might get something.'

Dad chuckles.

'You know, I'll never forgive myself for what I did to Pushkin,' Lucille says.

I stand up and snake my arm around Lucille's neck, giving her a kiss on the side of her head.

'What do you mean?' Elodie asks.

'You know how my parents were obsessed with finding Florian Dupont's will? Well, when you were staying here they cosied up to you in the hope that they could get access to the villa. That's why they had me sneaking around the library when you had that big supper, but I didn't find

anything. And then, when you gave Mum the cold shoulder
–'

'That's because I told Elodie I didn't want her being friendly with your parents,' Dad adds.

'Well then, my parents thought the best thing would be to try to get you to leave early, and then perhaps the house would be empty and they could search it when no one was here.' Lucille shakes her head as if she's finding the memories hard to deal with. 'It was so stupid, really, the silly stories about Margot's grandparents being murdered.'

'That wasn't true?' Elodie asks with surprise.

'Non.'

'And the dead squirrel up the chimney? Did you place it there?' she asks.

Lucille laughs. 'No. That was just one of those things. Sometimes animals get stuck in chimneys. Good or bad timing, however you choose to look at it. But the thing I really regret is giving Pushkin a sleeping pill. That was so wrong of me. I love animals and especially Pushkin, and I don't ever expect your forgiveness, but really I am very sorry.'

'And I'm sorry that we never found the will, although if we did – or if we do – I'm not sure what would happen,' Dad adds.

Dad and I have looked in the boiserie and found nothing, which is a relief really. He and the Moreaus will never be best buddies – there's too much history for that – but at least they're civil in each other's company, and they've both accepted that Lucille and I love each other.

I stack the plates and carry them through to the kitchen, placing them in the sink. Lucille and I will wash up later. Then I walk to the oven and remove my homemade clafoutis from the warming drawer. I whisk up some cream and put it into a blue and white striped jug and carry both back outside.

Elodie and Dad are talking business now. I'm so pleased for him, the way things have worked out. He deserves a bit of luck. When Elodie discovered that Dad used to work in sales and was rather successful at it, she suggested that he might like to act as her agent in France. I'll never forget that conversation, how his face lit up, how delighted he was at the prospect of ditching the garden maintenance business, something he only did because Mum wanted him to do it. He's closed a few deals over the past weeks, selling some expensive properties, and his healthy commissions are going a long way to paying off Elodie's loan. She wanted to give us the money to finish off the works on the villa, except Dad was too proud. He said he'd accept the funds only if it was a loan. André has been happy because he's actually been paid on time, and most of the works are finished now.

I place the clafoutis on the table and Elodie whistles. We tuck in and the groans of delight make me smile.

'This is so good,' Elodie says. 'Whenever you want to start your training in London, just let me know. I'll put you in touch with the top chefs.'

That won't be this year. First, we've got to get through Mum's trial and I've no desire to be anywhere near England when that happens. One of the many good things about being in France is that my friends don't know much about what has happened. Lucille and I are going to go travelling. I said I wanted to hang around to support Dad, but he says I should go off, enjoy myself, be on the other side of the world, far away from the horrors. Lucille and I are planning a trip to Southeast Asia and I can't wait to try out all the different cuisines. For a while, I wondered whether our relationship would work. I was gutted when she told me that her parents encouraged her to be with me, except now, all these months later, that insecurity has evaporated. We may not be forever, Lucille and me, but we're strong right now. And I'm happy. As Dad says, that's all that really matters.

A LETTER FROM MIRANDA

Thank you so much for reading *The House Swap*. I was in desperate need of a holiday when I started plotting this book and reckoned the South of France would be a great place for some rest and recuperation. Alas I didn't get to stay in a chateau in Provence or in a luxury town house in Knightsbridge, but my imagination took me there for the weeks I was writing this book, and it was a close second!

I know that house swaps are very popular, but I'm not sure I could do it. It would require too much clearing up and tidying away and worrying whether the strangers staying in my house might discover my writing notes and think that I was a monstrous murderer! Would you do a house swap?

As hopefully you know, I never cause animals any real harm in my books, and I can reassure you that Pushkin was absolutely fine! If you've read any of my other books, you might have noticed that Pushkin features in some of those too. I've named those dogs after our gorgeous Black Labrador,

Pushkin, who was my constant writing companion before he passed away last year.

Thank you to Ashleigh who won the naming rights in Sarcoma UK's fundraising prize draw. She chose to name a baddie character after her mum, Susan Lester. Sorry, Susan! Sarcoma UK is a charity very close to my heart as they supported me when I had bone cancer.

I give members of my Facebook Group the opportunity to name the characters in my books. Thank you to the following people who suggested names: Bob Fendt, Alyson Lucille, Nina Pleterski, Dawn Coulon, LaRae Hayes Galloway, Dannii Hutchinson, Nicolette Reite, Jill Sutheren and Noreen Dane.

If you would like the chance to name characters in my future books, I'd love it if you could join my Facebook Group, *Miranda Rijks Thriller Readers' Group*, where I post details of giveaways and bookish news. https://www.facebook.com/groups/mirandarijks

I am so grateful to the book blogging community and the wonderful bloggers who take the time to review my psychological thrillers, share my cover reveals and talk about my books on social media. If you love reading psychological thrillers, join Mark Jenkins' awesome Facebook Group, *Psychological Thrillers Book Club* or Raven Lynn Spalding's *Domestic Thriller Readers Book Club* or Sean Campbell's *Crime Fiction Addict*, or *Tattered Page Book Club*. There are many other great Facebook groups too, including *Psychological Thriller Readers*, *Thriller Book Lovers*, *Psychological*

Thriller Books, Crime, Thriller and Suspense Readers and Authors and *Fans of Psychological Thrillers*. In fact, too many to mention! If I've missed your favourites, please let me know.

I couldn't have written this, my twenty-fourth psychological thriller, without Inkubator Books. Thank you to Brian Lynch, Garret Ryan, Stephen Ryan, Jan Smith, Alice Latchford, Claire Milto, Elizabeth Bayliss, Ella Medler and the rest of the team.

Finally, and most importantly, thank *you*. If you have a moment to leave a review on Amazon and Goodreads, this helps other people discover my novels and I'd be massively grateful.

My warmest wishes,

Miranda

www.mirandarijks.com

ALSO BY MIRANDA RIJKS

Inkubator Books Titles

Psychological Thrillers

THE VISITORS

I WANT YOU GONE

DESERVE TO DIE

YOU ARE MINE

ROSES ARE RED

THE ARRANGEMENT

THE INFLUENCER

WHAT SHE KNEW

THE ONLY CHILD

THE NEW NEIGHBOUR

THE SECOND WIFE

THE INSOMNIAC

FORGET ME NOT

THE CONCIERGE

THE OTHER MOTHER

THE LODGE

THE HOMEMAKER

MAKE HER PAY

THE GODCHILD

EVERY BREATH YOU TAKE

THE HOUSE SWAP

The Dr Pippa Durrant Mystery Series

FATAL FORTUNE

(Book 1)

FATAL FLOWERS

(Book 2)

FATAL FINALE

(Book 3)

FATAL SERIES BOX SET

GASPS

A collection of psychological thriller short stories published by the author

Made in the USA
Monee, IL
11 December 2024